THE DECONSTRUCTORS

JUDE WALKEN

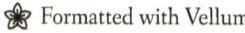

T(B)K – "Course I have."

CONTENTS

FOREWORD

All author profits generated by this work are to be donated to *Médecins Sans Frontières*, a charity providing humanitarian medical care to people affected by conflict, epidemics, disasters, or exclusion from healthcare. https://www.msf.org/

The author reserves the right to enjoy the irony in the unlikely event that this particular work goes on to sell millions.

In no way is any part of this based on a true story. Honestly.

To destroy the world you have,
is the only real form of art.

— Henrique Lausanne

TELLING STORIES TO STRANGERS

It wasn't my idea.

It wasn't my idea and that much is absolutely certain.

I can really only be accused of being part of its realisation. Does that make me responsible for the events that unfolded?

Jesus, what the hell is wrong with me? Am I a complete and total coward?

A woman is *dead*—almost certainly dead. Why can't I just accept that I share some of the blame?

Because, because—it was *his* idea, not mine. *He* is entirely responsible for this. Him alone. Not me.

Over time, yes, I was made to feel like I was part of its inception. But that was only because I was there from the start. Looking back, I think that may have been the entire problem. I was simply *there*. In the wrong place at the wrong time, lacking any sort of objectivity.

"That's me—Mr Zero Fucking Objectivity."

My mumbling alerts the middle-aged gentleman in the aisle seat beside me. He raises a weary eyebrow above his gold-rimmed reading glasses. I smile awkwardly and flush a little.

"Sorry, I..."

...may have had too much to drink. That's a given—talking to yourself in public pretty much confirms it, the only other valid excuse being genuine insanity. One or two to steady the nerves turned into four or five. Never mind. I needed it. God knows that's the truth. Besides, as my stepfather would say—*flying sober is a fool's game*. He's always had a rather unique set of life rules.

I close my eyes, try not to think about that poor, poor woman, and focus instead on regaining a degree of composure.

In the beginning I was sceptical. Highly sceptical. Part of me thought the whole idea was utter nonsense. Perhaps even a joke. Why, oh why, didn't I listen to that little voice of reason and turn away from it altogether?

I guess because a larger part of me wanted to believe in his vision. Believe it was the product of a genius mind—a unique conceptualisation—a genuinely original idea in a world where everything has been done before. That was the appeal. That's what blinded me.

Sometimes it's hard to see the obvious flaws in something. Sometimes we never really know what we've undertaken until it's upon us—and then it's just too late. And then you realise what you've done will hurt the few people in the world who may have cared about you...

Jesus Christ, I need to relax.

I need to stop thinking.

I need to sleep.

I close my tired, bloodshot eyes and become aware of how much they're stinging. I stretch my back with a view to settling into some quasi-meditation. At some point I knock my tray table, sending my complimentary gin and tonic over the aisle-seat man.

"Christ! I am so, so sorry!"

In a desperate and ineffective bid to mop up my faux pas, I begin dabbing at his gin-and-tonic-soaked crotch with my serviette. I stop abruptly as I realise I'm effectively touching him up.

"God! I'm sorry! I really... I didn't..."

The man smiles. Thank God—there's some warmth in that smile. He even looks vaguely amused by my inadvertent assault upon him. He's well dressed. Well, he *was* well dressed. His smile is framed elegantly by a greying moustache that is clearly maintained with affection. He begins to speak with a thick French accent. *Et voilà*—the look is complete.

"*Pas de problème, mon ami. Pas de problème.*"

"I'm so sorry, I..."

He shakes his head and hand in unison. "*Pas de problème.* Now, tell me—are you *really* okay?"

"Me? No... Yes! I mean, I'm fine... Just, erm, *jittery*... You know, with, erm, flying and that."

An expression of intrigue briefly drifts over the Frenchman's face. I'm now making a very conscious effort not to slur my words.

"Do you need a little something, maybe? I have a— tablet."

"No, no, I'm... I'm fine. I've... just had a bad week."

"*Bien!* I thought you were *really* not so keen to fly, eh? Those people are a super pain in the ass on such a long flight as this."

He chuckles to himself and folds down the corner of *Paris Match* or whatever magazine he's reading. I attempt to mimic his chuckle and end up making a strangled choking sound. Very composed.

"No, well, flying is fine—it's the landing I worry about."

"*Vraiment?* The landing is difficult, but I feel you should know most aeroplanes crash during the taking off. And, *mon ami*, we have already climbed that mountain."

"Right, erm, okay. It's strange they don't mention that in the safety briefing."

He laughs. "*Bon!* I am Claude. Here, let me get you another."

In one smooth motion Claude extends a hand over his head and heralds the flight attendant. This man has clearly flown long haul before.

"Gin and tonic, thank you," I say.

"I know, *mon ami*, I can smell it very well."

"God, I'm so sorry."

"Relax! A little joke."

"Right."

"Now please—your name?"

"Oh, sorry—Will."

"A pleasure to meet you, Will. A pleasure indeed. Now tell me—I have read this magazine and the movie is shit. There is something that troubles you, *non?* You have a little story to tell, maybe? Something to pass the time?"

Telling stories to strangers? This is definitely not in my limited repertoire of social skills. However, on reflection, it could be therapeutic. I'm normally a private person, but today has not been a normal day. It's not been a normal week. It's not been a normal year. I hesitate, then realise that I'm craving it—some sort of release, some sort of outlet for all of this.

And besides, I've definitely had too much to drink.

2

MR HUGO BOSS

Lucy and I pulled up outside a row of well-kept townhouses in Holborn. I carefully manoeuvred my trusty wreck of a hatchback into a typically inconvenient Central London parking space a number of streets away from our actual destination. Despite being purchased for significantly less than the cost required annually to get it through its MOT, I had plenty of affection for the old thing.

Still, if asked—we'd taken a cab. It simply wouldn't do to be seen pulling up in something that most terrorist organisations wouldn't even consider for car bomb material.

"For Christ's sake, Will, hun—people need *to know you're better than this!"*

Lucy's earlier heartening encouragement echoed in my mind as she giggled in the passenger seat next to me. The source of her amusement was my third attempt at paralleling parking; this time I'd come perilously close to a large, expensive-looking Mercedes. At least she was in a better mood now. She hadn't exactly tried to mask her disappointment in me earlier as I'd once again failed to sort out any cocaine for her evening. It wasn't my fault. I only knew a single *guy*, and he'd turned out to be unreliable. Unreliable drug dealers—whatever next?

I forced a smile, trying to remain good-humoured despite my rising agitation. I was tired and sober. This was in sharp contrast to Lucy, who had polished off a bottle of bubbles before announcing that she wanted me to drive to this wretched party. It was okay for her—she'd never had to deal with this sort of parallel parking bullshit. She moved through life with an effortless grace underpinned by the self-confidence of knowing that things would always be alright.

I should have been laughing too. The very notion of me trying to hide my automotive embarrassment in a side street should have had me pissing myself. However, after almost a year of working in the city, my sense of humour had begun to wither. Initially I attributed the culture shock of living in the capital to just being out of my comfort zone, but twelve months later, I still felt like a total stranger. Lucy was just about keeping me going. Her constant reassurance and persuasion had me still playing the game—keep up those appearances and you'll eventually be rewarded with some of the abundant bounty the city offers.

Lucy Kitson. We'd met while I was studying for my Master's degree at Durham University. She was an undergrad. I was trying everything possible to delay the inevitable working-for-the-rest-of-your-tragic-life stage. I'd stayed on at university to hold on to the good life, and Lucy, at the age of twenty, was the personification of this. She knew how to get by with as little effort as possible, reserving all remaining energy for recreational hedonism.

This was very attractive at the time. But now, in the cold light of the real world, I was beginning to see things differently. A continuation of the good life in the city could only be maintained by either coming from money or making significant amounts of it. It wasn't great that I'd been blessed with neither, but at least I had a job. A job with *prospects*.

We found the party at a townhouse six identical streets down from the parked car. As soon as we entered, we were enveloped by the warmth of loud voices buoyed by the self-confidence of alcohol, narcotics and the festive season in general. Desperate to get a drink in hand and begin dissolving my baseline social anxiety, I made a beeline for the kitchen with Lucy trailing behind, exchanging nods and *Hi, hun!*s with people she recognised.

En route, Toby, the party's host, stopped me in my tracks.

"Will! Will-i-am! My dear boy, how are you? You've met Nyles? Nyles *Henry* —the ultimate *en-tre-pre-neur*— just returned from the wilderness! Eh, Nylesy?"

An intoxicated Toby lazily thumbed towards an archetypal tall, dark and handsome stranger standing beside him. The stranger wore a loose, partially open white cotton shirt that signposted an impressive physique. He complemented this with elegantly chiselled features and perfect flowing jet-black hair. In comparison, my own look was very amateur—hair enthusiastically plastered with product and a salmon-pink Ralph Lauren polo. And yes, I had unfortunately succumbed to the collar-up mode.

"No, I don't think I have..." I smiled, shook Toby's hand, and extended the same gesture to Nyles, who stepped forward.

"Pleasure to meet you both!"

I had temporarily forgotten Lucy was by my side. Lucy, my most dependable social crutch, nodded politely. She smiled at Nyles for definitely a bit too long before seeing someone she recognised and disappearing. I was left stranded. Stranded and without a drink. Searching for something to say, I looked around desperately for inspiration. Thankfully, Nyles came to my rescue.

"I think we've met before, haven't we, brother?"

"Erm, we have?"

Toby's attention had now also been directed elsewhere. I weighed up the odds and decided it was probably okay to politely give Mr Hugo Boss the slip and find sufficient alcohol to tolerate this kind of interaction.

"Yes, brother, I'm certain—I never forget a face!"

Brother? Who says that? I gave up. *Nyles* was clearly intent on having a conversation, whether I liked it or not. I studied the smiling dark eyes before me. Nothing. Maybe a vague familiarity, but then again, he had the look of every male model in every advert for every Italian designer label.

"Curtis & Morgan!"

Shit! He'd got me there. That was my firm. My all-too-familiar sense of generic panic engaged. Adrenal glands gently flickering into action. Pulse quickening. Palms starting their trademark sweat. *Should I know this guy? Is he somebody important?*

"Yes, brother! I knew it! Outside JM's office. I passed you in the corridor on my way out, didn't I? Filthy old bastard that one!"

Nyles cracked a broad grin to reveal immaculate polished ivory. I struggled to return the smile, concentrating hard on not looking too panicked. JM's office? *Jeremy Morgan?* One of the firm's founding partners? Surely not. He had the reputation of an absolute gentleman—plus, I'd only ever seen the inside of his office once, a couple of weeks ago, to discuss rumours of a potential merger. I'd been a nervous wreck, waiting outside his office for what

seemed like hours... Hardly surprising that I'd no recollec-
tion of this guy.

"Ha! Relax, brother! You look genuinely stressed out."

"I'm sorry, I..."

"Don't worry, I've just got one of those memories for
faces. Now remember, this is a party—at least *try* to enjoy
yourself."

"Well, yes, quite." I looked around at the cavorting mass
of social exuberance and once again felt very sober.

"Well, listen, brother, shan't keep you. You look a little
parched. Have yourself a very Merry Christmas!"

I was saved from any further awkwardness by the standard graces of social etiquette. Smiling, I avoided offering
my sweaty handshake and squeezed past him, further into
the bowels of the party, desperate to find an antidote to
another godawful evening.

3

TWO WEEKS BEFORE CHRISTMAS

LIFE CAN BE a real bastard sometimes.

Over the next three weeks, I would lose everything. On reflection, this didn't amount to that much, but at the time, it was *everything*.

The credit crunch of 2008 bit me hard. As its teeth tore through the financial sector, my job was one of many to fall in tandem with stock markets around the globe. There were whispers in the corridors of job losses, but I foolishly decided to ignore them. Rumour is, after all, the backbone of any financial institution, especially one trading in futures.

Plus, I'd been given a major account. I'd also been involved, albeit peripherally, in discussions on the potential merger of our firm with a similar-sized Swiss outfit. I'd never complained, never grumbled, always arrived early, always stayed late. I thought I was the model junior employee. I thought I was indispensable—an integral part of the team.

Turns out I wasn't.

On Thursday, December 11th, I walked out of the marble-floored lobby of Curtis & Morgan, one of London's oldest financial firms, for the last time. I'd been there less than a year. I was told in no uncertain terms that those most newly recruited would be the first to fall. Nepotism, though, was alive and well, and a few held on to their jobs by virtue of their family names. It turned out that we, the non-connected, were only the beginning of the cull.

I blinked back tears as I nodded to Tony, the affable security-guard-slash-doorman loyally watching the threshold. He was a fellow Yorkshireman, and I'd liked to think there'd always been an unspoken mutual respect between us. That was the last time I ever saw him.

"Have a good 'un, Will lad!"

"Night, Tony, mate."

Alright for that fucker—his job was probably safe.

I was immediately ashamed of my venom as my anger subsided. Embarrassed, I stumbled through the polished chrome and glass of the revolving door, trying not to let it aptly hit me in the arse on the way out.

Dazed, I stepped into a cold winter's afternoon. The fading light created an ethereal high street. Disbelief turned off the early rush-hour soundtrack of the financial district. The roar of the city was silenced by a feeling of helplessness. Horns, engine noise and pedestrian chatter became a mumbled, distant whisper. I passed by the usual traders urgently tapping and barking into their Blackberrys while fiercely sucking snatched cigarettes. Their familiarity was now gone. I was no longer part of their world.

I looked up the street adorned with Christmas lights already switched on to light up the early smog of dusk. I felt like crying. I'd been made redundant. Sacked. Properly sacked. Two weeks before Christmas. What kind of bastard institution does that?

I'd played it safe and, with more than a little embarrassment, taken the two months of final salary rather than the stock options that were being offered. I had absolutely no savings to fall back on, so that was the only choice. Up until this point I'd not exactly been careful with cash. Once the money had started coming in, I'd seen no reason that it should ever stop. I'd ignored all warning signs and had been lording it over London with the best of them.

The final kick in the teeth was the cancellation of the lucrative Christmas bonus. To make matters worse, I'd already placed a significant portion of it as a down payment on a brand-new BMW. A payment I'd be desperately trying to claw back over the next few days through countless embarrassing conversations with smug and unsympathetic salespersons. One saving grace was that I hadn't yet paid for a trip to Vienna—a city break intended as the basis of a surprise proposal to Lucy. This was to be a very small stroke of luck in an otherwise extremely grim festive period.

I looked at the hurrying masses and felt so alone that I began to panic. I needed to speak to someone. I needed to confide in another human being—share the pain of the moment. I only really had two socially acceptable options. Lucy was one of them, and I couldn't face that. I had to tell her face to face, fess up, be a man.

I scrolled back over my phone's meagre recent call history until I found Max. A pint or two with Max, my only real friend in the city, would hopefully help put things into perspective. His eternal optimism was what I needed to be around right now. I knew I verged on being a shameless hope parasite at times, but right now I didn't care.

"'Sup, blud? How's tricks?"

"Aw mate, not good... I've been fucking fired! Proper fi—"

"Ha! Gotcha!"

"What?"

"Seriously though, unless you're a model or a smoking-hot air hostess, don't even thinking about leaving a message! *Awww yeah!*"

Wanker. The dial tone confirmed that he had indeed *got me*. Despite my mood, I had to concede this was actually pretty good for Max. I mean, anyone who phoned him outside of a social capacity might be less than impressed—his mother or boss, for example—but things like these did not really seem to concern Max.

Defeated, I briefly thought about calling my own mother, but I hadn't called her in weeks and I didn't want to risk upsetting her. As an only child, I was a bit of a shit son. Unsurprisingly, this thought failed to lift my spirits.

Clad in my newish Paul Smith suit, which was quickly to become my most expensive possession, I swallowed hard and headed towards the Tube. For the first time in my life I was tasting real failure. Unemployed in my mid-twenties, with very little on the horizon.

Facing the unknown at that age should be exciting, but I was terrified.

4

THE FULL HAT-TRICK

ANYONE WHO HAS EVER LISTENED to the lyrics of a blues record could probably tell you what happened next. This particular trilogy of misfortune I've come to think of as the full hat-trick.

Lucy. A six-year relationship collapsed under the weight of its own insecurities. Insecurities that were laid bare in the wake of a financially uncertain future.

I had assumed that my newfound unemployed status would just be one of those speed bumps on the winding road that is true love. I'd supported Lucy for a good few months when we'd first moved down to London while she looked for work that was "really her". I thought she'd reciprocate this unquestionable generosity, because that's what lovers do.

I was wrong.

I returned home the day I lost my job, cancelled our dinner reservation, and opted for the only slightly more frugal option of takeaway sushi. For some reason I decided that delicately sliced sashimi and Sauvignon Blanc were a safe choice over which to explain my employment hiccup.

That evening, Lucy was the perfect girlfriend: cuddles, a *we'll-get-through-this-together* reassurance speech, and a generous drunken helping of fellatio.

We lay wrapped in each other's arms in post-coital bliss on Egyptian cotton sheets with an unnecessarily high thread count. I'd lost my job, and the weather on the horizon didn't look great, but at least I had this. I was counting my blessings when Lucy interrupted my thoughts.

"Hun, you know what?"

"What? That I could perhaps turn tricks for a living?"

"Ha! You are *hi-larious*, but no. What I was going to say is that this might be the greatest thing to ever happen to you."

"Really? How, exactly?"

"Well, hun, let's be honest—you didn't exactly *love* working at CM, did you?"

"Well, true..."

"So then!"

"So then...?"

"*So then!* This might be *the* opportunity to find something that's *really you!*"

"Ah, I see."

Finding something that was *really me* wasn't a reality I could afford to entertain, even if I'd had a clue where to start looking. In the interests of harmony and sleep, I decided against pointing out the inherent differences with which we saw the world. We passed out entwined in each other's limbs. United. At that moment I thought we were invincible. Defiant lovers facing an uncertain future of austerity together.

Turns out I was wrong about that too.

The next morning, niceties were soon dispensed with and a thinly disguised annoyance emerged when Lucy realised that I wasn't up before her, making coffee. Yes, she'd had it pretty good up until this point. Of course, I recognised that she was now the breadwinner, but in my defence, this was my first day of being unemployed. I thought I was at least entitled to a lie-in before spending the remainder of the day wallowing in self-pity and contending with a mild hangover.

"So what are you doing for the rest of the day, hun?" she enquired icily, as though the day were half gone. I really should have made her that coffee.

"I'd not really thought about it. I—"

"Might be *wise* to, wouldn't it, hun?"

Sharp and painfully to the point. Delivered with the speed and precision of a prize fighter.

"Yes, I suppose so... It's just that I thought I'd take a few days to gather my thoughts and reflect on the poss—"

"That's one of your problems, though, isn't it, hun? You do like to obsess over things, don't you?"

I definitely should have made her that coffee. We'd gone from an absent latte to a deep-seated analysis of my character in under a minute. Impressive, even for her. She may have had a point, though—with respect to the obsessing over things, that is. Her expectations regarding coffee were probably unreasonable.

I wondered whether my new predicament would mean increased expectations on me in other domestic areas. Although I'd never bring it up, I thought it was pretty obvious that I already did the lion's share of the cooking and cleaning. And I was fine with that. But could my already limited masculinity cope with becoming her complete and total manservant?

I'd had vague aspirations of spending the morning in

bed amongst the pages of my favourite broadsheet, but these evaporated alongside my plan to finally perfect the Hollandaise sauce for my signature eggs Benedict. Lucy saw to it that I was brutally forced into action. I was instructed to phone a large number of her *chums* and *Daddy's pals* in order to eke out some sort of new career. So much for finding something that was *really me*.

In the run-up to Christmas, this was a task I was to bear with a significant degree of humility, even for me. Despite Lucy's presumption that festive jubilance would play in my favour, it didn't take long to identify a recurring theme: the sort of people who are contacted regarding jobs via a mutual *chum* or *pal* are not the kind to tell you straight—*there's no fucking chance of a job*.

I wasted the better part of two weeks lunching with posh idiots who had no intention of employing me. To make matters worse, the global financial crisis seemed to have a direct effect on people's willingness to front the unemployed a gratis feed. I finished the whole ordeal with significantly less of my two months' final salary and began nervously keeping a daily eye on my bank balance.

At home the atmosphere began to sour. I started to get the impression that I was singing for my dinner. I was impressing Lucy less and less with my tales of failure, regardless of how amusing I tried to make them. Each night I tried to soften the blow of again failing to acquire a job by making something incredible for dinner. I stretched my culinary skills to breaking point to no avail. She readily ate the food, but never seemed impressed or grateful. Neither empathy nor sympathy, it turned out, were things that Lucy did well.

Less than a month after I was sacked, she dumped me.

The warning signs weren't exactly subtle, but it still hurt. She'd copied my entire CD collection and had started to talk with extreme vagueness about the future, sometimes reluctant to even commit to the following evening's plans.

"Shall we just play it by ear, hun?"

I pretended that this lack of commitment was because my present employment status irritated her. She worked all day; I didn't. What right did I have to dictate our evening agendas? The CD pirating I simply ignored.

And then, there it was... I got dumped.

The familiar adolescent cocktail of panic and despair was back, and this time it tasted a lot stronger than I remembered. The cramping sensation in my abdomen, the unshakeable queasiness, my eyes beginning to burn every time I thought of her, of *us*. I felt like I was in free fall. Nothing was ever going to feel as good as it had with her again. Standard feelings that felt hopelessly unique at the time.

Looking back, I suppose we couldn't have been more poorly suited. They say opposites attract, but there's a limit, isn't there? She was never going to be anywhere near what I consider to be grounded in reality. I was worrying more than ever about things like the future, job security and the fluctuating price of fruit and veg. She worried about the most fashionable place to go skiing and the biannual upgrade of her wardrobe to ensure the most in-vogue labels.

At university, Lucy had found my South Yorkshire accent quaint and charming. Now, in London, when she introduced me to friends, I couldn't help feeling that she found the fact I was from Rotherham a little embarrassing. Maybe she had been looking to offload me for someone more becoming of an aspiring socialite for some time. Me becoming a financial burden as well just cemented my status as dead weight.

To add further insult to injury, our swanky East London apartment was not under a joint lease. Unfortunately for me, it was being rented from a friend of Lucy's father. It turned out that our cosy little love nest was not going to remain exclusively as such. A sledgehammer ultimatum was issued: I had seven days to vacate the premises. Lucy had a rent-paying *chum* lined up—her perennially single friend, Lotti.

Lotti almost certainly despised me. I cramped Lucy's style, and by association, that also cramped hers. She was a self-proclaimed modern-day It Girl—the perfect accessory for Lucy's new single lifestyle. It sent a clear message: I was out, and there was no going back.

"Look, hun, I just, need to, like, be around single people at the moment. It's a lifestyle thing, isn't it?"

She had barely even looked up from her *Cosmopolitan* while nonchalantly delivering the news that I would soon be without shelter. I thought about pointing out that techni-cally I was *single people* now, but decided against it.

I tried to leave the room quickly as my eyes began stinging once again. I've always maintained that saving face is an important element of self-preservation. Now it was all I had left.

I sat down on the single bed in the tiny box room I'd already been relegated to. I stared at the generic New York City IKEA print that hung on the wall like a big *fuck you* and began to cry as quietly as possible. Eventually the tears subsided. I reached under the bed, pulled out the one battered suitcase that *I* definitely owned, and began to pack.

And just like that, my life hit the jagged, unforgiving

surface that is rock bottom without the rest of the world even breaking stride.

Job, girl, house—the full hat-trick. All gone in less than a month. One pathetic fucking month.

Happy New Year, 2009...

5

SALVATION COMETH IN
LICENSED ESTABLISHMENTS

THE DAYS BECAME SHROUDED in a proper British January, darkness creeping into every relentless minute of the day. Ash-stained skies turned a heavy gunmetal grey as the winter wore on, and my mood worsened with it. Never-ending filth and sleet lashed down monotonously on London. I concede I was already miserable, but the weather didn't help.

I had never been a fan of winter, with its influenza and its stupidly short days, but London in the winter was partic-ularly grim. To me it lay somewhere between cold tea and public speaking on the joy index. I found myself allocating this pointless categorisation while sitting in a pub, trying to keep warm. I'd been doing a lot of that recently, though this time I was in the quirky and unfamiliar setting of Fulham, nursing a pint of lukewarm London Pride and once again trying to come to terms with it all.

I felt like a shell wrapped around a numb, lifeless host. Life had taken on a distant, dreamlike quality. I hadn't slept properly in over a week. Alcohol didn't seem to be taking the edge off things sufficiently anymore, although I seemed to be constantly hungover, which was at least some blessed distraction.

I was rapidly approaching that unfortunate financial position of *totally broke*. I had no savings, no rich relatives, and apparently no prospects. By the end of the week I was going to have to sign on to the dole. The only reason I hadn't done so yet was a desperate attempt at preserving what little pride I had left. My bank balance estimated that preservation would end on Thursday.

I looked around at the battered furniture and sighed at the generic shit pub décor that adorned the walls. A couple of career alcoholics sat at one of the other tables, listlessly staring out the window. Their presence was slightly at odds with the *Guinness is Good for You* slogan beaming down from a faded reproduced poster in a cracked frame.

The publican had disappeared down into the cellar, and there was almost total silence aside from the street noise. The oppressive greyness was breaking outside, permitting shafts of daylight into the pub to highlight the below-par cleaning job undertaken earlier that morning. It was probably time for a cigarette.

The fact I'd started smoking again was another source of self-loathing. Given the price of cigarettes, the enforcement of the smoking ban and the weather, I really couldn't have picked a worse time. Resolved to braving the cold for an expensive, unsatisfying cigarette, I downed the rest of my tepid pint without even wincing.

As I got up, Max walked in. The entire point behind my being in Fulham. He'd personally selected this fine establishment. He loved shit pubs, claiming they were more *authentic*.

"*Awww yeah!* Will, blud! *Amigo!* How's tricks, my main man?"

Maximilian Pearce was no longer just one of my most privileged and best friends; he was now also my landlord. I'd known Max since the first week of university, and fortunately for me, he seemed to feel an unquestionable loyalty towards me as a result. He was one of those people who managed to be highly unreliable and dependable at the same time. When Lucy had thrown me out, he had immediately come to my rescue.

Max had also pointed me in the direction of Curtis & Morgan following graduation. His father was a close personal friend of Jeremy Morgan. I got the feeling Max's most recent charitable offering of accommodation was born slightly out of a ridiculous feeling of responsibility. Ridiculous, but nevertheless highly welcome. It gave me the opportunity to use London as a location to wallow in despair. The alternative was to head back home to Rotherham and live with my mother and stepfather. A far, far worse proposition.

Max slammed a hand onto my shoulder and grasped me firmly with a grimace. This was him letting me know he was still concerned about me. "How the devil are you, eh? Salvation cometh in licensed establishments, eh?"

You'd think we hadn't seen each other in years. Max was one of those people capable of energising any situation simply through sheer unblinking enthusiasm. Blessed as an eternal optimist with buckets of self-confidence and a booming voice, he was the quintessential life of the party. We were absolute polar opposites in that respect, but we complemented each other well. I was the yin to his yang.

"Salvation would be stretching it, mate," I replied. "What about you? How was the interview?"

Max had lost his job around the same time I did, though you'd never in a million years have guessed it. His family connections hadn't quite been enough to save him from the fact that he was completely awful at his job.

"Superb, mate! Absolutely superb! You know, I think I may have nailed it. Two of the panel were friends with the old man. Two of the bastards! One of them, doddery old fart, even went off on some misty-eyed old anecdote about the old bugger. *Awww yeah!*"

I tried to appear pleased. Max, picking up on my air of desperation and checking himself for potential insensitivity, abruptly changed his maniacal grin to one of genuine concern.

"Chin up, Rodders, eh? Nuvva beer?"

"Sure. Cheers, mate."

Max returned from the bar with two pints of bitter and accompanying double whiskies. He downed one of the shots and thrust the other into my hand before raising his pint. "To the future!"

I nodded, downed the whisky and groaned. The pain of its slow scorching from throat to stomach lingered. I wondered briefly whether I might be getting an ulcer.

Max slammed his glass down on the faux oak tabletop and cheerfully took in his surroundings. "Good to get over to the other side of town, eh? Mind you, wouldn't want to bloody live here!"

"Why *are* we here, Max? I thought your interview was in the city."

"Because, geez, there's someone I want you to meet!"

"Right... Who, exactly?"

"Just an old chum, you know—an *amigo!*"

"Ah, a friend, then. Any chance you're going to tell me why?"

His raised eyebrow and the gentle stroking of his chin between forefinger and thumb told me he wasn't. I shrugged. I wasn't overly bothered; the booze was starting to soften my hangover quite nicely.

Max failed at subtly checking his wristwatch. He was clearly more excited than usual. His rhythmic head-nodding and foot-tapping had him on the verge of actual bouncing.

"You seem pretty… stoked to be seeing him again?"

"Yes! Yes I am, Rodders! How could you tell?"

"Well, Del Boy, I'm extremely perceptive."

"You know me, mate—just love meeting up with old bros. But this chap is something special! He's without a doubt one of the most interesting people I've ever met —and I've met a shit-tonne of people."

"I see. And does he have a name, this *chap?*"

"Nyles Henry! We were at school together. Well, he was a couple of years ahead, but, you know—cut from the same cloth. Anyway, he's been AWOL for some time and I can't wait to find out what he's been up to—he's an absolute ledge-bag!"

I stared blankly, waiting for some sort of justification for this accolade, but none came. The name did have a vague ring to it, though, and just as I was about to seek further clarification, he appeared as if from nowhere.

Nyles stood before us, carrying a tray with a fresh round of pints. As he sat it down, we both stood up. He and Max immediately clasped in a manly embrace with plenty of back-slapping while I stood awkwardly to the side, awaiting the obligatory handshake. Even with my relatively poor judgement of aesthetics, my immediate impression was that Nyles was extremely handsome—smooth, sculpted features and a strong jawline. And there was a familiarity to him, as if I'd met him somewhere before—and recently, too.

"Maximilian, brother! It's good to see you."

"Nyles! Mate! How the devil are you, you absolute fiend?"

"Good, brother, very good."

"Still causing mayhem with the ladies, no doubt?"

"You have to have some competition!"

Max turned to me. "This is Will—a dear friend of mine from uni."

"Will, yes, brother—we've met before, no?"

I blinked in surprise. "We have?"

"Some godawful party in Holborn, wasn't it? Just before Christmas?"

A-ha—Mr Hugo Boss!

Nyles clasped my hand between both of his like an old friend. His dimpled smile continued with a hint of a smirk that suggested inexhaustible amounts of raffish charm. The man oozed confidence from every pore. I could see why *causing mayhem with the ladies* was the status quo.

I wasn't exactly in a place to be seduced by him—in fact, I was pretty sure I hated him. Having said that, I warmed to him. Rapidly. It was impossible not to. I don't think I'd ever met anyone quite so... *engaging*. The guy was just so interesting—he reeled you in immediately. He was witty and articulate, and he'd done so much. Once the stories began to flow, minutes galloped towards hours and the three of us became progressively more inebriated on a continued procession of Scotch and pints.

Nyles was a reasonably successful entrepreneur who had dabbled in a number of fields including finance, tech and media. This provided him with an almost endless stream of slanderous anecdotes involving celebrities, Premier League football players and politicians. If even half of what he claimed was true, he was a walking tabloid journalist's wet dream.

Nyles was egged on by Max, who for once seemed more than happy for someone else to be the centre of attention. In comparison to his highly detailed anecdotes, Nyles remained pretty vague about what he'd been up to recently and why he'd been AWOL. After a while, Max gave up and stopped haranguing him about it, pressing him instead for more dirt on catwalk models and reality television stars.

I was in danger of forgetting my entire miserable predicament when Nyles directly enquired about it. Just as I'd decided I genuinely liked him.

"And yourself, Will? How are these lean times treating you, brother?"

"Erm, well, not so great... I'm—well, I'm out of work."

"Perfect! You should go and work for Nyles-ey!" Max's outburst was almost cut short as he overbalanced on his chair's two back legs, but he caught himself just in time and managed to regain some composure. "Seriously, though, it could be perfect! Think about it, Rodders—if there's anything going on, of course?"

I laughed at the notion. Me, a desk jockey at best, suddenly catapulted into the mainstream of the rich, powerful and famous as Nyles's awkward sidekick, doing whatever it was he did. I could see it now—tripping over the red carpet and landing on flat on my face in full view of the cameras. No chance!

"*Seri-arse-ly!*" Max roared, alcohol having removed what little self-regulation of volume he had.

Nyles smiled and shook his head. "No, I'm afraid I'm out of all that glitz, brother. I'm taking a break—it's become... unfulfilling."

"*Unfulfilling?*" Max barked incredulously. "What exactly is *unfulfilling* about having access to a constant supply of smoking-hot famous women?"

"Well, I admit I wasn't specifically referring to that aspect. It's just—well, I've been working on a new project."

"A-ha! I knew it! You have yet another *cunning plan?*"

"Something like that, brother."

"Well? Go on, then!"

For the first time that afternoon, Nyles seemed hesitant, giving me a sideways glance. Was he working out if he could trust me or whether I minded? I nodded enthusiastically, which seemed to reassure him.

Despite the staggering amount he'd drunk, he spoke clearly and deliberately. It was bizarre—there was a clarity to his speech that was mesmerising, almost hypnotic; it sounded as though he hadn't touched a drop.

"I want to help people deconstruct their lives—and take back control."

Nyles paused, perhaps for dramatic effect, but possibly just to see whether we were in a fit state to fully understand him. Max and I sat, gently swaying, and waited for him to go on.

"People have lost control of every aspect of their lives. We think we're free—but the modern world generates nothing more than a second-rate illusion of freedom."

Another pause.

"We have never been more trapped. We're restricted *every* waking hour by some aspect of our lives: our jobs, our relationships, our health—the newspapers we read, the websites we visit."

I had no idea where Nyles was going with this, and judging by Max's poorly disguised expression of total confusion, I wasn't alone. The messiah was preaching to imbeciles.

"And you know what? I think underneath it all, people are sick of it. I believe evolution is the answer—and that's exactly what I'm going to offer! I'm going to offer people the chance to evolve."

"Now you've lost me..." I slurred quietly, while Max raised both hands in surrender.

Nyles nodded and gave us both a kind smile. Apparently it was okay that a new world order had been announced and neither of us quite had the nous to grasp it. "I am going to set people free! Help them transcend whatever elements of their life are holding them back."

"Like a life coach or something?" Max asked.

"No, brother, not like a life coach."

"Well, what then?" Max was now looking more confused than ever. Even more than the single time I'd seen him leaf through one of his economics textbooks at university.

"I'm going to offer something far more radical. I'm going to offer people the chance to undergo their own *Deconstruction*."

"*Deconstruction...?*" I echoed.

"Yes. I'm going to help people *Deconstruct* their lives to allow them to regain control. And for those who want it, I'll give them the greatest opportunity of all."

"Which is...?" I asked this more to look like I was still following him than anything else. Max had tapped out some time ago.

"A blank canvas."

"A blank canvas...?"

"Yep. Freedom to start all over again, but with a brand new hand—maybe even a different pack of cards altogether." Nyles clapped his hands together.

Taking his cue, Max began nodding enthusiastically. "Sounds revolutionary, mate!"

"All revolutions are doomed, brother. The very definition of a *revolution* is steeped in irony—a circular movement of an object around a point of rotation. You'll always end up where you started. History is crammed full of examples of this: political persuasions drifting to and fro, ideologies swinging from left to right..."

"I just meant it sounds like a great idea, old boy..."

"It is, brother—I'm just saying that *evolution* is the answer. Society needs new ideas, not old ones rehashed!"

"Either way—bloody awesome stuff, mate!"

Nyles returned Max's praise with another smile. It was hard not to be pleased with him. After all, he'd entertained us for the best part of an afternoon and an evening. I hoped it worked out for him, whatever *it* was.

"Now, who's for another pint?" he asked. "One for the road?"

As Nyles headed off to the bar, Max turned to me excitedly. "*Awww yeah!* What about that?"

"What about what?"

"Farkin' 'ell, Rodders! About his *idea*?"

"Aw, mate, I haven't a clue—it didn't make any sense to me," I admitted. "But then again, I'm absolutely hammered, and for once I'm bloody glad I don't have to get up for work tomorrow."

6

LIFE-STRUCTURING

THE DAY AFTER MEETING NYLES, I woke with a continental-sized hangover. The evening's final conversation was archived deep in the recesses of my subconscious while I concentrated entirely on the more important task of self-loathing. Hangovers took on a new dimension when you were depressed. I don't think I even managed to get dressed for the rest of the week.

It was mid-February. I had finally reached my nadir. It had been four weeks since I'd moved into Max's place. I had used everything at my disposal to fill my excessive amounts of free time slumped on his vintage designer chaise longue. I read his extensive collection of *Men's Health* magazines. I flicked through the minimal collection of coffee table books —obscure, but clearly carefully selected for their potential to impress visiting women. I watched DVD box sets—a great deal of them: American sci-fi, English comedies, Scandinavian dramas.

I rewrote my CV repeatedly. I applied for the meagre smattering of jobs that were on offer, knowing that they'd already selected the recipient in-house or that there was no actual job available. The *fake job* was particularly irritating —everyone seemed to be doing it. Appearing to be actively recruiting helped companies create the impression that things were not quite as bad as they were. The illusion of waving, not drowning.

After a day spent staring into the abyss, I'd genuinely look forward to Max arriving home—to human contact and possibly even something that could pass for actual conversation. It was the highlight of my day. Unfortunately, being a wealthy bachelor in his mid-twenties, Max was seldom home, and his presence became a rare treat. Time with Max was now essentially the entirety of my pathetic social life. The vast majority of my "friends" had been mine *and* Lucy's. They sided with her. It was fair enough—given her social standing and my present predicament, she was by far the more attractive option.

If Max wasn't home by seven, I'd throw on my battered trainers and ageing thermals and hit the streets. The more depressed I became, the longer I ran. At least I was doing something to offset all the calories from comfort food and alcohol. Running became almost meditative, to the extent that sometimes entire blissful seconds would pass where I'd forget everything.

I spent hours pounding the streets south of the river. They became my one dependable constant. Streetlamps and houses drifted by as the damp tarmac passed beneath me, bathed in an amber glow. The streets were deserted. At times it was hard to believe I was running through a capital city. Occasionally I'd pass houses where the curtains hadn't been drawn—I'd catch glimpses of living rooms shrouded in the holy warmth of central heating. Fleeting moments of other people's happiness.

On the rare occasions when I caught Max, he seemed to

have something on his mind. An aloof distance had infected his usual outgoing self. I tried confronting him over it, but he dodged questions or changed the conversation. Finally, on a particularly wet and miserable Tuesday evening, Max broke his silence over a Chinese takeaway.

"*Aww yeah!* Dinner is served!" He dumped the assortment of overflowing white plastic bags on the coffee table and bowed ceremoniously, allowing the annihilation to commence. "Will, mate, I've been doing some thinking..."

"Hmmm?"

"About Nyles' idea."

"Hmmm?"

"It's funny, isn't it? You don't see someone for years and all of a sudden they're absolutely farkin' everywhere!"

I nodded in encouragement while chewing furiously. Mr Chan's Szechuan beef, while presenting extremely good value, required some fairly intense mastication.

"I suppose he *may* have sought me out... but then again, there's nothing actually wrong with that, is there? Besides, you don't get far without being a bit resourceful, do you, Rodders?"

"Hmmm?"

"It's just—his idea, it's like... It's just so good! Really fucking good! And that's a rare thing these days. You know, sometimes it's like there isn't a single original thought in the world..."

I choked the beef down and wracked my brain for what Nyles' *really fucking good* idea was. I remembered something about giving people a blank canvas—some vague spiritual-sounding life-structuring rubbish. But surely this wasn't what Max had been stewing over and was now talking so wistfully about—was it?

"Seriously, mate—what are you on about?"

"His *Deconstruction* idea! The one he talked about in that shite pub—the one where people Deconstruct themselves and start again fresh! It's pretty neat. I like it! And it's got a certain altruism about it too..."

"*Altruism?* Do you even know what that actually means?"

"Fuck off, of course I do! Anyway—it's the *idea* that's important. Nyles' idea is solid! Especially right now—these are desperate times. People everywhere are looking for a new start."

Max was grinning and nodding like a Labrador puppy on amphetamines. This all-consuming enthusiasm was a large part of his character, and it was pointless not letting it run its course. I sat back, picked up another spring roll and let him go on.

"So a couple of days ago I bump into Nyles in Georgio's —my absolute fave coffee shop off The Strand. You know the one?"

"The one you incessantly bang on about with the über-hot baristas?"

"Precisely! That's the one! Anyway, we get chatting, and out of nowhere I remember his new venture—the Deconstructing thing. So I bring it up. Anyway, he seems surprised—starts getting all coy. I've never seen him like that! He even gets rather ratty, as if he's upset I'm mentioning it."

"Maybe he regretted telling you about it?"

"Maybe, maybe! But that got me thinking—why would that be?"

"Maybe he's worried you'll steal his idea and make millions...?"

"Nope! The exact opposite, in fact! I called him on it,

and he asks how long I've got. Coffee then turns into a fairly spectacular boozy lunch."

This was not the most surprising thing in the world. Max lived for a boozy lunch.

"Anyway, turns out Nyles is absolutely obsessed with this idea. He's living and breathing it twenty-four seven. He's just frustrated he can't turn it into reality quick enough!"

"There's a surprise."

"Turns out all his money is locked up in three or four of his enterprises, and pulling any of it out in this climate would be fatal."

"Ah, I see... But surely—no pain, no gain?"

"Will, for fuck's sake! We're talking about people's livelihoods here—you of all people should be able to sympathise with that!"

I flinched. That was true, but a little close to the bone.

"Sorry," Max said. "I didn't mean to..."

"Don't worry about it. It's cool. I'd just never had you pegged as anything less than a ruthless capitalist."

"Wanker!"

"It's true."

"Yeah, to be fair, I am! *Aww yeah!*"

I declined his high-five.

"But that's the thing," Max went on. "This *is* a good opportunity to make some money! And doing a little good at the same time is an absolute bonus."

"Yep—important to remember that bit."

Max gave me one of his trademark winks. "Anyway, basically, Nyles doesn't have the cash end quite sorted, and that's what's stalling him. But! I'm pretty sure I can sort something out..."

"You're going to invest in this—*thing*?" I knew Max was

loaded, but pouring money into some vague, idealistic start-up in this climate was an insane gamble, even for him.

"God, no! I'll just have a chat with one of the old man's chums at one of the clubs. Maybe Beaconsfield's... I'll just wheel the dashing Nyles in—*et voilà*! You'd be amazed at how quickly the coin flows when they think there's even the remotest chance of buggery in the air."

"Right, well, thank God you're not going to piss away your own money at least. What does he need the cash for, anyway?"

"You know, the usual bollocks—office somewhere decent, somewhere central, etcetera, etcetera."

"Just an office, then?"

"Well, obviously a bit of petty cash to float things—publicity, wining and dining clients—all tax-deductible stuff. Oh! And a secretary! He even said I could help choose one. Which is something I think I'd be pretty exceptional at. *Aww yeah!*"

So *that* was how he'd hooked Max. From the way Max was grinning, you'd be forgiven for thinking that this particular aspect of Nyles' proposed venture *was* the opportunity.

"Anyway, mate, there was one other thing."

"Uh-huh?"

"Well, I sort of need to protect the investment a little, don't I?"

"I'm not sure you really can, mate."

"Look, I know nothing comes without risk, but I don't want things to spiral into some sort of horrific mega-debt, bankruptcy type situation."

"Right."

"Well, what I mean is, while I do admire Nyles, he does come with something of a reputation..."

"A reputation?"

"Yes, nothing too shady, of course—but I know of at least one person who's had their fingers badly burned with him... But everyone's had a bad stock tip from someone at some point—you can't hold grudges forever! And besides, I know of at least ten people who've come away from the table very much up."

"I see. So what's your plan?"

"Well, I rather thought I'd see if you were up for some temporary to permanent employment? You know—with benefits, of course."

"Are you serious? But I don't know the first thing about —whatever this is!"

"Does it matter? All I need is for you to watch the money side of things—make sure it doesn't get out of control, be my man on the ground. You're pretty good with numbers, aren't you? And besides, it's not like you're particularly busy around here! Every day I come home and expect to find you in some sort of wanking-induced coma."

"Thanks."

"Seriously! Why not?"

"Well, if you put it like that."

"So you're in?"

"Mate, you're offering me a job! I almost handed my CV in to McDonald's today, for fuck's sake—of course I'm in."

We finally high-fived over the remains of the egg fried rice.

The fact I had absolutely no idea what working with Nyles would entail didn't matter in the slightest. Right now, any job was better than none.

7

A STUNNING PANORAMIC

THE FOLLOWING week I met Nyles at Georgio's. Max's incessant prattle regarding the establishment had worn me down. Nyles was keen to look at a couple of potential office premises in the area and I was delighted to help. Leaving the house for once, with some sense of purpose, was something to be cherished.

Nyles didn't seem the type to be punctual, but nevertheless, I left the house early. Punctuality was one of the few things I did well in contrast to the rest of the world. I was surprised to arrive to find Nyles already seated and halfway through a coffee. He was early. Very early.

"Will!"

"Nyles." I extended my hand and he clasped it firmly in his trademark grip.

"Good to see you, brother!" Nyles beamed. He genuinely seemed pleased to see me.

We exchanged pleasantries and I enquired as to how the new venture was progressing.

"Yes—good! Really good, brother! I'm busy, though—

insanely busy. You know, always takes a hundred times longer to get something up and running than you think!"

"So, you've done something like this before?"

"Well, something similar—and certain things are universal: office space, secretaries, etcetera." Nyles pointed to a couple of highlighted properties on an A4 printout on the table. "We'll look at both of these, then grab a quick bite—and then maybe head over to a fantastic little tailor's I know, just off Savile Row."

"A tailor's?"

"Yes! Look, brother—you've got to look the part if we're going into battle."

"But I have suits!"

"I'm sure you do. But, ahem, how do I put this—I want us to reflect a particular type of image. Image is everything. And I mean this with absolutely no offence intended, but that suit is not quite the image we need to portray."

I looked down at what I had considered to be my best suit. Nyles' sympathetic smile mitigated any offence. I shrugged. "None taken, I guess. But..."

"What?"

"Well, I'm not exactly flush with cash at present. Things are a little..."

"Nonsense! Company expense, brother—I couldn't expect you to pay a penny."

"Really? Are you sure?"

"Brother, do soldiers buy their own armour, weapons, uniforms?"

"Well, I've no id—"

"Of course they don't. Now, you want a coffee to go?"

❧

THE FIRST POTENTIAL office we viewed was an overpriced basement: dimly lit with tobacco-stained yellow light and a strong odour of generalised dampness. Nyles did little to disguise his irritation that the estate agent had even brought us there. We made our excuses and left.

The second office was worlds apart. Hidden in a side street off The Strand, it was a beautiful five-storey building complete with Romanesque pillars standing sentry beside the entrance. The property's suave letting agent greeted us in the marble-and-oak ground floor enclave. He gestured us towards an old-fashioned steel grated door lift, which we rode to the top of the building.

"As you can see—classical architecture furnished in a contemporary style throughout," the agent purred. Nyles and I nodded approvingly.

The elevator jolted to a halt with a reassuring cast-iron thud. The concertina door opened onto the top floor's marbled hallway with an imposing dark wooden door at the other end. The agent paused outside, and once he'd milked the moment sufficiently, he exchanged glances with each of us.

"Brace yourselves, gentlemen."

As the door opened, Nyles stepped past him and derailed any further rehearsed sales pitch with a polite smile and firm handshake. "Many thanks, brother. We'll meet you back in the lobby."

The agent looked stunned. Nyles may as well have patted him on the head.

I followed Nyles into the office and he shut the door behind me. It was impressive, occupying the entire top floor and furnished by someone who knew what they were doing. Two large rooms were minimally decorated with a subtle nod towards modern Japanese design.

"Hmmm! How very, very Zen."

It was unclear if Nyles was being sarcastic, but he was definitely sold. The large south-facing windows gifted a stunning panoramic view overlooking the Thames. Nyles slid the heavy wooden window up in its frame, threw his head out and sucked in a great lungful of cold London air.

"Oh yes, brother! Now this is more like it!"

"It's unbelievable." I couldn't help smiling. The view was amazing. Open-mouthed, I followed Nyles into the next room.

"So *this* will be your office! I might occasionally use it for the odd meeting, but predominantly it's yours, brother."

This room was significantly bigger, with even larger windows. It was crazy—you could work for a lifetime and never even get close to having an office with a view like this.

"But where will you...?"

"I prefer to conduct business out-and-about, brother. There'll be a lot of logistics to sort out behind the scenes, so you'll need the office—you'll see! Besides, I'm no good at being cooped up. Just as long as I can use *that* chair whenever I want, I'll be more than happy." Nyles gestured to a deliciously worn leather armchair positioned in a corner of the room with a prime view out of the largest window.

"Sounds reasonable to me, mate. So, are we going to take it?"

"It'd be rather rude not to."

"Well, I mean, can we afford it?"

Nyles began to say something, then paused. He surveyed the room a final time and made for the door. "You leave it all to me, brother. Enjoy the view and I'll meet you on the ground in five."

Thinking Nyles didn't want me party to his negotiating skills, I gazed out of the window before taking the stairs back down. It would be incredible if we ended up working here.

The stairs seemed safer than the ancient lift, and my cowardice paid off. On the staircase, I briefly paused to let what was hopefully going to be one of my future office neighbours past: a pretty brunette in her mid-twenties with cropped hair and dark-rimmed glasses. She was dressed in an elegant and expensive-looking business suit. We politely exchanged smiles, and I was smitten. By the time I reached the lobby I had planned our entire life together.

I was yanked back into reality by the sight of Nyles gesturing dramatically to a distraught and flushed estate agent.

As I joined them, Nyles quickly turned to me and whispered, "Grab a cab and wait outside, brother." He spun back around and continued airing whatever grievances he had regarding renting the office. "It's just a little—crass. Yes, crass—there, I've said it."

"*Crass?*"

Ten minutes later, Nyles exited the building, shaking hands firmly with the estate agent at the entrance steps before surveying the street. I wound the window of the cab down and he walked over with an amused look on his face.

"Brother, it's time to celebrate—with at least a half-decent drink!"

"It is?"

"Indeed!"

"So you, erm, negotiated—well? We have the office?"

"Abso-fucking-lutely! Managed to drop the rent down by roughly fifty percent as well."

"Wow! How did you do that?"

"Simple, really. Bit of good-natured banter and a promise of couple of tickets to some gig."

"Wow, nice work! Which gig?"

"Oh, just some new up-and-coming French techno outfit he was fan of."

"Who?"

"Oh—so you're fan of French music?"

"Well, no, I've never really—"

"Don't worry, brother, no one really likes French music." Nyles gave me a wry wink as he jumped into the backseat with me. "Now—on to Soho!"

8

BRAND-NEW TAILORED SUITS

AN HOUR later I was standing in front of full-length mirror, having measurements taken for a single-breasted charcoal grey suit—Nyles' suggestion for battle dress. He was sprawled over one of the tailor's armchairs, sipping a very high-quality Scotch while idly leafing through a magazine.

I'd spent too long deliberating over the exact cut of the lapels and was now worried about the colour again. Perhaps it was a little too shiny. I didn't want to look like a Premier League footballer on a night out. I asked an extremely patient Nyles once again for his opinion.

"Relax, brother. A little flash and show never hurt anyone. Besides, how many suits do you own?"

"Two."

"*Two*? Genuinely—two?"

"Yes, two—that one and, erm, another one..."

"My God—how'd you ever manage at work?"

"I... I had a shrewd choice of shirts."

"Wow! Okay, look, brother—you can tell a lot about a man from the company he keeps and the clothes he wears.

You must remember that." Nyles smiled gently. *Here endeth the lesson.*

"Well, it looks like we're going to be spending a little more time in here than I'd anticipated."

On cue, the tailor's assistant appeared out of nowhere and topped up Nyles' glass and then mine with another healthy measure of single malt. This was definitely the way to buy clothes.

When it finally came to settling the account, Nyles was revealed to be a valued customer, managing to place the entire bill on credit. The Scotch had dampened down my frugal sense of concern and I didn't even ask what the damage was. This was incredible—after a second fitting I was to be the proud owner of three beautiful, brand-new tailored suits.

I barely felt the cold as we marched from the tailor's towards the heart of Soho. Nyles' appetite for decent Scotch had been whetted and we kept a brisk pace, heading towards one of his favourite whisky bars. As we walked, he passionately extolled the virtues of various Islay single malts. It was absorbing. Nyles seemed to have an inexhaustible amount of interesting facts about whatever topic he was talking about.

THE BAR HAD a modern Scandinavian feel, sparsely furnished with a light pine floor and matching tall pine tables and stools. An impressive array of whisky bottles loomed orchestrally behind a beautiful barmaid, also Scandinavian-looking.

"Samantha, *er det ikke?*"

The barmaid nodded, her face lighting up with Nyles' flash at her native tongue.

"*Ja!* And how are you today, sir?"

"Very, very well."

"Great! And what will you be drinking?"

"I'd like to introduce my good friend Will here to some of my usual favourites."

Samantha smiled and blushed as Nyles engaged her with small talk. There didn't seem to be any defence for his particular blend of charm and wit. It was like watching a hypnotist play with a submissive punter for the pleasure of the crowd: slightly uncomfortable, but absolutely mesmerising.

Nyles settled us into two minimalist armchairs in a corner within eye-catching range of Samantha. He then embarked on a grand tour of his favourite whiskies. Drinking spirits was something I did chiefly to get drunk quickly or fit in somewhere. Savouring their character for pleasure was new to me, but after a number of generous measures, I could see the appeal.

I was in a good place and happy to play audience to a skilled raconteur, but booze plus warmth does tend to make the mind wander. Nyles, perhaps sensing that he was losing me to a Scotch-induced slumber, excused himself. I became so lost in thought that I scarcely registered him returning. I was wrenched from a daydream by him grabbing my hand and shoving something into my open palm.

"Wakey wakey, brother! This ought to pick you up!"

"What? Oh, erm, thanks. Erm, what's...?"

"What do you think it is?"

"Ah, well, yep, I've got some idea..."

I slowly fingered the small oblong piece of cardboard

that been dealt by Nyles' sleight of hand. This was almost certainly a wrap of cocaine. Oh God. Cocaine. *Do I really have to do cocaine?* I wasn't huge fan of drugs in general—the sensation of not feeling quite in control was something I disliked immensely. But then again, I didn't want to appear ungrateful, or worse still, rude...

I'd only taken cocaine once before. It hadn't worked out well. At university, I'd been offered a similar-sized wrap by one of Lucy's visiting friends from London. I'd never taken the stuff before and certainly didn't want to look provincial by asking further questions. Unfortunately, my entire knowledge of cocaine consumption at the time was gleaned from *Scarface*. Subsequently, in a Tony Montana-esque move, I consumed the entire wrap's contents in one confident snort. I promptly had an anxiety attack so bad I thought I was going to die, as well as making an enemy for life of Lucy's visiting friend.

That was the sum total of my hard drugs experience. That and now this—another shiny cardboard wrap pressed between my already sweating fingers. Being in the same social circles as Lucy, I'd been presented with ample opportunity to reacquaint myself, but had always politely declined. Cocaine and I were not suitable bedfellows.

That was before, though. There was something about being in Nyles' company that made me feel more relaxed—why not try a little again? Maybe this time simply do less?

Nyles had gone back to tapping furiously on his Blackberry. If he could still be productive on the stuff, then really, what harm could there be in moderation? Expensive Scotch was a great catalyst for decision-making. I slowly got to my feet and carefully strolled to the gents', trying my hardest to appear sophisticated-drunk and not yob-drunk.

I locked the toilet cubicle and unfolded the wrap of

cocaine. The carefully folded rectangle was constructed from a flyer advertising a gentleman's club in the East End. Did suave Nyles have a more sleazy side? I cautiously tapped out a small quantity of the white powder on the top of the cistern—safely about a twentieth of the amount I'd consumed previously. I pushed a line together with the edge of my NatWest bank card, rolled a five-pound note into a hollow cylinder, placed it to my right nostril and inhaled.

No turning back now.

My nose burned with the battery acid–like searing that was immediately familiar. I sat down on the closed toilet seat and waited. *Enjoy the sensation.* My heart rate began to rise and I managed to quell a brief flicker of panic. *Enjoy the sensation.* I felt okay. I was definitely feeling okay. In fact, I felt pretty good. My Scotch-induced stupor was lifting.

This was already better than last time. A lot better. I briefly thought about doing more and decided against it. I didn't want to overcook things. Pleased with this decision and myself for making it, I flushed the toilet for appearances' sake and left the cubicle. I was still firmly in control.

I returned to the table to find Samantha delivering a fresh round of drinks and being captivated once again by Nyles' chat. We were now drinking some sort of whisky-based cocktail. My heart raced as Samantha smiled warmly at me and winked before excusing herself. As she walked off, I felt a surge of promise amplified by newly installed confidence. She had definitely winked at me!

"Lovely girl—and off at nine! I said we'd meet her and a friend for drinks. Every celebration should be blessed with female company when possible—don't you think, brother? By the way, what's your situation?"

"You mean with women?"

"Yes. You're unattached?"

"I—erm... Is it that obvious?"

"Haha! Only because most people in a relationship need to tell you about it, and you haven't."

"Well, yes. You're spot on. I'm single. Broke up with a long-term girlfriend at the beginning of the year. Still getting over it, I guess. What about you? I take it you're not off the shelf yourself?"

"Wouldn't dream of it, brother! I intend to live out my days as a content bachelor. I'll leave relationships for those who need them."

"I see."

"You've gotten back on the horse, though, so to speak?"

"The horse?"

"Yes! You know, back in the saddle?"

"A-ha! No. Not, erm, yet. Truth is, I haven't really met anyone. Haven't really been looking. Guess I just can't face it at the moment. I'm not great at the one-night-stand thing, anyway. I just think too much."

That was an understatement.

"Nonsense! You need to get laid, brother! Only way to get over *anyone* is to sleep with someone new, full stop. It doesn't even matter who! Same rules apply for both men and women."

"Right. Well, that sounds—definitive."

"Seriously! Give it a go, brother. If I'm wrong, then it's a terrible tragedy, but at least you got laid."

"Well, it's not like I'm averse to the idea. I just haven't really had the opportunity."

"Right! That's settled, then—tonight's the night."

"Well, if you're sure it's really going to be that easy..."

"That's the spirit, brother! By the way, while I remember—I have something for you."

"You do?"

Nyles reached into his wallet and pulled out a pearl-white business card, which he thrust into my hand. He rubbed his hands together in anticipation. "Well? What do you think?"

```
┌─────────────────────────────────────┐
│                                     │
│          DECONSTRUCTION             │
│                                     │
│            WILL HARPER              │
│         - EXECUTIVE DIRECTOR -      │
│                                     │
└─────────────────────────────────────┘
```

"*Executive Director?*"

"Ha! Thought you might like that! Everyone needs a title, no?"

"But I thought I was just going to look after the accounts..."

"Is that really all you want to do?"

"Well, no—I mean, I just thought, you know, it's just—Max said..."

"Max of all people will be *delighted* to see you take a more involved role. Now—what do you think of the *card*, though? It's only a mock-up—thought I'd run it by you before I go and get them printed."

"It's cool! Really cool. Simple, classy—but where're the contact details?" Were we really going to be so elusive and contemporary that we couldn't be contacted by conventional methods?

"On the back, brother! I thought we'd go for a rather more subtle approach."

WILL.HARPER@DECONSTRUCTION.CO.UK

I had to squint to see it, but the bar wasn't well lit. It was cool, but I was terrible at judging that sort of thing. It was definitely a lot slicker than the dull, soulless, standard-issue business cards I'd been given at Curtis & Morgan, now destined to remain forever in their cellophane.

"Nice! So, I've got a new email address too?"

"Yep! Registered the domain name ages ago. Quite minimalist, don't you think?"

"Yes. I like it, mate. Very cool."

"It's an exercise in branding, you see, brother! A sleek piece of personal publicity never did anyone any harm. I'm glad you're a fan." Nyles grabbed my forearm and squeezed it tightly. "I'm really glad you're on board with this! It's really good to have met you, Will."

We clashed glasses and enthusiastically entered into more frantic cocaine-fuelled chatter. A chemically enhanced Nyles was even more entertaining and animated with his anecdotes delivered like stream of bullets from a machine gun.

Nine o'clock came around remarkably quickly. Time was punctuated only by Nyles' frequent trips to the bathroom. I'd even cautiously decided to have another line myself. I still felt good. Perhaps even better.

Nyles was in the midst of a story from his time in India involving a sadhu, some type of holy man who spent his entire existence high on marijuana, when Samantha and her friend Hilda appeared by the table out of thin air. We both jumped to our feet, as good men should.

Samantha now wore her hair down, shoulder-length blonde locks of sunshine. A change in make-up made her look even more stunning. Hilda was taller and perhaps even more beautiful, looking as though she belonged on the runways of Paris or Milan. Next to her Samantha became girl-next-door-esque—which she most definitely wasn't. Well, not if you're from Rotherham, at any rate.

Nyles insisted we share a bottle of the bar's very best champagne before the four of us piled into a cab and skirted east along the Thames. We arrived at a club and Nyles nodded to the doorman as we strolled past the waiting queue like celebrities. We were greeted by a dimly lit, predictably good-looking bohemian crowd cavorting to a heavy minimal electro beat. The club was clearly *the* place to be seen, and looked like it might even remain so for at least a couple of months.

After a fresh round of champagne, we hit the dancefloor to join the sweating masses. A short while later, Nyles grinned at me as he turned to slide his arms smoothly around Hilda's waist. She reciprocated and leant into him. Nyles kissed her gently on the neck while winking at me, and Hilda melted into his arms. *How did he do that?* Nyles grinned at me again as he handed me another wrap of cocaine, albeit now with far less stealth.

I looked around for Samantha. She'd disappeared, hopefully only temporarily. But if I was honest, she'd probably found someone better-looking and sweating far less than me. It was hard to feel too disappointed, infused by cocaine and champagne. This club was cool and I was in a mental state of constant high-fives and back-slaps. I strolled off to the toilets, wrap in hand, with a confident swagger. One foot in front of the other. Still just about in control.

I collided with Samantha as I enthusiastically surged back out of the gents' towards the dancefloor. I was delighted—she genuinely seemed pleased to see me! I then made the mistake of presuming all Scandinavians must be liberated recreational drug-taking party animals and offered her the remainder of Nyles' cocaine. Unfortunately, my stereotyping missed the mark, and I was met with a sobering look of disapproval. She shook her head and walked away.

Shit! Shit! SHIT!

I finally caught up with her at the bar. "Look, I'm sorry —really sorry! I don't usually do this sort of stuff, honestly. This is only the second time I've, y'know, and I don't really even like it. I was just trying to fit in, with, erm, Nyles. We're celebrating, you see! I didn't mean any offence. I'm really sorry!"

"That's okay. I thought you were a good boy—not like the Nyles!"

"I am, mostly—well, compared to Nyles I probably am."

Samantha broke into a grin and took my hand. "I accept the apology. Come on—you can buy me a drink."

Sometime later, the two of us were dancing together like our lives depended on it, driven by feel-good harmonies and euphoric basslines, right in the heart of the dancefloor's throng of heaving bodies. There was a moment when Samantha pulled me close and tried to tell me something. I couldn't make out what she was saying, but it didn't matter. She started kissing me.

This is fantastic! This is better than fantastic—this literally never happens to me!

An explosion of self-confidence ripped through me as it dawned on me that Nyles might be right. I might even get lucky tonight.

9

ON FIRST IMPRESSIONS

THE FOLLOWING MONDAY, March 2nd 2009, we moved into our new office.

I collected the keys from the same suave, mildly irritating letting agent's office promptly at eight o'clock. We'd arranged to begin interviewing potential secretaries within a couple of hours of gaining access to our new premises. Max had been particularly insistent that this was of paramount importance and required immediate attention prior to anything else. He remained keen to play a pivotal role in the process.

I arrived outside the office armed with a tray of large coffees. Max was already there, excitedly pacing up and down on the pavement, talking loudly on his phone and completely oblivious to the volume of his voice, as per usual. He mouthed *Cheers, mate* while deftly selecting a coffee from the tray. I grabbed his newspaper off him and motioned that I'd meet him upstairs.

I climbed the stairs, still wary of the lift and vaguely hoping I might bump into the same pretty brunette from the previous week. It wasn't to be. I did manage to sneak a look at the brass plaque that hung outside the offices on the first and second floors: *Dixon & Sons*—a law firm. In my head, the brunette became a highly intelligent lawyer—one of the good ones: a public defender fighting just causes for the downtrodden man.

By the time I got to the top floor I was breathing hard. My ancient-lift phobia was possibly going to kill me. My exhaustion evaporated as soon as I opened the office door and once again saw the incredible view across the South Bank. I collapsed into Nyles' leather armchair and sat mesmerised until Max finally entered, still glued to his mobile. He grinned, rolled his eyes and mouthed, *For fuck's sake!*

I spent a pleasant hour idly leafing through Max's papers while he used the reception area to attend to his multiple phone calls. This was the type of start to a working day I could get used to. Max stuck his head around the door at frequent intervals, presumably to check no secretarial candidates had snuck past him. Each time, he gave me the same manic grin and another roll of the eyes. I caught snatches of frantic, important-sounding conversations. Max was clearly meant to be at his actual job.

Presumably having temporarily appeased his employers, Max came in to interrupt my daydreaming. *"Awww yeah! No-ice* view, Rodders!"

"Not bad, eh?"

"Christ, you can say that again! Hang on—how much are we paying for this fucking place?"

"Fifty percent less than we should...?"

"Awww yeah! Fair play! Hang on, what the fuck is going on with these chairs?"

"What do you mean?"

"Well, they just look a bit… Did you set them up like this?"

"Yeah, why?"

"Well, it just looks a bit like the poor girls will be facing a firing squad or something."

"Or—an interview panel? I suppose you thought the candidates would be sitting on your lap, did you?"

"Right, yeah. Okay. Fair point, mate. No, it's good actually—professional, I guess. Top work, mate!"

I'd set the office up with what was available. The minimalist approach to its design meant we weren't exactly blessed in the furnishings department. I'd moved the desk into the centre of the room and placed a chair facing it for the interviewees. In the absence of anything else, the leather armchair was on the other side of the desk, flanked by a much smaller chair and an ottoman. It was some stretch to describe it as *professional*.

Max became increasingly agitated as the time for our first interview approached. He paced like a greyhound on heat and at times I thought he might actually break into a slow jog. His idle chatter switched to a frantic monologue, a stream of consciousness spilling out completely unchecked. It would seem he had been looking forward to today for some time and was now very, very excited.

"What time is it?" he demanded.

"Quarter to ten, mate."

"Christ! Where the fuck is Nyles?"

"Jesus, Max, I don't know! He said he'd be here."

"Yes, but—*when* did he say he'd be here?"

"For the interviews."

"Well, when does the first one start?"

"Ten! Jesus, relax, mate."

"Exactly! That's in five fucking minutes!"

"It's in a quarter of an hour."

"Fuck's sake, that man!"

The front door's buzzer rescued me and I jumped up to answer it. The first secretarial candidate had arrived.

Perhaps I shouldn't have been surprised—it was Hilda. Nevertheless, caught off guard, I welcomed her in the most awkward manner possible. I offered to take her coat, realised there was nowhere to hang it and handed it back, red-faced. Coffee was then proffered, despite me having no method of producing any. Thankfully she declined. A coat stand and coffee machine were urgent priorities.

I was saved from further embarrassment by Nyles, who breezed through the same door a minute later—a little shy of fifteen seconds to ten. It was clear the pair had shared a cab, but Nyles shook Hilda's hand and smiled warmly as though meeting her for the first time. She beamed brightly and followed him through to the main office, where Max and a worn carpet were eagerly waiting. I smiled to myself. If Hilda and Nyles were going to keep up this ridiculous appearance, then I would as well. It was nice being in on a joke for once.

Max had strategically positioned himself in the central armchair and was attempting a contemplative look while surveying the view over the river. Nyles ignored the embarrassment of seating options and leant up against the wall by the window. I caught his eye and he returned a brief wry smile. Did he really want Hilda working for him?

Max enthusiastically devoured Hilda's CV, and after a brief round of largely unnecessary introductions, he launched into his questioning, which also soon transpired to be unnecessary.

"So, Hilda! I see you grew up in Denmark, of all places?"

"Yes. This is true."

"Fantastic! In Copenhagen as well?"

"Yes. This is also true."

"I've *always* wanted to go there! Tell me, what would you say are the highlights?"

"It depends what you like. What you are into."

"Oh, you know, the usual—art, culture, fine dining—generally letting one's hair down."

Max was oblivious to the awkward silence that followed. Hilda was less comfortable with a question that couldn't be answered with a binary response. She twisted a strand of hair and began to look irritated. From then onwards, the interview dragged on like a slow-motion bus crash into an abattoir. Max did the talking; I occasionally tried to steer him back on track, but eventually gave up. Nyles smiled warmly throughout the interview without saying a word—a masterclass in impartiality. Hilda's responses became shorter and shorter until every question was basically answered with a nod or a shake of the head. There was a predominance of head-shaking.

Thankfully Nyles decided to interject on account of the time and asked her if she had any final questions. She didn't. I showed her out and enthusiastically assured her that we'd get back to her. I suspected that despite her less-than-groundbreaking performance, she'd probably already gotten the job. I decided it probably wasn't the best time to ask about Samantha, and besides, she hadn't returned either of my text messages.

Back in the office, Max was grinning manically while slowly swivelling round on the chair. Nyles hadn't moved from the window. His arms remained folded.

"I quite liked her," Max said.

"Really? You don't say."

"Yes, Rodders—I *do* say! *Awww yeah!* Whatcha think, Nyles?"

Nyles was gazing out the window and seemed to be couple of time zones away. That view was seriously going to hamper our productivity.

"Nyles! What do you reckon?"

"Sorry, brother—reckon about what?"

"Her! The Swedish chick—Hilda!"

"I thought she said she was Danish?"

"Right, whatever, same diff, no? So, what did you think?"

"Ah, well, in that case, I'm afraid I'm in for a *no*."

"What? Why?"

"Well, brother, I think she just lacked that—*je ne sais quoi*, didn't she? Not always the warmest of people, the Scandinavians—particularly on first impressions, and first impressions are going to be extremely important for us."

Immediate shock, followed by an expression of careful consideration, crept over Max's face. Eventually he nodded. Nyles gave me a wink, which was presumably meant to suffice as an apology for wasting three quarters of an hour interviewing one of his prior conquests who he'd never had the slightest intention of employing.

The day wore on and the interviews quickly became relentless. But not for Max. He greeted each candidate with the same boundless enthusiasm, and after each interview, argued hard to give them the position. I was beyond caring, and by mid-afternoon would have happily given the job to just about any pathological sociopath. I began to wish I hadn't decided to pick this week to quit smoking again.

Nyles had vetoed every secretary bar one so far. The global financial crisis meant we had no shortage of applicants. Fifteen interviewees had been put through their paces, largely by Max. The only *maybe* from Nyles had been Veronika, a bright and cheerful Czech girl with generous breasts and a similar statuesque supermodel appearance to Hilda. Nyles clearly had a type. I thought Veronika's poor grasp of basic English should probably have counted against her, but apparently no one else shared this opinion.

By late afternoon I'd lost all hope and had accepted the prospect of daily stimulating conversations with Veronika, or, as Max gleefully referred to her, *Tits-on-a-sticka Veronika.*

A single candidate remained. Ms Adriana Fae.

Adriana came from a different dimension to the other interviewees. I suspected Nyles had done this deliberately —saved the best until last, but dismissed the idea, as it seemed like an elaborate waste of time without any obvious benefit to us. Well, with the exception of Max.

Adriana was and still is one of the most striking and elegant women I've ever met. She floated confidently into the office with the air of somebody who didn't take life too seriously. Her relaxed smile lit up the room as she greeted each of us in turn. My heart skipped a beat; I sensed Max's skipping several and possibly flatlining briefly. Even Nyles was no longer gazing out the window.

"Good afternoon, gentlemen! Hmmm... wow! A *bela vista*, no?"

She was the only interviewee to comment on this so far. She spoke with a soft, staccato accent and a huskiness likely owed to a lengthy appreciation of full-strength Marlboros.

"*Awww yeah!* It most certainly is!"

Adriana raised an eyebrow at Max's affectation as she possibly tried to work out whether he had some sort of brain injury. Max, unperturbed, hammered straight in there with the small talk.

"Do I detect some sort of accent there, Ms Fae?"

"Yes, you do—Brazil."

"South American, eh?"

"Yes. You are well read, Mr... Max?" She delivered the putdown in a jovial manner, making Nyles and me laugh out loud for the first time that day.

"So, erm," Max went on, "do you... have many Brazilian friends?"

"No. I only make friends with the Argentinians."

"Ah, I see... Argies, eh?"

"No. I am joking. Of course I have many Brazilian friends."

"Ah, I see..."

Finally at a loss for words, Max had met his match. It fell to myself and Nyles to fly through a couple of relevant questions, and we managed to wrap the interview up in half the time.

In addition to being both witty and charming, Adriana was undeniably beautiful. Possessing a statuesque body and an olive complexion, she had the most amazing emerald eyes that sparkled brilliantly against her thick, dark hair, as luscious as any shampoo advert. She was the type of woman that men would covet and women would want to be. Why on Earth did she want to work for us? Where had Nyles found her?

When Nyles brought the interview to a halt this time, it was unwelcome. "Any further questions, Ms Fae?"

"Yes. When do I start?"

"Ha! We'll be in touch soon. It has been a pleasure."

"The pleasure was mine, gentlemen."

We stumbled over enthusiastic goodbyes and fumbled handshakes before Nyles saw her to the door. He returned wearing a satisfied grin.

"So, gentlemen, I believe that concludes today."

"*Awww yeah!* Oh my God, man! What an incredible woman! And what a stunna."

"And Will? What do you say, brother?"

"I'm sort of forced to agree with Max for once."

"With our *Managing Director*, eh?"

"Yep, 'fraid so."

"How about we wrap this up so we can go for a drink? Let's put it to a vote, shall we? It would appear our two front-runners are the lovely Veronika, the Czech, and Ms Fae, the Brazilian. Can I have a show of hands for the lovely Veronika?"

Max and I exchanged glances. Nyles looked at both of us individually before shrugging and slowly raising his hand.

"Seems only fair."

"Really?" Max and I echoed in unison.

"And now for the equally lovely, although perhaps a little more so, Adriana? I see. Good. Well, two beats one, and thus, in the interests of upholding the principles of democracy—Adriana is our secretary."

Elated, Max punched the air. "Ha! *Awww yeah! Joga bonito*, as they say! That is awesome. And you know what—I've never actually *had* a Latina."

"Jesus, Max!" I exclaimed. "For fuck's sake, mate."

"What? It's true! There's a *huuuge* space on my list there."

"Will has a point there, Max, I'm afraid. As the Managing Director, it's hands off—you're in a position of superiority, brother. We don't want a sexual harassment lawsuit on our hands."

"No, of course. I just meant—well, look, she has *Brazilian friends*—she told us! Surely they're not off limits?"

"*Friends* is a different story. No problem there at all, brother."

Max, reassured, grinned with renewed delight.

"Right, gentlemen, I feel we should adjourn till tomorrow. Will, would you mind giving our successful candidate the good news? Max, could you possibly let the unsuccessful ones know?"

"*Awww yeah!* Absolutely! I'll let them down gently, of course. Possibly over a drink, or maybe even a meal. Surely that's okay? I mean, they're not employees, per se, and there's no chance of them getting the job now... You know, just to say 'Thank you but no thank you'. We've got to maintain a good reputation, after all. And besides, it'd be a tax-deductible expense! Either way, I don't mind dipping my hand into my own pocket..."

"Whatever it takes, brother. Whatever it takes. Now, shall we go and find out which watering hole is actually closest to this fine office? I believe there are a few."

I walked beside Nyles on the way to the pub. Max trailed behind, probably doing mental cartwheels to calculate just how many dates he could potentially fit into the next week.

"I was a bit surprised Adriana wasn't your first choice, mate," I told Nyles.

"Ha! Indeed—case of Czech-mate, eh?"

"And Hilda...?"

"I just thought it'd be nice for Max to meet her, brother. I think she and him would be a good fit—you don't mind, do you?"

"No, no—not at all."

It would seem the man had a plan, and in the grand scheme of things, it didn't seem too unreasonable.

10

DERRIDA, MY BROTHER

Thursday evening a couple of days later was intended to be our first business meeting. Nyles was keen to have these twice weekly to maintain focus. Monday mornings would be used to discuss upcoming business, and Thursday afternoons to reflect on the week's activity and discuss future strategy.

Following the interviews, Nyles and I had spent a tedious week working on publicity. Nyles' detailed strategy involved multiple adverts on the internet and in a broad range of the city's printed publications. I had spent the day following his instructions and liaising with the various advertising departments of said publications. It wasn't the most enthralling work. But it was work.

Max, setting a precedent, was unable to attend this first meeting and sent his apologies via courier. An expensive-looking crate of Belgian beer arrived at the office at quarter to five. The meeting kicked off five minutes later as Nyles cracked the caps of two generously sized long-necks and thrust one into my hand.

"Cheers! Looks like it's just you and me, mate," I said.

"True, but we have a quorum, and that should be chalked up as a success. Don't you think, brother?"

I nodded in vague agreement while admiring the beer's ornate label—7.8% alcohol! Jesus, this was essentially drinking wine by the bottle.

"Still, on the plus side, brother—it means there'll be a little more of this stuff to go round!" Nyles reached into his jacket and produced another meticulously folded wrap, tossing it onto the desk between us. This time the Essex origami was constructed from plain old vanilla card and not a strip club flyer.

My raised eyebrows gave away my disapproval—it wasn't even Friday, for God's sake.

"Steady on, brother! This is only because it's our inaugural business meeting. It should be at least a little celebratory in nature. Don't worry—it most definitely won't be happening on a regular basis."

"But we've got beer—very strong beer."

Nyles grinned and waved away my protest, and began carefully arranging a couple of generous lines of white powder on the desk with his credit card. "I'm told this is some of the finest Charles the capital has to offer."

"Mate, I think I might pass..."

"Really? How come? You planning on hitting the gym tonight?"

"There's no need for that! I just thought I should keep a clear head. Someone's got to keep a record of things..."

"Nonsense! Just tape it, brother. The desktop has a microphone. Adriana can type it up on Monday—it'll give her something nice and easy to do on her first day."

"But what about the drugs?"

"Simple: don't mention them—point and shoot. Besides,

do you think she's going to render her only source of income null and void on her first day?"

Sniffft. Nyles enthusiastically inhaled a considerable amount of cocaine and began tapping on the desktop's keyboard. Another line lay on the desk, temptation incarnate. My heart pounded in anticipation. I wished I hadn't had that three o'clock espresso. Was I really going to do this? Might this be the start of—a habit?

Oh, fuck it! You only live once.

Sniffft. The now familiar searing burned my nose. I sat back. It felt as though half my face was already numb.

"Good stuff, hey, brother?"

"Wow! Yes, it seems—strong."

"Good, good! Right. So let's recap." Nyles clapped his hands together and pressed a button on the keyboard. "*Voilà!* We are recording!"

"Great. So?"

"So! We've made a sizeable dent in this publicity and advertising bollocks. We need to concentrate a bit more on branding—probably need some sort of lo-fi website. Something really, really simple. A point of contact in case people are too wary to pick up the phone."

"Wary? Why would they be wary?"

"Trust me, brother—people are fragile beasts, and we'll be dealing with some very sensitive areas of their lives."

"Okay, cool. No problem. Do you want me to look into that?"

"Not at all! I know a guy—bit of a tech-geek, owes me a favour or two. What we need will take him no time at all."

Nyles nodded with conclusive satisfaction. Was that it? He confirmed proceedings had been brought to a head by tapping more cocaine onto the desk.

"Jesus, Nyles!"

"Relax! We've pretty much covered everything, haven't we?"

"Really? But, erm..."

"Something on your mind, brother? Speak!"

"Well, I guess, maybe... Well, what about—Christ, this stuff is strong!"

"Good, isn't it? Got it from a friend who buys it wholesale off some local Colombians. God bless globalisation, eh?" *Snifft.* "So! You were saying?"

"Right, yes. Well, I guess we've not really discussed how all this is going to work, have we?"

"How what will work?"

"This process! This —"

"*Deconstruction?*"

"Yes! I mean, well, how exactly are we going to—*Deconstruct* someone's life?"

"Well, brother, that's a good question." *Snifft.* "Fancy another?"

"No! Really, I'm good. Thanks. So, you were saying...?"

"Right! Yes! Deconstruction."

"What does it mean?"

"To dismantle! To take apart!"

"Yes, I know. But how the fuck are you going to do it?"

Nyles smiled and leant forward. "Well, brother—*we* are going to be guided, to some degree, by a certain twentieth-century French philosopher."

"I'm sorry?"

"You ever heard of a chap called Jacques Derrida?"

"Erm, no. Definitely not."

"Well, Derrida, my brother, was essentially *the grandfather of Deconstruction!*"

"Right..."

"I'm serious! Without him I'd never have come up with

any of this. Derrida taught me dismantling, taking apart, deconstructing anything—any idea, any concept, anything— can give us a greater understanding of it. Deconstruction allows us to look at something's individual parts and see whether the solution lies within it or within its reflection." *Sniffft.*

"Right. No thanks, seriously—I'm still good. You've, erm, lost me though—what reflection?"

"Look, brother, it's like this—Deconstruction removes all those pesky subconscious biases we have. Look at it like this: we constantly emphasise the importance of one concept over another: money over poverty, power over humility, light over dark. However, nothing is that simple! Deconstruction teaches that true understanding requires considering the object in question and its opposite—what is money without poverty, or light without dark? Savvy?"

"Erm, I think so..."

Nyles leant forward in his chair, locked his eyes on mine and grabbed my knee. My thigh spasmed as if a jolt of electricity had entered me. I got it.

"Deconstruction acknowledges that the solution to anything is not simple. Any idea or concept is complex, and can be contradictory in nature. Acknowledging this and embracing it can allow a true understanding."

"Okay. So, erm, how are we going to do this?"

"Well, that's it, brother! It's simple, really. Deconstruction is already there within us—we're just going to unlock it!"

"But *how*, exactly?"

"Well, clearly a universal approach to each individual just isn't going to be possible. We'll assess each client on a case-by-case basis. We'll conduct a highly specific, tailored Deconstruction for each individual. We'll meet with them, and over a series of consultations, we'll gather enough information to Deconstruct them as an entity—every aspect of their life: their problems, their past, their present will all be Deconstructed in order to focus on their future."

"So, essentially we *are* offering some sort of counselling service?"

This hit a nerve. Nyles launched himself out of his seat to tower above me. "NO! Not at all! This isn't a *counselling service*. I want people to Deconstruct everything in their lives to the point where they see nothing matters—only the moment in which they exist. Once they reach this state, they'll be able to see what elements within their lives underpin their misery and disillusionment. And *then* they'll be able to move forward!"

"Right. I just don't see how we're going to do that, practically speaking."

"Well, brother—let me give you an example! Take Mr Smith. Now, Mr Smith is your archetypal twenty-first-century British success story. A self-made successful businessman! An entrepreneur! Own business, hot little housewife. Lunches and tennis lessons, kids doing well at some reasonable private school. Nice house in Surrey, holiday home on the old Costa del Scorchio. All the trappings of success! But that's it—they're all just trappings. Mr Smith is *trapped!*"

Nyles paused to take a half-bottle swig from his beer and wipe his lips with the back of his hand.

"Now, Mr Smith begins to feel it—a gradual suffocation that creeps into those quiet moments. These moments get longer and longer, becoming a perennial uncertainty, until he realises one day that he's been unhappy for years. On the outside, yes, he appears the very picture of success—but on the inside he's drowning. Probably at the very least consid-

ering having an affair or taking up base-jumping or something drastic—anything to change the situation. But he can't
and he won't, because there's too much at risk. And that's
just it—he's fucked! Trapped by the trappings of success!
And then he cracks—BOOM!"

Sniffft. Crash.

I jumped as Nyles punctuated consuming yet another
line by violently slapping the desk with as much enthusiasm
as humanly possible.

"Fuck! Jesus, Nyles, take it easy."

"*Fuck* exactly! *Fuck* exactly, brother! And do you know
the best thing?"

"What?"

"I'll wager that there's hundreds, perhaps even thousands of people out there like this. People who appear to
have it all—but are *trapped!*"

Nyles sat back down, straightened his collar and took a
moment to compose himself, perhaps realising that his
wide-eyed maniac routine might be losing me.

"Look, brother, right now we have a tipping point—this
global financial crisis has given us a unique opportunity.
This perennial uncertainty is now on the front page,
exposed in all its ugly glory! People are scared—they've seen
just how fragile the apple cart is."

"Right. But, erm, aren't we targeting people at their
weakest?"

"At their *lowest*—yes! But we're setting them free. Don't
you see? We're going to turn all their introspection into
something real!" *Snifft.* "These are lean times, brother, lean
times. People in general are more uncertain and scared than
ever. In times of crisis, everyone questions everything—
people are questioning whether it's all worth it! And these

people, brother, these people we will set free before they do something worse."

"Worse?"

"Worse—overdose, suicide, acts of random violence. People do insane shit when they're scared! We'll actually be doing society a service."

Nyles got up again and walked over to the window, helping himself to another beer and handing me one too.

"Look, Will, I'm okay with you being cynical about the process. Questioning things is fine—healthy, even! I just need you to be completely on board with this. I need your full support if we're going to make this work. Can you do that?"

Of course I could. I would support anything if it kept me in a job, and who knew—maybe Nyles had hit upon something here. I'd heard worse ideas.

"Nyles, mate, I promise you've got my one hundred percent support."

11

BRAND-NEW COAT STAND

For as long as I could remember, Monday morning had generally been a horrific concept. The anxious, nagging idea of it creeping into a perfectly pleasant Sunday afternoon. A mild fever that insidiously progressed to an overwhelming septic state by the late evening—sometimes severe enough to prevent sleep itself. Except this Sunday, things were different.

Late afternoon saw me sprawled on the couch in post–pub roast bliss, actually looking forward to Monday morning. I felt inspired, enthused and ready to throw myself fully into this venture, even if it did seem a little crazy. Admittedly, I was also looking forward to meeting Adriana again. I hadn't quite managed to get our extremely striking new secretary out of my head. I'm sure I wasn't alone.

The weekend had been a good one. It felt as though I was beginning to surface from the darkness that had swamped me after getting fired and the break-up with Lucy. Max had been away for the entire weekend after organising a last-minute trip to Paris with one of the unsuccessful applicants that he'd had to *let down gently*. I'd had the flat completely to myself and had spent the weekend indulging in clean living: avoiding booze, eating well, running and lazily leafing through a couple of books on Buddhism Nyles had lent me. The books had a lot of appealing ideas, but I couldn't help finding them all a bit too idealistic. Perhaps it wasn't for me, but I could see the ideological appeal, and perhaps that's all that mattered.

On Monday morning I caught the first Tube on account of being wide awake at four a.m.—the downside to having a stupidly early night. The Underground was still sleepy, with a gradual trickle of bleary-eyed commuters avoiding the chaos to come. I let myself into the office building, hesitated in front of the archaic lift and decided once again to take the stairs. Completely out of breath by the time I reached the top, I froze as I saw our office door ajar at the end of the corridor.

Shit! Had we been robbed? Did we even have anything worth stealing? The computers, I suppose... My heart raced as I gently eased the office door open a little further and peered around it.

Instant relief. An immaculately dressed Adriana sat behind the large wooden reception desk, organising papers.

"Good morning, Will!"

"Hi! Erm, good morning. Erm, how did you get...?"

"Through the door—the normal way, no?"

"Ha, I see. I, erm, suppose it is."

"Coffee?"

"Wow, we have coffee? Coffee would be great! But please, don't get up," I protested. "I mean, I can—it looks like you're busy..."

Adriana smiled and walked over to the small kitchenette inside the walk-in cupboard cordoned off from the rest of the office by a sliding door. "Relax, Will, this is okay. It's just coffee, and besides, it is in the job description, no?"

"You have a job description?"

"Of course no—you want me to write you guys one?" She smiled again and shook her head. She was running rings round me! But then again, why shouldn't a Brazilian have a better grasp of sarcasm than me?

"So, erm, how *did* you get into the office?"

"I used a key. C'mon, Will!"

"Of course you did. Did you bring the coffee machine?"

"Do I look like a delivery man?"

"No, it's—"

"The machine came over the weekend and they leave it outside. Not so careful. You take milk?"

"Please."

"Foaming?"

"Excuse me?"

"Do you want the milk with the foaming? With the bubbles? How do you say this?"

"Yes please. Erm, frothed, I think."

"Sugar?"

"No thanks. Amazing—thank you!"

The coffee smelt and tasted incredible. This was a magical moment—I was never going to need the services of Canary Wharf's Costa Coffee again.

"And, erm, how'd you get a key?"

"Nyles—he dropped it to me yesterday."

"Ah, of course he did... How very kind of him."

"Urgh! *Não quero!* He is not my type, thank you!"

"Sorry! No, of course, I—I didn't mean to..."

"Ha! Relax, Will. You are just thinking that I cannot defend myself against his charms, no?"

As if on cue, Nyles swept into the office. I immediately

panicked that he'd heard our exchange and a wave of guilt-edged anxiety swept through me. He nodded to both of us before dramatically throwing his overcoat on to the brand-new coat stand—another new feature I'd failed to notice.

"Morning, all! I trust we all had fantastic and fulfilling weekends?" Nyles winked at Adriana, who mockingly returned an exaggerated one. Maybe even Nyles had met his match. He grinned amorously and nodded towards the coffee machine. "Excellent—coffee already brewing! Will, I need a quick chat with you in the office, brother."

"You mean before the meeting?"

"I'm sorry?"

"The meeting—given it's Monday?"

"Right! Yes, of course! Sorry—totally forgot. Adriana, can you join us in five?"

I followed Nyles into the office. The early-morning sunlight of a beautiful spring day was already pouring through the half-closed blinds. Shards of bright light caught dust motes in their lazy dance of perpetual slow motion. The building's central heating had already brought the room up to a toasty temperature.

Nyles motioned for me to shut the door behind me. "Good weekend, brother?"

"Yep, nice and quiet. Max was... *away*."

"Ha! That old devil! So—how did you get on with those books?"

"Good, yeah—really good! There's a lot of good ideas in there."

"Excellent. Some of those *good ideas* are over two and a half thousand years old."

"Really?"

"Indeed, brother! So, quick cheeky line?"

"*What?*"

"Jesus, Will—relax! Just a little joke!"

It was hard to tell. I wanted to believe him, but I wasn't good at hiding my residual uncertainty.

"Honestly—I am joking! I'm actually planning to have a bit of dry week—ended up having a fairly boozy weekend lubricating a couple of potential investors. One of them I've got to shoot out and catch up with again this morning."

"More investors? But I thought we already had some pretty decent capital behind us from Max's *connections?*"

"I know, brother, I know. But a lot of people are getting excited about this! It doesn't seem sensible to turn down investment—especially given the current climate."

"But we haven't actually done anything yet!"

"It's the concept, brother, the idea—people are seeing it as something fresh, something new."

"Right, well, erm, okay. So, do you want me to come along?"

"To be honest, it's going to be fairly dull. I've just got to head across town and get some documents signed—legal stuff. It'd probably be more productive if you stayed here and followed up on some of this publicity."

This was fine by me. I was pretty sure it meant I could legitimately get stuck into the morning's paper for at least an hour or so.

"Okay. Cool, no problem."

"Great! It'll also give you chance to get to know our new colleague a little better."

"Right, of course. I hear you paid her a little visit yourself over the weekend?"

"Yep, thought I'd drop off a key and her contract—get it signed and sorted."

"Couldn't have waited until Monday?"

"What? And had no coffee for us on arrival?"

"Right. I see."

"What?"

"Well..."

"*Well* nothing! Adriana and I are, and will stay firmly, on professional terms. I've been there, brother, seen it, and bought a collection of T-shirts."

"So, not something you'd recommend, then?"

"On the contrary, I couldn't recommend it more! But once you're one of the more senior chaps in a business venture, then—well, it's a little crass, a little... *cliché*."

"I see."

"*You*, on the other hand, could probably get away with it. I'd say the option's open—I take it you're still trying to get back in the saddle, no?"

"Well, yes, that's true, but that wasn't what I—"

"Good! Well, that's that sorted. Adriana! Could you come in now?"

Nyles gave me a lecherous wink and I felt myself blush instantly. Adriana entered, clutching a notepad, and I did everything possible to avoid eye contact.

Our first Monday morning meeting turned out to be a fairly brief affair. Nyles half-heartedly gave out some guidance regarding publicity while occasionally flirting with Adriana. His efforts were met with a nonchalant dismissiveness that was both amusing and refreshing to witness.

After twenty minutes or so, Nyles decided to call it a day and excused himself. On his way out, he made sure to deliver a set of parting instructions dripping in innuendo.

Adriana rolled her eyes as he left the room. "*Oh meu Deus!*"

"I'm sorry," I said. "He can be pretty relentless, can't he?"

"Yes, all the time, but he is harmless, I think."

"You don't mind?"

"His powers will not work on me."

"Really? You don't think he's...?"

"Ha! No! I am very happy with my girlfriend for now."

"Oh! Really? I'm sorry, I didn't mean to..."

"To what?"

"I mean, I, erm, didn't know... that you were, erm..."

"With a woman?"

"Erm, yes. Sorry."

"Relax, Will. I am not one hundred percent. At one time I could eat a man like that for breakfast! But I am not so hungry now."

"Wow, really? Well, I'm not entirely sure Nyles has picked up on that."

"Of course he knows, Will! He meets my girlfriend on the weekend."

"Really? The cheeky bastard..."

"Cheeky why?"

"Ha! Erm, no reason."

There was an awkward pause while Adriana seemed to try to work out what I was getting at, but then gave up. She shrugged and stood. "So, will we go to breakfast?"

"I'm sorry?"

"Breakfast—you know, to eat?"

"Right! Of course! I haven't eaten, but shouldn't we—"

"There's always time to eat! Come. There looks a nice place on the corner—I think maybe they have the croissants!"

"Georgio's?"

"I have no idea of the name, Will. Come on, let's go before it's the lunch!"

Georgio's was still fairly empty. I ordered coffee and croissants while Adriana retreated to the comfort of one of the new old-leather sofas.

There was no small talk during the croissant consumption. Adriana went straight for the conversational jugular, assessing my socioeconomic and personal status within the first five minutes. Normally, with my ridiculously uptight sense of privacy, I would have felt violated by her line of inquisition, but something about her warm, relaxed character made me open up easily. I gradually reclined on her psychiatrist's couch and began divulging everything—all the details of my relationship with Lucy and the subsequent pain and misery I'd been wading through. She was a fantastic listener, encouraging me to talk by pressing for extra details and constantly reassuring me that she was still genuinely interested in my outpouring of grief.

Looking back, in return I only ever really managed to coax the most meagre reciprocal details out of her. Her life to date and how she managed to end up working for a small, peculiar start-up venture in Central London remained a mystery. Any enquiries I made were deflected as she turned the conversation back to me until I gave up. The only things I still really know about her are that she grew up in São Paulo and that she'd moved to Europe a couple of years earlier, following a relationship break-up. Since then she'd lived in number of capital cities and done a number of odd jobs.

I made my way back from the counter with our second round of lattes in a good mood.

"And what about now?" Adriana asked when I returned.

"You mean—am I looking for a girlfriend?"

"Yes, for sure!"

"Not really. I mean, erm, I've not really met—"

"*O meu Deus!* You have not got laid since you are breaking up?"

I attempted to laugh this off as I became acutely self-conscious of my inadequate sex life being shared with the rest of Georgio's clientele, which had now increased significantly in numbers. True to form, I began to blush heavily while nervously looking around the coffee shop.

"Relax, Will! No one cares. And besides, there is no problem with this. It will come for sure! You are a handsome man, no?"

"Well, I don't... Look, it's just—well, I'm just not very good at that sort of thing."

"I think maybe you are too nice, no? It's okay, Will. Women sometimes just want to fuck."

"Jesus! Is that so?"

"Look, if you have no one in a month, I will introduce you to a friend."

"Really? I'm not sure that—"

"For sure, for sure! I have a friend, Isabella. She is a total slut—it is almost disgusting."

"*What?*"

"Relax! Again, Will, I am joking!"

"Ah, I see."

"She would eat you alive. So, you really have met no one you like—even a small bit?"

Inevitably, after significant cajoling and partly in desperation to move the conversation on, I mentioned the girl I'd passed on the stairs.

Adriana shifted up a gear. "This will be the first office romance! So, what is her name?"

"I literally haven't a clue! I just passed her on the stairs —nothing more."

"Well, I shall be the detective!"

"Detective?"

"Yes, you know—the one who solves crimes, like the Sherlock Holmes."

"Yes, I know what a detective is, I meant—*how* will you find out about her?"

"Simple! A law firm has secretaries too, and us secretaries—we talk. I already know where they go to smoke."

"But I don't know if she even works there!"

"This is true, but if she does—you will need help. I think you may be a bit shit at this, no?"

"Thanks."

We sat and talked until the early lunch crowd started to filter in and the staff began to give us irritated glances. My hyperawareness of such things contrasted beautifully with Adriana's nonchalance, but she reluctantly agreed that we should head back to the office and at least attempt some form of work.

12

STRICTLY BUSINESS

MONDAY AGAIN. This time a little late. I'd gambled on the snooze button and lost. Not that it really mattered, but I still prided myself on punctuality being one of my strengths. I jogged through the unrelenting drizzle from Max's flat to the temporary sanctuary of the Underground. The train's presence on the platform urged an obligatory sprint out of me down the remainder of the escalator. I arrived just as the sliding doors slammed shut with a loud *fuck you*.

Sweating and panting, I tried to catch my breath. The uncomfortable closeness of the underground climate was amplified by my too many clothes. The train pulled away after an unreasonably long moment with a self-satisfied swoosh.

As I slowly brought my eyes down from the heavens, I was greeted by a new advertisement billboard bathed in the anaemic glow of artificial light.

DECONSTRUCTION ?

I took a sharp breath. A strange mix of excitement, tinged with the ever-so-slightest amount of panic, passed through me.

This was becoming real.

Up until this point I'd naively thought that I'd been kept abreast of all the publicity and advertising we'd done. This was clearly not the case. Despite feeling a little put out, I couldn't help but be impressed. It was eye-catching. It was intriguing. It was cool. And I was only slightly irritated by how it left no way for the reader to find out any further information. A wry smile crept onto my face—had Nyles chosen this Tube station specifically?

Jogging from Southwark to the office saw me shave valuable minutes off my margin of lateness. The subsequent small amount of self-satisfaction completely evaporated when I was greeted by an immaculately presented Adriana while catching a whiff of my own body odour. Acutely aware of our office's lack of shower facilities, I vowed to head out mid-morning to buy some deodorant from the nearest Boots.

"Morning, Will—*café*?"

"Morning, Adriana! Please. Sorry I'm late—bloody snooze function."

"Snooze function?"

"The snooze, on the alarm clock. Never mind. Good weekend? I don't suppose you've seen Nyles this morning?"

"Ahem, no. But he called and he will meet you at the lunch with Max."

"Lunch?"

"Yes—the meal we have between breakfast and dinner. It is normal to eat this in the middle of the day, no?"

"Thanks, Adriana."

Adriana grinned to herself as she poured a couple of mugs of piping hot coffee and handed me one.

"Hmmm, thanks!"

"It is my pleasure."

"So did Nyles mention where or why we're having lunch?"

"He did. And it is somewhere very, very nice! You may want to change your shirt..."

"Really?"

"Yes, really. And maybe some cologne would be good also..."

"Yes, sorry, I know—I ran because I was... Anyway. Where am I heading?"

"The lunch? Somewhere very nice—*the Savoy*! At one o'clock, and drinks before at twelve o'clock at the lobby bar."

"Wow! The Savoy, eh?"

"Yes, I know. Very nice, no?"

"And you? Are you coming?"

"No, this is a *strictly business* lunch, but Nyles—he is

very kind and tells me to take the afternoon off. So I will get a facial, a manicure—have some time to myself."

"Right! Well, that's excellent. Not a bad start to the week for either of us, eh?"

My God—lunch out! What a blessing. My self-enforced economy drive plus lack of culinary imagination meant I was getting extremely sick of sandwiches and Super Noodles. It was like being a student again—that first paycheque could not come soon enough.

I sipped my coffee while dreamily gazing out of my office's large bay windows across the river, a swollen torrent from the recent rain. A sip of the Colombian blend slapped me in the face, injecting me with a surge of enthusiasm. The trouble was, I didn't have anything to do with it.

All the books were up to date. Though admittedly, I had just discovered another of Nyles' outlays, but I could ask him about that at lunch. I should probably enquire about any other unaccounted spending, but it didn't really matter too much—I'd have the month's credit card bills by the end of the week. The damage done would soon be clear enough.

Now restless and caffeinated, I wandered back into Adriana's office. "So, I take it the Monday morning meeting is, erm, cancelled?"

"Not *cancelled*—moved to the lunch."

"Right, I see. Well, erm, is there anything that needs doing?"

Adriana twirled her chair round to face me loitering in the doorway. She stuck her bottom lip out in an impressive mock pout. "Oh, *poor* Will—you are so bored and have nothing to do?"

"Well, erm, yeah."

"I will make a deal. You come and keep me company for one cigarette and I will give you the news I have."

Immediately intrigued, I obediently followed her out to the lift, forgetting to grab my jacket. Outside, I politely declined a full-strength Marlboro while tucking my hands into my armpits and bouncing on the balls of my feet to try to generate some warmth.

"You should try one for the heat, no?" Adriana prompted.

"Really, I'm fine. So, you mentioned some news?"

"*Sim*, I did—but you must try to be relaxed when I tell you, okay?"

"Well, I can definitely *try*."

"Good! So—I have you a date!"

"Sorry?"

"A date, Will! You know, you go out with somebody nice and spend some time..."

"Yes, yes—but who with? And when?"

"With the girl!"

"Which girl? With your friend, the, erm..."

"*O meu Deus!* Isabella? No way! She would destroy you. With the girl you talk about last time. The girl on the stairs! The one you meet the other week!"

"But I didn't *meet* her! I can't just..."

Adriana shrugged and blew on the lit end of her cigarette in an exaggerated gesture of indifference.

"Fine—apparently I can. But how did you...?"

"Will, this is a women's secret—you know I will have to kill you before I tell you."

"Look, that's very kind, but I'm not sure I feel entirely comfortable with—"

"Relax, Will! I just take a little smoke with one of the secretaries from the office downstairs—Melissa is her name. Nice girl—a little boring, but nice. Anyway, I investigate like I said, and—ka-boom!"

"Ka-boom?"

"Yes, *ka-boom!* Explosion! I find out everything about your girl. Well, everything important. She is single and her name is Catherine—Miss Catherine Harding! Good, strong English name, no? Anyway, so Melissa and me, we talk and talk—almost every day now—mostly just the bullshit. Anyway, I ask for a date for you. She thinks a while, then she says—*Fuck, okay! Why not?*" Adriana paused to expertly light a new cigarette from the dying embers of the one she was smoking. "You see—*ka-boom!*"

"Right—well, yes, I mean, great. No, it's great! I guess I just wasn't prepared..."

"So, where will you go?"

"Erm, Christ! I've no—"

"Up to you. But I have plenty of ideas. Here, I have her number. She is awaiting the call from you!"

"Thanks, Adriana, that's, erm... great!"

"*O meu Deus!* Will, you mess this up, you make me look bad, and I will kill you—for sure!"

Adriana grinned emphatically, extinguished her cigarette and opened her expensive-looking purse. She retrieved a business card from the law firm downstairs—Dixon & Sons. On the back in elegant biro scrawl was a mobile number. *Catherine's* mobile number.

HAVING ABSOLUTELY nothing to do afforded me a decent couple of hours of solid daydreaming before arriving extremely early to lunch. I was in good spirits, having mentally played out a dozen or so detailed eventualities that *could* slash *would* occur with Catherine, formerly *the girl*

on the stairs. Things progressed well in each fantasy, all resulting in some combination of a nice house somewhere in the home counties complete with 2.4 children, plus or minus a dog.

The Savoy's lobby was as regal as I'd expected. I strode through it towards the bar. I planned to start a tab, order something appropriate to the surroundings, and soak up said surroundings sufficiently enough to appear completely at home by the time the others arrived. Annoyingly, though, Max was already sitting at the bar, enthusiastically chatting up a smartly dressed waitress. My irritation dissolved upon seeing his eager, beaming grin.

"*Awww yeah!* How are tricks geez?"

"Very good, mate, very good! How was Paris?"

"*Formi-dable*, Rodders! *Formi-dable!*"

Max ordered two old fashioneds from the waitress, who nodded and smiled with an impressive degree of profes- sional patience. She walked off gracefully with Max's eyes following her. I waited until her tight charcoal skirt was out of view before attempting to engage him in any form of conversation. Eventually his nods of approval stopped, leaving only a lecherous grin behind.

"So, good trip, then?"

"*Awww yeah!* Absolutely splendid! Top, top bird. Did it all—walks along the Seine, good food—*beaucoup de* banging."

"Great, I've really got quite the sordid picture there. So, will you be seeing Hilda again?"

"Well, maybe—I dunno, mate. Beautiful little Scando thing—very much my cup of tea, but..."

"Yes?"

"Well, I sort of made plans with Elizabeth in Berlin for next weekend..."

"My God, really? That ridiculously intense art student? The one who likes to sculpt mutilated female genitalia?"

"*Awww yeah!* That's the one, old boy!"

"Jesus Christ. I thought she was..."

"Gay?"

"Well, not gay, just not quite pro-male... Regardless, I just didn't quite see the two of you hitting it off, that's all."

"I think the jury is still out on that one, Rodders. Plus, she's a massive Bowie fan, and turns out, so am I."

"David Bowie?"

"Yeah! I love that 'Rocket Man' tune."

"For fuck's sake, mate—that's Elton fucking John!"

"You sure about that?"

"Dear God. So, is there anyone we interviewed who you *aren't* taking for a weekend away?"

"Of course there is—some of the less promising ones I'm just having dinner or coffee with. So! Tell me—how are things at the old HQ?"

"Good, mate. We're ready for action, I think."

"Excellent! And what about that fantastic secretary-ologist creature?"

"You mean Adriana?"

"Yes! Are things evolving there? Office-based romance and all that?"

"No, it's all strictly business at the office. Not for want of Nyles' trying, though."

"Really? He's trying to sneak a piece of the pie, is he? Crafty blighter!"

"I don't think so. He's encouraged me to, though, despite the fact he knows she has a girlfriend."

"*Lesbian*, eh?"

"Well, right now she has girlfriend."

"*Bi?*"

"Yes. Do calm down, mate."

Our old fashioneds arrived and we were informed our table was ready. We arrived to find Nyles at a table smartly laid for multiple courses, aggressively chewing a cocktail stick while tapping furiously on his Blackberry. He was dressed in a burgundy suit with matching shirt. He looked sharp, but there seemed a reasonable chance this was a man who had already done significant amounts of cocaine today.

"My brothers! Good to see you both!"

"Nyles, you rascal!"

"Max, my man! Long time no see. I hear you've been gallivanting around Europe?"

"*Awww yeah!* Well, one tries..."

Dinner descended into a champagne-fuelled orgy of degustation excess, garnished with lobster and Kobe beef with truffle stuffed into almost everything. Somewhere between the entrées and mains, a highly polished silver-plated matchbox was duly thrust into my hand. The champagne had smoothed out any conflict of conscience I had regarding my involvement in the escalating lunchtime excesses.

During one of Max's many trips to the gents', Nyles was jibing me for not making a pass at Adriana. I played along for a bit in order to turn the conversation.

"Don't you think you should tell Max about you and Hilda?"

"Hilda? Ha! Brother—what's to tell?"

"Well, you know, you and her!"

"Oh, that! Nah—why? What purpose would it serve? You can, if you like. Do you really think it'll do any good?"

"Well, what if he finds out?"

"How will he find out?"

"She might mention it!"

"Trust me, brother—women like her don't mention it."

I sat back. Perhaps he had a point. Would Max care anyway? It was doubtful. I resigned myself to telling him if things got really serious.

"Okay, well, can I ask you about something else?"

"Sure, brother! What's on your mind?" Nyles focused on me with sudden, intense, almost sober concentration.

"I saw one of our billboards! On the Tube."

"A-ha! So, whatcha reckon? I was a touch worried I may have gone a little overboard on that one! I wanted maximum impact."

"Overboard?"

"With the number!"

"Oh! I was going to ask if you specifically chose that Tube? How many..."

"Never mind! More importantly—did you like it?"

"Well, yeah! It was awesome."

"Exceptional!"

The lunch rolled on into the evening, and by nine o'clock proceedings had begun to falter. We had been relocated to the hotel's cigar lounge and continued drinking Scotch in a blurry atmosphere of Cohiba smoke. I was beginning to feel queasy. The silver matchbox had been enthusiastically emptied many hours ago. Max was now slumped unconscious across a chaise longue, empty Scotch glass in hand. Nyles remained an energetic hunter, scouring his phone book in an attempt to find more drugs.

"Gentlemen, will there be anything else?"

The conscious members of our group had been completely oblivious to the waiter standing by our table. This was clearly a cue to leave. Nyles seemed to acknowledge this and placed his phone back on the table, accepting defeat.

"I've got this, brother."

Clearly one to never check the bill, he casually flicked the waiter one of our company credit cards. These bills were going to be colossal. But I was too wasted to care, and besides, it was technically a tax-deductible expense.

13

WINNING AT MORE THAN ENOUGH

My ANXIETY-RIDDEN HANGOVER following the Savoy lunch lasted most of that week. During that time I felt again like I was teetering on the edge of a colossal depression. Something had to give—an intervention was needed.

I vowed to take things easy: no more drugs, and no—well, far less—booze. In reality, this wasn't actually going to be that difficult. My options for socialising were being curtailed more by my greatly reduced circle of friends than the atmosphere of austerity that permeated the city.

I decided not to call in sick the day after the Savoy, feeling it wouldn't reflect a work-hard-play-hard mentality. I dragged myself to work and wished I hadn't. Having a full-blown panic attack while trapped in the suffocating abyss of a London Underground train is not something I want to relive. Sandwiched between fresh-faced commuters and feeling like death warmed up, I began to find it hard to breathe. Impending doom gradually enveloped me to the point of total panic. I had to get out.

At London Bridge, I pushed through the swarm of commuters in a less-than-controlled fashion. I eventually collapsed in a hyperventilating mess on a bench outside the station. The cold air calmed me down and I immediately vowed to adopt a monk's lifestyle from there on. This was to be one of many moments of clarity.

I arrived at work a shaking, sweaty mess. Adriana smiled and intuitively gave me a sympathetic hug. Instead of our mid-morning trip to Georgio's, she appeared with a blanket and pillow and suggested a mid-morning siesta.

As I lay cocooned on the office floor, I cursed myself for turning up to work. Why had I bothered? It wasn't until Thursday that I actually saw Nyles, and when I returned home from work, Max hadn't made it further than the couch. I found him watching back-to-back episodes of *Lost* in his hat and scarf with the faux fire blazing.

"Evening, Max."

"Sweet Jesus, man! You look like shit!"

"That's better than I feel. Take it you didn't quite make it to work?"

"God, no! Worked from home—thought it might be best in the interests of career preservation."

"Right, fair point. Actually quite a smart move. Why is it so fucking hot in here?"

"Attempting to sweat out the toxins, old boy. Old Scando trick—Hilda recommended it."

"Is it working?"

"Maybe! I still feel godawful, but who knows—maybe I'd feel even worse without it. Can't believe you actually went in, you absolute ledge-bag! What time did you roll in?"

"For fuck's sake, Max—we came back together! I half carried, half dragged you from the cab to the lift. I'd say your doorman wasn't exactly impressed."

"Ned? Nah, he's cool, man—he's seen me worse. Much, much worse. *Awww yeah!*"

"No, not him—the other one."

"Oh, well, he's, erm, less cool. But anyway, same rules apply. What happened to Nyles?"

"He caught a different cab."

Max gave me a manic grin with raised eyebrows and began nodding slowly.

"What?"

"Well, I expect that wasn't the end of the night for him."

"I dunno, mate. He was pretty far gone."

"One is never quite far gone enough for hookers, is one, eh, Rodders?"

"*What?*"

"Almost certainly! There's always been more than a fair few rumours flying round about that boy."

Max was still nodding, but now with the assured conviction that comes from accepting one's own theory as fact. I was too tired to argue that he lacked any form of evidence and gave up. "You eaten?" I asked.

"Not a thing, mate. Nothing all day—couldn't face it! Just water to help with this insatiable sweating."

"Chinese, then? The usual?"

"Uh-huh! Say, Will, I forgot to mention something..."

"Hmmm?"

Max sat up suddenly, immediately looking as though he regretted the shift in posture. "Ugh! My head is still wrecked. Right—I meant to talk to you about our little start-up fund."

"Jesus, Max. I don't think I can right now."

"No, it's nothing—it's all good news, in fact! I just meant to tell you about another donation I secured at the club."

"At Beaconsfield's?"

"Uh-huh—one of the old boys there was pretty keen to lend a hand. Bent as a nine-bob note, of course!"

"A genuine donation?"

"Well, sort of—somewhere between a donation and a loan. Good chance he'll have passed away before it's time to repay it."

"How much?"

"Solid six figs!"

"Holy shit! A hundred thou?"

"Double it, baby—*awww yeah!*"

"Holy shit! That's a shitload of money. What about repayment? What's the interest?"

"Don't worry about that—it's a fairly casual agreement. These things always are. And besides, it's pocket change for old boys like that."

"Casual...? Are you completely sure about that?"

Max gave me a look of complete incredulity.

"Fine. Well, at least I should probably chill out about these credit card bills..."

"Ah, I see. They've, erm, arrived, have they?"

"Not yet. Why?"

"Well, I may owe the company a little there—not a great deal, mind! I've, erm, I've just given the old chap a gentle spanking on a couple of those *business* trips."

"You mean *dates.*"

"Well, yeah, okay. Fine. Look, I'll pay it back, of course—things are just a little tight in the personal account, you know, after the festive season."

"Right, well, cheers for letting me know at least. We'll sort it out another day."

When the credit card bills did arrive, they were impressive. *Five figures* impressive. But given our large amount of capital acquired by Nyles and now Max, it was hard to get too worried. We were haemorrhaging money, though, and with no revenue being generated, there was no sign of this changing soon.

I tried suggesting to Nyles a more rationed approach to spending until we actually turned a profit. It wasn't a popular idea. Nyles remained confident and wasn't at all concerned that we'd yet to perform any sort of Deconstruction whatsoever. I'd never met anyone so self-assured. Every concern I had was alleviated as soon as I brought it up, as though he'd already considered it. He didn't exactly have a hard time convincing me.

On an individual level, I was enjoying the ride. The exhilaration I felt upon receiving my first paycheque in three months was fantastic. Nyles had given me an extremely generous wage considering how little of what I was doing felt like actual work. A combination of being recently very broke and socialising less meant for once I hadn't blown my paycheque by the end of the month. Even after managing to get Max to reluctantly accept back-paid rent from me, I'd been able to save money. This had been a previously alien concept to me, and it felt good.

I was in an incredible position. I wasn't having to work hard, I was getting paid, and even if Deconstruction imploded, I hadn't personally invested anything in the company. I'd just be back to square one again—job-seeking with the masses—but it wasn't like I had any sort of reputation that would be tarnished from having been involved with a failed venture.

Things were bad in the city. The job market was getting tighter. There were rumours about suicides, and I knew of at least one attempt by a reasonably senior partner at my old firm.

I began to receive calls. Very soon, around one a day was coming through from an old colleague or a friend-of-a-friend, scratching around as I had in the meagre hope of finding a job. Word had gotten out that I'd been one of the few to regain some sort of employment. Knowing how devastating false hope can be, I was careful to avoid giving those who enquired any optimism about gaining employment with us. Presently there was none, and I downplayed any future prospects as speculative, even if things took off. I knew if our present form continued, we wouldn't last long. I was still keeping one eye on the classified section in the morning papers and reading the same job adverts as everyone else.

My day-to-day activities at the office were mainly centred around what Nyles liked to call *galvanising exposure*. I wouldn't see him for days, and then he'd appear in the office unannounced, looking fresh in an immaculate suit I'd never seen before. Each time he'd have some new idea about promoting the company, which he delivered with the same infectious enthusiasm. I'd then liaise with various IT companies or advertising firms to make his ideas a reality.

Our publicity was excellent. Completely over the top, but excellent. At considerable cost, we paid an IT firm to manipulate search engines. When a disillusioned individual keyed in search terms such as *life changing, new life* or *new direction*, they were directed to our minimalist website. The site had been up and running for over a month and did nothing to lift the veil of mystery we'd created. And that was the idea. Apparently. Users were greeted with a banner once again positing the question of *Deconstruction?* and an email address for further enquiries.

Nyles rationalised this unhelpful approach of depriving the user of actual information under his theory that information is power, and thus seeking out information is an exercise in empowerment for the individual. I didn't buy it, but Nyles was adamant that this would weed out those lacking the self-motivation to undergo Deconstruction. There was a weak logic there, but ultimately it was far easier not to challenge Nyles.

Information was provided to us on a daily basis regarding the number of hits our website had received, as well as the number of what Nyles called *conversions*. Conversions were hits that had gone on to send an enquiry to the email address. Nyles alone had access to these emails, and claimed to sift through the enquires from wherever he was. Occasionally I asked about them, but was reassured that we hadn't yet found a suitable client.

"We're looking for a very particular type of individual here, brother."

"A *very particular* type?"

"Yes—someone willing to transform themselves, to undergo a true metamorphosis."

"Right, that type."

"And, well, there's other issues."

"What kind of issues?"

"Well, most of the enquiries are a load of shite. One hundred percent pure shite. People really do have a tremendous amount of spare time on their hands—it's quite remarkable."

For the overwhelming majority of my time in the office, it was just Adriana and me. Our friendship grew stronger as we spent more and more time on the couch at Georgio's. Despite this, I still failed to find out much about her. Every attempt at extracting any sort of information about her past was met with vague responses or a change of subject. I couldn't work out whether she was actually hiding some dark secret or genuinely had no interest in talking about herself. I decided it didn't matter.

All aspects of my life were looking up apart from my love life. This remained firmly non-existent. My date with the-girl-on-the-stairs, Catherine, was cancelled at the last minute. We'd been due to meet for a drink at a newish wine bar in Covent Garden. I'd looked forward to it all week. I'd carefully selected a Thursday in order too not look too keen and disguise the fact that I'd no plans for Friday night again. I'd been instructed to go shopping by Adriana, and purchased a well-fitted shirt that she subsequently approved. I'd even remembered to bring my best cologne with me to work.

However, at four o'clock, I received a text message that sent me into a spiral of plummeting disappointment.

Really sorry - not
going to be able
to make tonight

EMERGENCY AT WORK
PROMISE I'LL MAKE
IT UP TO YOU! Cx

I felt my hopes of lifelong romance draining away. The feeling of being let down gently was something I'd not experienced for a few years—since before Lucy. But now it was a familiar friend turning up again. I slumped in my chair and angrily tossed my phone across the desk.

At five o'clock, Adriana stormed into to my office to enquire as to why I hadn't left yet. "Will! It is the worst manners to keep a lady waiting! I thought this *you* would know!"

"The date's off. She's got to work late."

"Oh, well, okay. Good! That is better."

"What?"

"Chill out, Will! She has to work late. These things happen. She is an important lawyer, no? Did she send you the text? Let me see!" Adriana slowly read Catherine's text, but then, with flurry of fingers, shot back a reply before throwing my mobile back. "*Aqui!*"

NO PROBLEM!
LOOK FORWARD
TO IT! Wx

"*Adriana!*"

"Will, this is not a big deal! She is still keen!"

"I've heard that before."

"Relax. Go home, take a glass of wine. Forget it for the weekend—then text her next week to make another date. *Comprendo?*"

"Right. Next week?"

"Yes! Of course—don't look too keen. So that is that! You will be okay? You will survive? I have to go."

"Thanks, Adriana, really. I'll be fine."

"*Boa! Tchau!*"

I watched Adriana grab her packet of Marlboros from her desk before sashaying gracefully out of the office. She was no doubt heading off somewhere cool and interesting to hang out with befittingly chic and fascinating people.

But I was fine. Completely fine. You can't win at everything all the time. I was winning at more than enough, and I was extremely grateful for that.

14

TEZZA

Our first Monday meeting in May had gotten off to an even slower start than usual. Nyles was late; Max was going to be even later, and if past form was anything to go by, probably wouldn't show up at all. Max seemed more and more content to keep things at arm's length despite being the company's sole other partner. This suited Nyles down to the ground, as it gave him the final say on any decision.

I was uncharacteristically irritated by the slow start. I just wasn't myself. I felt unwell. A late winter virus had decided to resurface and do the rounds, providing a cocktail of headaches, chills and general misery. I'd seriously toyed with idea of not coming in, but the Monday meeting was the only chance during the week where I could physically talk to Nyles.

I needed to talk to him with some urgency about his ever-increasing expenses, and about whether the company —now officially *Deconstruction Ltd*—was in fact about to implode. I'd heard that twenty percent of new businesses fold in the first year. With a global financial crisis in the mix, I didn't fancy our chances.

I'd not seen Nyles since the previous Monday. In an effort to appear busy, I'd spent every day reading the newspapers cover-to-cover, ensuring our adverts had been strategically placed—crucial work that I performed while listening to the soundtrack of Adriana, who had begun to deal with an exponential number of phone calls. Nyles had grown tired of being the sole individual handling enquires, and so a phone number had been placed on the website. The resulting deluge ranged from abusive crank calls, to genuine individuals, to those with no desire for Deconstruction who'd just had their curiosity piqued.

Adriana was not exactly delighted by her new role. I was once again about to rescue her with a trip to Georgio's when Nyles burst through the door.

"Morning all! Good morning! And how are we? I trust excellent weekends were had by all!"

I wearily blew my nose in acknowledgement. Adriana looked up from her phone call to flip him the finger, accompanied by her most sarcastic smile.

"*Adriana!* Excellent stuff! Nothing better than a bit of healthy contempt for one's seniors. Can you bring some coffee through for Will and myself in ten? Will—shall we? Jesus! What's wrong with you? You look like hell, brother."

"Thanks."

"No, genuinely, are you okay? Should you even be here? Christ knows I don't want to catch whatever the hell you've managed to pick up."

"Nice—self-preservation masked as concern."

"Ha! Precisely, brother—that's the spirit! You've got to look after yourself—no one else is gonna."

Inside my office, Nyles kicked the door closed behind me and vaulted into his armchair. Even his high spirits failed to lift my mood.

"*Jackpot!*"

"Jackpot?"

"*Yes!* After weeks of hard graft we've finally done it!"

"Hard graft?"

"Yes, brother—hard graft. Just because you've been sitting on your arse doing sweet F.A., it doesn't mean I have! I've been sifting through literally hundreds of emails for potential Deconstructees, and I've *finally* found one."

"You have? And?"

"*And*—his name is Terrence Armstrong." Nyles settled back into his leather chair and began to stroke its smooth, worn arms, seemingly for dramatic effect. It wasn't necessary. He had my full attention. "Now, sit down and let me introduce you to—*Tezza!* Terrence Armstrong is who we've been searching for—the ideal debutant."

"Right—I sort of thought just about anyone would be a good option at this point."

"Nonsense! Terry is our Holy Grail! Our *pièce de resistance.*"

"How, exactly?"

"Tezza is the *perfect* candidate for Deconstruction—he has the desire *and* the resources. Don't you get it? We absolutely can't let our first Deconstruction fail—the selection has to be perfect."

"So, what's his situation?"

"Well, since the eighties, he's almost single-handedly built up an engineering franchise that's now based in almost every major city in Europe. But! Success has come without real satisfaction. Outside of his work, he feels trapped—in a loveless, childless marriage, without any real sense of direction or purpose. In short, he hates his life and is desperate for a way out. He *is* perfect, brother! Savvy?"

"Right. So how will we go about this?"

"First, we're going to meet him."

"When?"

"In about five minutes."

"Fuck! Five minutes?"

"Yes, five minutes. Slightly less than ten."

"*Here?*"

"Yes, Will—Jesus! Relax!"

I leapt into action, frantically tidying the office—a task that thankfully didn't take long due to our continued approach to sparse furnishing. I placed the chairs in the *open-space arrangement* suggested by Nyles and pushed the desk to the side of the room to remove any obstacles between us and Terrence. Nyles helpfully assisted with the preparation by remaining in his chair and nonchalantly flicking through emails on his Blackberry.

Almost exactly five minutes later, Adriana knocked on the office door to announce that Terrence Armstrong had arrived at the building's front door. Nyles sprang from his chair, adjusted his tie and walked out to the reception area with gladiatorial strides to wait for Terrence's entrance. I elected to remain in the office, figuring a welcoming committee might look a little amateurish. I looked out of the window and practiced some controlled breathing techniques to slow down my heart rate.

This was really happening. *Finally!* My excitement had even lifted me out of my virus-ridden stupor. For weeks, what we'd been doing had seemed like an exercise in fantasy. Now Deconstruction and Deconstruction Ltd were being placed into the realm of actual reality. I was a bag of nerves. I closed my eyes and counted to ten. This was my entire arsenal of anxiety management techniques. They had now all failed.

"Mr Armstrong," I heard from the reception area. "A

pleasure to finally meet you in person. Nyles Henry—please, do come in."

A tall, well-dressed man in his late fifties slowly shuffled into the office, followed by Nyles. He wore a grey suit, well-tailored but shabby, the same colour as the many flecks in his black hair. His features were thin, verging on gaunt, and seemed to hang off his tired, bloodshot blue-grey eyes. His appearance was anything but intimidating. I began to relax.

"Mr Armstrong, this is one of our Executive Directors—Will Harper."

"How do you do?"

I smiled broadly and reached out to shake a very limp hand accompanied by a meagre smile.

"Please, call me Terry, lad." He spoke in a quiet but deliberate manner with a soft Lancashire accent.

"Pleasure to meet you, Terry. Please, have a seat." I smiled and pointed to Nyles' chair. The key seat, placed strategically facing the window so clear sky was visible.

Nyles nodded approvingly as Terry half sat and half slumped into the chair and folded his arms. Nyles smiled and signalled for Adriana to bring coffee. Adriana acknowledged him with a distinctive mouthing of the words *fuck you*, to which Nyles returned an affectionate wink.

At this point I only knew what Nyles had briefly told me about Terry. However, from this point on, I would become permanently connected to him. I would eventually come to know the most intimate details about this tall, softly spoken man in front of us. Terry didn't just look mentally shattered; he looked entirely broken. Nyles needed to convince him that we could reassemble him for the better—it seemed a big ask.

Following a few pleasantries, Nyles assured Terry of total confidentiality and produced a legal-looking document to reinforce this, which the three of us signed. I was impressed. I hadn't even considered this, but it achieved the desired effect, and Terry appeared to relax. Nyles opened up with small talk, encouraging Terry to tell us about his background before moving on to talk about his present-day life and what was causing him such misery.

Terry had grown up in a small town in Derbyshire, raised by his widowed mother. His father had been killed in an industrial accident before his first birthday. The resultant handsome financial compensation package allowed Terry to be brought up in relative comfort and receive a solid education. At the age of eighteen, despite significant maternal pressure, he'd made the decision to start his own business rather than attend university.

This turned out to be an excellent choice. Initially, Terry rented a warehouse just outside of Nottingham and started buying and selling machine parts. His new company had weathered the first few years with modest profits, but when the eighties arrived, things really took off. The company had gone from strength to strength and now boasted warehouses across Europe, making it one of the larger providers of industrial supplies.

Terry was still worth millions, even after the global financial crisis had torn off a significant chunk of his company's value. However, for the company to survive in the present economic climate, something had to be done. This included sizeable staff redundancies, another burden weighing heavily upon Terry's mind. He was yet to actually sanction any redundancies, and each day the company was losing more and more money.

"So what's stopping you from making these redundancies?" I asked.

Terry fixed me with a patient stare, sighed deeply and

shook his head. "I'm going to guess that you've never actually employed anyone, have you?"

"Well, that's true."

"Well, if you ever do, lad, you'd do well to remember that every employee you have is your responsibility—and that man's family relies on him. That food he puts on the table ultimately comes from you. Your responsibility goes way beyond that man. Do you understand?"

"I do. Sorry."

Nyles nodded sympathetically. "An extremely difficult and delicate situation—and one that sounds as though it needs to be tackled with a degree of urgency. But tell me, Terry, what's life like away from work? Is there any respite? Any relief at all?"

"I have few pleasures, Nyles. Me work has always driven me."

"But you're married, are you not? Is there no support to be found there?"

"My wife—ha! God help me, that bloody woman..."

Things on the home front were also not going well for Terry. It didn't sound as if they ever really had. The woman who'd had the most positive effect on his life, his mother, had passed away before she'd seen his success. The death of his mother and therefore his only immediate family had a profound effect on Terry. Seeking solace in the relationship he'd been in at the time, he'd mistaken companionship for love and subsequently entered a marriage that never really had a chance.

For many years Terry had suspected his wife, Gloria, was having an affair, or perhaps a string of them. This upset him, as he'd always remained faithful, and from time to time even attempted to salvage what was left of their loveless marriage through romantic gestures that always fell short.

Terry was pretty sure his wife hated him. Things had now reached their nadir, and lately Gloria had even given up on the snide remarks and despising glares.

Terry's marriage had never produced children, and while this simplified the situation a little, it constantly caused him to wonder whether it was the cause of his relationship's failure. Would having children have united them —brought them closer together? Would children have made their lives more complete and maybe happier?

Terry had married Gloria before his company had achieved any meaningful success. He'd previously dabbled with the idea of separation and divorce. He confided in a friend, a lawyer, who advised him that Gloria possessed the legal position and vindictiveness to ruin him.

Terry finished describing his state of marital misery and took a slow sip from his coffee, shoulders drooping. Nyles had appeared to listen intently to everything Terry said, and now looked deep in thought. He sat leaning forward, elbows on knees with his fingers interlocked and index fingers held to his lips.

After an appropriate period of contemplation, he cleared his throat. "Thank you, Terry. That level of detail is vital, and of course, during this process, it may be necessary to delve a little deeper into some of those aspects."

"I've told you all there is to know, lad—it's nowt more complicated than that. There's just no solution..."

"I know that's how it seems, but it *is* possible to see things from a different angle."

"Hmmm..."

"Look, the way I see it is that your life and all the stresses inflicted upon it can be viewed independently—as discrete entities. For example, your relationships with yourself, your wife, your work and colleagues, your leisure time can all be thought about individually. Now, while all these elements need to be in balance for a happy life, it's often easier to improve the balance by isolating them first."

"Aye, I hear what you're saying—go on."

"Okay—we're going to attempt a basic exercise in Deconstruction. I want you to close your eyes and try to clear your mind."

Terry looked at both of us, then, with an air of resignation, slowly closed his eyes.

"Good. Now, I want you to completely separate out each of those components I've just mentioned. Firstly, isolate your work—try to view it as a separate object. Sometimes it's easier to perceive it as something physical. For example, think of it being contained within a box. Once you've done that, I want you to move on and think about another element of your life. Think about your marriage—view it as a separate entity—place it in another box."

Nyles gave Terry a few moments to attempt the exercise.

"Now, were you able to do that easily?"

"Erm, no, not at all."

"Precisely! You see? You're so trapped by these elements that it's impossible for you to assess them from an external viewpoint. You have become totally immersed in your problems and can't view them with any degree of objectivity. With the way you view things at the moment, there is no hope of a solution."

Nyles spoke slowly and sincerely and was even more engaging than usual. Terry appeared to be following what he was saying. I was fairly captivated myself. There was just something about Nyles' energy and enthusiasm. It was hard not to hang on to his every word.

"I can see that your work and relationship with your

wife have become interwoven. They have become symbiotic —but they are both draining you. Do you think there's any truth in that?"

"Aye, well, I suppose..."

"Every day they'll feed just a little bit more. The question is—how much of you is left? And we haven't even discussed the most important element of your life."

"What do you mean, lad?"

"Well, what you do for enjoyment, for love, for fulfilment. Call it *leisure*, call it *recreation*—it doesn't matter. When was the last time you did something you enjoyed? Something that made you pause and acknowledge how wonderful life is?"

"I..." Terry looked thoughtful for a moment, then shook his head, defeated.

"Exactly! Your life as it is right now is only filled with elements that cause you stress and pain! This is common. We see it all the time—it's become an unfortunate but acceptable normality in the modern world."

"Look, I know all of this. I know there's nothing in me life that I enjoy or look forward to. None of this is news to me, lad! I just want to know how you can help—if indeed you actually can..."

Nyles nodded as if welcoming the challenging tone of Terry's voice, which had started to shake a little with irritation.

"Okay. Very simply, in order to improve your situation, each individual element that makes up your life needs to be assessed in isolation. This is next to impossible for an individual to achieve by themselves. That's where we come in. We offer an objective, neutral perspective with only one bias—towards you as the individual, to improve your life. To improve *you*."

"And how exactly do you propose to do this?"

"Through the process of Elemental Deconstruction—a highly specific programme tailored to the individual. Once we Deconstruct an individual's life, it places them in a unique position. From here it's possible to realise a better, more fulfilling existence. We are with you through this process—once your life has been Deconstructed, we will help provide the raw materials to rebuild you."

"Raw materials?"

"It's likely that you already possess these in some form. In general, a new start requires new scenery and new surroundings, but most importantly, a genuine commitment from you."

"What do you mean by that?"

"Well, if Deconstruction is successful, the end result is you being in a life that genuinely fulfils you—physically, mentally and spiritually. If you end up being in a position where your past is accessible, then Deconstruction has failed. Your life as it is now needs to be made permanently inaccessible, and we need you to be committed to that."

"I'm not sure I—"

"I'm sorry, but without this commitment, Deconstruction is impossible. I'll shake your hand and wish you good luck—I'll even waive the initial consultation fee as a show of good faith."

"I didn't realise I was being charged..."

"Well, in that case, you'll not be charged either way. We are only interested in helping those who want to be helped. I can tell that you need help, Terry, but the decision to access it is entirely yours to make."

Terry didn't say anything for a while. He sat gazing out of the window, far off into the distance. His eyes looked tired and weary. He chewed on his bottom lip. He had a distance about him that made him hard to read. I tried to empathise with him and imagine how it might feel to be so disillusioned with your life that you'd be willing to place it in the hands of total strangers for a chance of improvement. I tried, but I couldn't.

At the point where the silence was becoming uncomfortable, Terry rubbed his face with both hands, stood up and slowly walked over to the window. Nyles watched him with a patient smile. Terry placed his forehead on the cold glass and closed his eyes.

"Fuck it—I've nothing to lose, and things can't exactly get any worse."

Nyles smiled, pumped his clenched fist in victory and gave me a wink.

15

DECONSTRUCTION LTD

OVER THE NEXT FEW WEEKS, Deconstruction Ltd focused on its first client, Terrence Armstrong. Under Nyles' direction, I became immersed in every aspect of Terry's life. It became all-consuming. Every working hour and plenty of those outside it were taken up by Terry and his problems.

Terry's main sources of misery were his company, which needed to be rapidly downsized, and his relationship with his wife, which needed a similar strategy. Nyles was adamant that with both these problems rectified, everything else would fall into place. Terry would be able to paint whatever he liked on his blank canvas.

The trouble was that Terry had absolutely no idea what he wanted to do instead of being miserable. The time when he'd actually had hopes, dreams and aspirations was so distant that he was now effectively a different person. Realising he was getting nowhere fast, Nyles encouraged a reluctant Terry to take two weeks of leave and entered him into a personally tailored *rejuvenation programme*.

Terry's two-week programme, as far as I could tell, basically consisted of common-sense healthy eating—though at the expense of a dietician; regular exercise—requiring the services of a personal trainer; and an introductory course to meditation—to be taught by a spiritual advisor, whose fee was almost double that of the personal trainer and dietician combined. Despite this, Nyles seemed more than happy to outsource what I'd previously considered to be his role of spiritual guru.

"I see it as a sort of *Buddhism lite*, if you will," he told me.

"Buddhism lite?"

"Yes—less doctrine-based, a bit more secular. Don't want to push the religious connection too much, do we?"

"Erm, I guess not...?"

Halfway through Terry's fortnight, Nyles suggested the two of us pay him a visit at the health spa he'd been temporarily relocated to in deepest, darkest Surrey. I jumped at the chance—any opportunity to get out of the office was welcome, as I'd spent the entire week trawling through the unending accounts of Terry's machine parts empire. Exciting work it was not.

In fact, I'd started to become pretty jealous of Nyles, who breezed in and out of the office in between meeting an array of individuals all involved in rearranging some aspect of Terry's life. Nyles had a knack for managing, delegating and outsourcing just about everything imaginable. I couldn't understand why it wasn't possible to outsource the particularly dull process of verifying the legitimacy of Terry's in-house accountants as well.

I ended up bringing up my fairly uninteresting role in Terry's Deconstruction with Nyles in the car on the way down to Surrey. I was driving. I'd insisted. This was mainly because I couldn't be entirely sure whether or not Nyles was under the influence of high-grade cocaine.

"I just don't think I'm the best person for it, mate. It's not even really my field."

"Nonsense, brother! You were some sort of accountant, weren't you?"

"Yes, but not this kind, and I've got fuck all experience."

"Okay, brother, okay. I'll look into it. Regardless, we still need two independent financial assessments of the company. And it's not as if you're up to much else, is it?"

"True—but why two assessments?"

Nyles paused. I switched lanes to avoid the traffic, which was slowing for the M25 turnoff.

"Reassurance, brother. Firstly for our client, but more importantly, for potential buyers."

"Well, maybe I could help with finding potential buyers?"

"Well, I may already have some good news on that front."

"Really? Already? Terry's agreed to sell the company?"

"Well, let's be honest—Terry is still considering his options. I'd rather get things a bit more concrete before divulging any details."

"Even to me?"

"Especially to you, brother—you're my most trusted confidante! I wouldn't want to let you down. Now, how about we pull in at the next service station? I've a little something I could do with from my bag in the boot."

"A little something…?"

"Well, brother, as you absolutely insisted on driving, I thought I'd make the most of our day out."

"Jesus Christ, Nyles, we're going to a fucking health farm! There's probably people coming out of rehab and shit there. The last thing they need to see is you coked off your face, bounding around like a lunatic."

"Brother, I am *always* discreet—you should know that by now. Look, see that sign? There's one in five miles."

We arrived at the health spa to find Terry in the library, a sort of converted Victorian conservatory with leafy palms and a total absence of any actual books. The gentle May sunshine was generating a subtropical atmosphere that made my shirt's high polyester content acutely apparent. Terry was sitting in a comfortable-looking armchair with a paperback novel opened face down on his knee. He looked better, far more relaxed than the last time I'd seen him. Dressed in a towelled dressing gown, he was freshly shaven with a recent haircut.

"Excellent! Simply excellent to see you!" Nyles greeted him. "How are you, Terry? This is exactly how we hoped to find you!"

"Good, Nyles. A bit more... relaxed, at any rate. Will—how are you, lad?" Terry nodded towards me as I fingered my collar in a desperate ventilatory effort to adapt to the conservatory's climate. I attempted to reciprocate a relaxed smile while Nyles continued.

"So, how has the programme been going?"

"Good, lad. Some bits better than others—food isn't up to much, mind."

"I'm really pleased with the feedback I've received about you, Terry. You seem to have been engaging well in all aspects of the programme—it's very promising."

"Well, I won't lie, it has been a pleasant change."

"Excellent!"

Nyles and Terry exchanged pleasantries for a good five minutes. I zoned out. The heat was becoming unbearable. I'd loosened my top button, but rivulets of perspiration were beginning to merge into raging torrents down my back. Thankfully, one of the spa's staff emerged with glasses of iced water. I enthusiastically gulped one down, immediately wanting another.

The conversation had moved on to the state of the company.

"Look, it's not in *terrible* shape," Nyles said. "There's definitely huge potential to sell it, allowing someone else to take on the burden of restructuring."

"You mean sell it off and allow someone else to sack me staff."

"Absolutely not! If we find the right buyer, they may actually want to expand on what you've built—use it as a foundation, a global platform, even!"

"I won't lie to you, Nyles, I've often thought about moving beyond Europe. But me wife would never go for it. She'd actively oppose it. Anything that might bring me satisfaction, she'd oppose. There's a lot of hate in that bloody woman."

Nyles sat back in his chair, looking contemplative, giving a considered smile. How the hell was he not sweating? He'd consumed half of Colombia's export market since stopping at Clacket Lane services. Maybe he had a purely cotton shirt and some vastly superior antiperspirant, probably specially selected for these surroundings.

"Don't worry about your wife," he told Terry.

"Easy for you to say, lad—you've never met the damned woman!"

"Well, if you'll permit me to talk to her..."

"Fill yer boots, lad!"

"Sometimes having an external individual highlight certain advantages can be very persuasive."

"As I said—fill yer boots. She'll never go for it."

"She'll still stand to make a reasonable amount of money."

"She'll demand half, and she can afford decent lawyers..."

"She won't get half, Terry, don't worry."

"How can you be sure?"

"It'll take some work. Considerable work, but I'm sure I can convince her."

"I don't like this..."

"Terry! Listen, did we not agree that you have to relinquish control of certain parts of your life? Certain areas that are controlling you?"

"Well, I suppose..." Terry dropped his shoulders and raised a hand in resignation.

"There is one thing I want you to do over the next few days."

"What's that, then?"

"In addition to your meditation, I want you to spend an entire hour a day somewhere quiet outside, just thinking."

"Thinking? About what?"

"About what genuinely makes you happy."

"Right..."

"Terry—I'm serious! This is fundamental to you and your future."

And with that, the meeting was brought to a close. Nyles stood up and buttoned his jacket. Relief flooded over me as we shook hands and said our goodbyes. I followed Nyles out of the conservatory, vowing never again to purchase another shirt with even a suggestion of polyester in it.

OVER THE NEXT week and a half I continued to trawl through Terry's books. Nyles kept his word, and the accounts were also handed over to an external firm for review. In reality, the company was not in great shape—debts were clearly mounting, and I was sceptical about a successful sell-off in the present climate. Nyles looked disappointed in me when I suggested this might be the case.

"Look, brother, at the moment I really only need you to have a look at the company's accounts—make sure everything's above board and legit. Leave the sale side of things to me, okay?"

"I know, I just thought I'd—"

"I've already told you that this is being handled, brother! You need to trust me. The company can and will be sold without liquidation. I know some very good guys in this field."

"Okay, sorry... I—"

"Don't worry about it—I should be the one apologising. I'm just a little stressed with this being our first client, that's all. I just want everything to work out perfectly—absolutely everything!"

Nyles had endless contacts who could get things done quickly and efficiently, and he patiently explained to me who was handling what. However, the situation with Terry's wife was a different story. Nyles felt that this required a delicate touch and wanted to be personally involved in any negotiations. He was reluctant to share any details of his plans, and naturally, that made me more intrigued.

Terry's wife held the key to any potential sale. Adriana and I had chatted about it at length, and even she was out of the loop. Knowing that Max would love the mystery and therefore do his utmost to find out what he could, I brought it up with him one evening.

"So he's told you *nothing* at all about what's going on with the wife? Zero?" he asked.

"Absolutely fuck all. I've tried prying, but you know how Nyles is when he doesn't want to talk about something."

"A touch—*aloof?*"

"Yep. He's pretty good at changing the subject."

"*Awww yeah!* A true master!" Max grabbed a Heineken from the fridge and offered me one.

"Cheers."

"Well, I guess he probably has his reasons."

"What possible reasons could he have?"

"Jesus, Will, I don't know—maybe he's banging her or something? Is she a hottie?"

"Well, she'd be pushing well beyond fifty..."

"And?"

"No way! Even *you'd* have an age limit, surely?"

"What? Why? True beauty is timeless! Besides—it *definitely* wouldn't stop Nyles. That man is driven *way* beyond the cause."

"I doubt it. She's not exactly his type, judging by her photo..."

"Well, let me be the judge—got it on you?" Max pulled one of his classic lecherous grins and licked his lips.

"Fuck off—what's wrong with you? I mean, I just hope he's not doing anything illegal, you know, like threatening her..."

"Threatening her? Don't be ridiculous! With what? His excessive charm and charisma? He's good at what he does, but he's not fucking oo7!"

"I don't know. He knows *a lot* of people, that's all."

"Look, relax. As long as you're not aware of anything super dodgy going on, then it's fine. You want me to talk to him?"

"You can. Doubt he'll tell you, though."

I had planted the seed and was watching it grow. Max nodded thoughtfully before his mind turned to more practical matters.

"Right! Well, how's about getting some Chinese in? Han's for a change, maybe?"

"We've already had that this week!"

"Well, Will, maybe just go a bit fucking off-piste for a change—there's a hundred and twenty different dishes on that menu, for Christ's sake! Live a little—go for something else!"

"Fair point."

Even off-piste, I decided to play a fairly straight bat, going for sweet and sour pork with noodles. Max chose something neither of us could pronounce that looked awful when it arrived. Stubborn as ever, he turned down my offer of going halves and tucked in with feigned enthusiasm.

"Not—*bad!*"

"Yeah, right."

"No really—it's genuinely okay!"

"Despite looking like the contents of someone's bowels?"

"If you don't believe me, try some!"

"No thanks. But I'll grab you another beer to flush out the taste if you like?"

Nights in with Max generally went down like this: a Chinese and a gradual descent into a beer-soaked state of obliteration. Tonight was no different. With his voyage of culinary discovery abandoned, Max concentrated on getting drunk.

"So, you still making steady progress through those secretaries?" I asked him. "You never told me how Berlin went with Beth."

"Ah... *Elizabeth*... Ahem. That, my friend, was not a weekend that worked out well."

"Really? I am genuinely shocked."

"Well, the flight over was okay—but things went downhill rapidly as soon as we got to the hotel. I'd splashed out—gotten us a suite at the Grand Hyatt. She was immediately offended by the *opulent* display of wealth and sneered at everything—including the fucking bellboy!"

"Not the *fucking bellboy!*"

"Fuck you very much, Rodders. Anyway—I decided that everything'd be smoothed out as soon as she had a couple of drinks in her... but she refused to drink anything unless it was *fucking organic!* And in case you didn't know, organic booze is pretty bloody hard to get hold of in Berlin. I mean, they've still got chunks of that fucking wall everywhere. Parts of the city still actually look like a fucking war zone..."

"I think it's meant to serve as a historical reminder."

"Fuck that! They should get rid of the damned thing."

"Right, anyway, so you're saying she stayed teetotal?"

"Well, yeah, she did—girl of her word, I'll give her that much."

"What about you?"

"Are you fucking kidding? I had to cope somehow! And you know what? After a few drinks I actually began to enjoy things. You know me, mate—with a bit of booze I can tolerate pretty much anyone. That's actually quite a skill."

Max paused, looked me straight in the eye for comedic effect and took a half-pint gulp from his open beer.

"So, what happened next?"

"Well, we were in this vegan café thing and some crusty cretin in a military jacket hands her a flyer for a free party. We ended up there. I was all for it, thinking it would... *appease* the situation."

"Did it?"

"Well, long story short, she got hold of some grotty drugs, which were way too strong. I took one pill and thought I was going to die. I also decided it was a good idea to urinate into my Armani jeans."

"Ha! Brilliant!"

"Fuck off."

"Look on the bright side—it's slightly better than shitting in them."

"True."

"So, what happened next?"

"Well, I managed to socially isolate myself from the rest of the crusty Berliners on account of smelling strongly of urine—pretty ironic, I'd say. But basically, no one would come near me."

"But what about Beth?"

"Well, she fucked right off, didn't she! Last I saw her, she was walking off with two Aryan-looking chaps, arm-in-arm! Didn't see her for the rest of the weekend."

"Holy shit! Didn't you get the same flight back?"

"Ah, well, I conducted some invasive manoeuvres—changed my flight for an earlier one and left her ticket at the concierge with her bags. God knows if she ever went back for them—she could still be there, for all I care."

"So Berlin doesn't, in fact, rock?"

"No, it's shit. Good beer, though."

16

THIS DECONSTRUCTION BUSINESS

It was fast approaching the end of May and summer was almost in sight. I felt a newfound sense of optimism, enhanced by the buzz of London anticipating summertime. The impending finalisation of selling Terry's company was requiring a lot of work, though. Long hours with very few breaks had become the norm. Boozy lunches were now very much a distant memory—though one of fond reminiscence.

Upon completion of Nyles' tailored two-week Deconstruction programme, Terry was to meet up with us again in London. That day had arrived. Nyles decided we should bail from the tidal wave of paperwork we were surfing in order to prepare the office for Terry's imminent arrival. The mountains of paper were hurriedly filed away under Adriana's desk and Nyles donned his freshly pressed jacket. He'd managed to extend Adriana's remit of tasks to include his personal dry cleaning.

Terry still had to agree to the sale of his company, which meant the massive amount of work we'd undertaken over the last two weeks could all be for nothing. Nyles was as supremely confident as ever, though, and fully believed he would agree. Either way, it was impressive how we'd managed the whole thing and what we'd achieved in just two weeks.

Max was very much taking a back seat in the whole affair and was once again in a continental European city, attempting to woo one of the candidates we'd interviewed for Adriana's job. It was an arduous task, like he said, but he was coping well, and he hadn't let the Berlin incident put him off.

Terry arrived at two o'clock sharp. He looked well. Very well. Clean-shaven and lightly tanned, appearing far more at ease in his own skin. Perhaps there was even a hint of self-belief exuding from him. He wore a new-looking ash-grey sports jacket and slacks—new threads for a new man. He could have passed for ten years younger.

He shook both our hands with fresh conviction. "Lads—good to see you!"

"Terry! Looking very well indeed, brother! And I see you've even been shopping."

"Aye, Nyles, indeed I have—took yer advice and used that Savile Row tailor you recommended."

"He is rather good, isn't he? A fine cut he's given you there."

Terry gave a mock half-bow before sitting down in the same seat he'd used a couple of weeks before. He took a few moments to admire the river view. Nyles and I waited patiently for him to start talking.

"So, I've had me accounts man have a look over those figures you sent me, and I've got to say, we were both pretty bloody impressed!" he began. "You've managed to get a fairly decent price for the old girl."

"Thank you, Terry. A lot of blood, sweat and tears has

gone into the negotiations. Myself and Will have worked very hard on this and we're glad you're pleased."

"Aye, well, credit where credit is due, lad. I'm also right impressed by these Russians' intentions to expand the company further into Eastern Europe."

"We're particular pleased by that, and we've actually gotten one more thing that you're going to like even more..."

"Really? Go on then, lad—I'm all ears!"

Nyles produced an envelope and began to slice it open with an expensive-looking letter opener. Its silver blade sparkled brightly as it caught the sunlight that streamed through the window. Nyles slowly placed the envelope into Terry's outstretched hand. He caught me with my eyebrows raised and gave me a subtle wink.

Terry read the envelope's contents. "Sweet Jesus! How on God's green Earth did you get that woman to agree to this?"

"Well, simple, really. A case of facts and figures. The figures speak for themselves. We showed her how much she stands to make from the company's sale and conversely how much she stands to lose if she opposes it."

"But what about this—*legal separation?* I take it that means divorce?"

"Yes, and an amicable one at that—providing that's what you want, of course?"

"God, man, yes! I want nothing more! Have for years. But how did you get her to agree? And to accept the financial settlement?"

"You're asking why she's settling for such a small amount of money?"

"Yes! I mean, it's more than she deserves... but still, how?"

"Well, certain facts came to light. Our legal negotiators

came into possession of some freely available information regarding your wife's fidelity."

"You didn't blackmail her, did you? She's an evil cow, but that's plain wrong."

Nyles chuckled. "Terry, there really was no need. The information we had was available in broad daylight, exactly as you suspected. Credit card bills can be very... enlightening."

"Right, well, if you say so, lad."

"It's clear to me that neither of you were happy with your present predicament and you're both better off out of it."

Terry beamed. He looked like he'd just been told he'd won the lottery. "God, I wish I'd brought some champagne!"

I smiled back at him. "I'm sure that can be arranged."

It was good to see Terry happy. He seemed like such a decent bloke. Compared to the man who'd sat in that same chair a few weeks ago, he was now unrecognisable. Now he was looking reborn.

But Terry slowly stopped grinning, a sombre demeanour gradually spreading over him. Eventually the silence in the room grew awkward. He looked out the window and began to frown.

"Everything alright, Terry?" Nyles had a look of genuine concern on his face.

"Look, lads, I really appreciate all you've done... Really! It's unbelievable. I feel like a new man. You've given me a new sense of perspective. It's just this last step..."

"You can talk to us, Terry—about anything. What is it? What exactly's causing you grief?"

"It's me staff, lad. All the folk who've put a shift in for

me day in, day out. I can't help thinking putting their future in someone else's hands is... just not right."

"Terry, brother—*R.S.T.* is a very large, very well-established Russian company that has *significant* assets—assets not only vital to your company, but essential to keep those very people employed."

"I know, but..." Terry trailed off, rubbing his temples wearily and staring into space. Some of the old self-doubt and uncertainty seemed to be creeping in. If I could sense that, I was sure Nyles could too.

For once, though, Nyles seemed at a loss for words. He shot me an exasperated look. I felt obligated to say something. Anything.

"Look, Terry, I'm no expert in the field of engineering hardware..."

"Aye, you can say that again."

I swallowed hard. The last thing we needed right now was Terry becoming irritated or annoyed and undoing all that inner Zen he'd worked so hard to achieve. I smiled sympathetically at him and waited.

"Sorry, lad, I didn't mean to snap—that was uncalled for. Go on."

"No problem, thank you. It seems to me that any company intent on expanding, especially in the present climate, would be highly unlikely to make staff redundant."

"Why?"

"Well, sacking staff right now would seem like a show of weakness, which would be detrimental to the actual expansion of the company itself. What's more, if there's one thing I know about Russian business, it's that appearing weak is absolutely the last thing they'd want to do. They see business like warfare. I'd say presently your workforce is a lot safer in Russian hands than in those of a British bank."

I finished talking and waited. Nyles was smiling at me; he almost appeared impressed. Slowly, Terry began to nod, and the smile began to creep back onto his face.

"Okay, fine—fair point. I hadn't thought of that. Well... we might as well just bloody do this, then! It's not like I've got any other decent option, after all. Where do I sign?"

"Not so fast, Terry!" Nyles interjected. "There's one thing we really need to discuss first."

"Nyles, lad, I'm serious—I've thought about this a hell of a lot. Any more thought and I'll probably change me bloody mind again."

"I know, I know! But we need to decide what you're going to do after your Deconstruction is completed. You've now got a blank canvas in front of you—a unique opportunity. You remember that I asked you to spend some time thinking about what you wanted to do based on what fulfils you and what gives you a sense of purpose. Hopefully you had ample time to do that and to discuss it with your spiritual advisor?"

"Aye, I did."

"And...?"

Terry shifted his posture. Nyles and I both leant forward in anticipation.

"Well, I like some of what you've said—a new start and all. I like it a lot... Doing something different, somewhere different and all that..."

"That's great! So, what do you think might give you a more *fulfilling* existence?"

"Well, I guess... something helping people? Looking back, it's probably the only thing I can say I really enjoyed about running this bloody company."

"Helping who, exactly? There are a lot of people more disadvantaged than yourself, Terry."

"Aye, definitely... You know, growing up without a father often made me feel disadvantaged, like... but then I'd think about how lucky I was to have my mother compared to some kids who have nowt."

"Perhaps working with an NGO that works with disadvantaged children?"

"Maybe. I guess I've always been good with kids. I always felt I'd have made a good father... maybe even a teacher..."

Terry drifted off, looking whimsically into the distance over the river.

"Well, I'll make some enquires and see what's out there. It's important to try something like this. To give you a sense of purpose in your day-to-day existence. Even if you find that you're not enjoying the work, it won't be too hard to organise something else. There will always be lots of options for a man of means such as yourself. Have you thought about where you'd like to go?"

"Well, somewhere different... Maybe out of Europe for a change..."

"That's great, Terry—really great! That gives us plenty of options to work with."

Terry was smiling dreamily when Adriana knocked at the door and, before anyone could answer, stormed into the office. Terry appeared briefly startled before breaking into a grin. Nyles had once told me that the appearance of a beautiful woman can work wonders on the male subconsciousness in terms of suggesting potential. My first thought was that Nyles had staged Adriana's entrance to somehow obliterate any lingering doubts Terry may have had, but then she spoke directly to me.

"Excuse me, gentlemen. Will, you have an appointment, no?"

"I do...? Shit! I do!"

I'd totally forgotten. Tonight was the rescheduled date with Catherine. I'd taken Adriana's advice and casually enquired via text message the following week. We'd set the date ages ago. It'd been on my mind for most of the week, in fact, but focusing on Terry's visit today had allowed it to evaporate from my thoughts.

"Excuse my French. I'm really sorry, but I'm afraid I've got to go. Thank you, Adriana!"

"Really, William? How intriguing!" Nyles sat with one perfectly raised eyebrow and gave me an approving wink.

I rose and shook Terry's hand firmly. Terry smiled back warmly. It was true—he had changed. The dishevelled husk of a man we'd met six weeks ago seemed gone. Maybe for good. Although he didn't know exactly where he was heading, he had undergone a metamorphosis, and almost certainly for the better. Seeing him smile felt really good, but what felt even better was the fact that I'd played a part in it.

Maybe there was something in this Deconstruction business after all.

I'D ARRANGED to meet Catherine at the same wine bar in Covent Garden. Now I cursed the decision not to meet somewhere closer to the office, given that we worked less than ten vertical metres from each other. Having said that, despite our initial passing on the stairs, I'd failed to *accidentally* bump into her again, despite my best efforts.

I managed to grab a cab as soon as I stepped outside the office. I uttered a silent prayer to the gods of London's rush hour traffic and was trying to compose myself when I felt the vibration of a text message.

NO fucking way! If she was cancelling again, then that was it. I was completely done with her—possibly completely done with women all together.

NICE WORK
BROTHER! TOP JOB!
I THOUGHT WE'D
LOST HIM THERE!
SHARING A BOTTLE
OF CHAMPS WITH
OUR FIRST
DECONSTRUCTEE.
ENJOY YOUR DATE.
;-)

Ha! Relief swept over me. The potential of lifelong love, marriage and 2.4 children was back on.

I jumped out of the cab and entered the bar. I picked her out instantly. Catherine was sat at a window-side table at the front of the bar, watching the world go by with the deepest of brown eyes. Christ, she really was beautiful...

"I am so, so sorry I'm late!"

Catherine smiled with an almost professional air and firmly shook my hand. Textbook British formality. You had to love it.

"Forty-five seconds late, to be precise, Mr... Harper? I was actually about to leave." She cracked a grin, her handshake breaking the ice while helping her avoid having to kiss a perfect stranger. Impressive work—she was most definitely the ONE.

"I can assure you it won't happen again."

"No, it won't—given that you're talking to a lawyer."

"Ah yes, of course... Consider it a sort of verbal affidavit."

"Very good, Mr Harper."

"Right, well—I suppose given the venue, some wine is in order?"

"A fine choice, Mr Harper. We don't want to go too off-piste on a blind date, do we?"

And genuinely quite funny too. Were *all* my preconceptions going to be proved correct?

"Ha! Well, in that vein, something conventional and refreshing, perhaps? A nice Sauvignon Blanc, maybe...?"

"Another solid decision there, Mr Harper. Well, this is really going quite well, isn't it?"

"Please, do call me Will—Ms Harding."

"Christ, I never thought you'd ask!"

And with that the evening kicked off well. In fact, things went so well that I even nailed that potentially awkward end-of-first-date conversation as we stood saying our goodbyes outside the entrance to her East End flat.

"So, what about... meeting up again sometime?"

"Hmmm, maybe..."

"No pressure, of course."

"I'll have to check my diary."

"Of course."

"No, seriously, that'd be great, Will. I'd love to!"

Catherine's eyes sparkled and smiled at me under the amber glow of the streetlight. She had the sort of eyes that you happily lost moments in. My heart skipped a beat as butterflies began to unfurl and flap their wings somewhere deep inside me.

"Cool! Well, I've heard about this restaurant where all

the waiters are blind and you eat in the dark—it's meant to heighten your sense of taste so the food is incredible..."

"Wow! Really?"

"It might just be a unique way of serving average food, but at least you wouldn't have to spend the entire evening looking at my ugly mug—I couldn't possibly put you off your dinner."

"Ha! Are you fishing there, Mr Harper?"

And with that, she gently kissed me on the lips before walking up the steps to her front door. After unlocking it, she looked back and gave me one last smile. I was still standing on the pavement grinning from ear to ear like a complete simpleton.

The first perfect moment in a long time. It was too good to be true! The entire way back home, my wine-fuelled internal monologue kept asking the same question—*is this really happening?*

17

SMALL MOUNTAINS
OF BELUGA CAVIAR

THE NEXT DAY I woke up early as my head kindly reminded me I'd drunk far too much wine the previous evening. I thought back to the night before and immediately felt elated. I took advantage of the early start and high spirits by taking an early Tube, jumping off at London Bridge to enjoy a longer walk to the office.

I strolled at a leisurely pace, taking in great lungfuls of the late spring air. I felt better than ever. I couldn't stop thinking about her. Catherine, Catherine, Catherine. Even her name was a beautiful mantra. Surely this was more than just routine infatuation? I was sure I hadn't felt like this after my first date with Lucy, and before that was too far back to remember.

There was just something so completely fantastic about her. She managed to tick every box important to me: fiercely smart, beautiful, funny—she even laughed at my awful jokes. She was ambitious with a genuine drive to do something with her life for the benefit of other people—I mean, she wanted to be a human rights lawyer, for God's sake! She was a much better person than me in so many ways, and despite that, still seemed interested in me.

As I floated along past the Thames, it was still early. I picked up coffees from Georgio's with a couple of the almond croissants that Adriana was so fond of and arrived at the office as she was unlocking the front door.

"William! Wow—for me? Thank you!"

"My pleasure."

"So! So! How was the date? You get a little action?"

"Adriana, please! No, I didn't. Jesus—can you keep your voice down? We're literally in the hallway."

"Relax, Will! You Englishmen—*so* uptight."

"Look, I'm sorry, but it's just—I mean, she works ten feet away, for God's sake!"

"Right, and she has the *super hearing* as well. C'mon in and tell me everything—I want to know *all* the details!"

Thankfully, halfway through my in-depth cross-examination with the Brazilian Inquisition, the office phone rang. Adriana cursed violently in Portuguese before picking it up. I could tell immediately from the way she switched to her slightly flirty, slightly condescending patter that it was Nyles. After a couple of minutes of regular banter, Adriana gave a high-pitched whistle while shaking her head. She strolled over to the window to look down at the street before returning to the phone.

"Okay! Very, very nice, Nyles. I send him down straight away."

She rolled her eyes and slammed the phone down.

"*Filho da puta!* Will, you must go downstairs—Nyles is waiting for you outside. You have to go with him."

"What? Why?"

"To finish the paperwork!"

"What paperwork?"

"The paperwork with the investors—for the Mr Armstrong deal! I dunno how you guys do anything. You are both without a clue, all the time."

"Nyles wants me to come along? Why?"

"I dunno—maybe he thinks you will enjoy the ride!"

"Right. I guess I'll head down—"

"Not so fast! You must promise me to finish this later!"

"Finish what?"

"The story! About last night—the walk home, the kiss—and then what?"

"Well, that's it... Really—I went home."

"What? That is all? Oi-yah! You too are a *filho da puta*! All that talking for this ending of shit! You are also full of shit! Get out!"

I shrugged and left Adriana shaking her head to await the day's barrage of phone calls. I took the stairs two at a time to the ground floor, pausing briefly on the first as had become routine, but as usual, the frosted door was closed and there was no glimpse of Catherine.

On the street I was greeted by Nyles, dressed in a plaid dark-blue three-piece suit and a pair of unnecessary Armani sunglasses. He was nonchalantly leaning back against a jet-black Cadillac limousine.

"Ah, Mr Harper, good morning!"

"Jesus! What the hell is this for?"

"This old thing?" Nyles patted the car's roof and opened the back door, motioning for me to get in. I jumped inside. "A friend of mine owns a fleet. Small side business of his—always suspected it was a front for something... Still, comes in handy from time to time."

"But why the limo? Where the hell are we going?"

"The limo is simple, brother. You don't ride into battle on a donkey."

"Battle?"

"Metaphorically speaking—where we're heading, a stretched Caddie is almost the very least thing we can turn up in. Now, how about some champagne?"

"It's a little early for me, mate..."

"Nonsense! Never too early for a spot of Dutch courage! No? Really?"

"Dutch courage—for what? Where exactly are we going?"

Nyles finished pouring himself a glass of champagne and sat back on the leather seat opposite me. "Will, my brother, we are heading to meet *ze* Russians!"

"So? Why do you need me? Are you worried? Is it for moral support?"

"Not at all! It's just the done thing—you don't turn up having orchestrated a multi-million-pound business deal by yourself. It'd just look strange."

"Why not bring Terrence?"

"*Tezza?* Are you mad? He's going through his Deconstruction—he's trying to move on! This would be the worst thing possible for him to experience. Being present at the selling off of his only child isn't likely to do anything positive in his quest for enlightenment, is it?"

He had a point there.

I tried to relax and enjoy my debut ride in a limousine. Streets slipped by as we gracefully meandered through the late rush-hour traffic. Pedestrians craned their necks to ogle a look inside the car, trying to catch a glimpse of a potential celebrity. Nyles grinned and shook his head in mock disgust.

"Go on, then," I said after a while. "Perhaps I will have just one glass..."

"That's the spirit, brother! It's not bad stuff, either!"

I took the glass Nyles was proffering and spread out on the wide leather seat. I hadn't really had time to take stock of the situation. Following yesterday's meeting with Terrence, I hadn't given him a second thought. Catherine had occupied my mind entirely, and the fact that Terry's Deconstruction was now almost complete hadn't registered. We were on the verge of actually achieving something here! We had taken his life full of misery and removed him from it—hopefully changing him for the better. The two big stresses in his life were about to vanish. Permanently. A masterstroke from Nyles that he seemed to have pulled off easily.

Rather too easily, perhaps.

"So, Nyles, I do have a question..."

"Shoot, brother."

"I understand you've put a lot of graft into finding these investors..."

"Ze Russians? Thanks for the recognition, brother—in all honesty, I haven't worked so bloody hard in years. Generally I've always gotten someone else to do this sort of tedious legwork."

"While I'm impressed, the thing I don't understand is how you managed to convince Terry's wife to get on board with all of this."

"Ah, Gloria..."

And there it was—a glint in his eye alongside that self-assured smug grin. I fucking well knew it! There was no way this was as straightforward as he'd made out.

"Fucking hell, Nyles! What did you do?"

"Will, brother, relax. Seriously. Everything was—and still is—completely above board, as it always is between two consenting adults."

"Fuck, Nyles! What the hell?"

"Seriously—relax!"

"How can I? Surely that's totally illegal."

"Nonsense! How on Earth can it be *illegal?*" Nyles continued to shake his head while draining his champagne flute.

"Well, what happened? Tell me!"

"A mere fleeting romantic involvement—that is all, brother."

"When?"

"Look, you don't think I've just been sitting on my arse doing nothing when I'm not in the office, do you? Okay, okay, full disclosure, seeing as you're not going to let this one rest..."

Nyles topped up his champagne glass and offered the bottle. I shook my head. I was pissed off. This was beginning to look pretty messed up. Nyles shrugged, settled back into his seat and switched to full storytelling mode.

"Gloria and I *met* seemingly by chance in a shabby hotel lobby somewhere off the M1. She was there to meet someone she was romantically involved with—as we know, she tends to have a couple of chaps on the go at any time. She has quite the—*appetite...*"

"Nyles. Seriously—just tell me the key facts!"

"Okay, okay. So I *engineered* it so that we met, and I worked a little charm. She decided—*of her own free will*— that I was a better option than the poor chap waiting in room sixty-nine... *And!* As luck would have it, there was a two-star Michelin restaurant down the road from the hotel. So I wined and dined her, turned the charm up a little further, and *voilà*—Robert's your father's brother!"

"Right. So that was it? You went back to the hotel, had sex and—"

"No, no, no! That was just the beginning of what was a

rather sordid three-week affair. Her—*appetite*—was insa-tiable. Especially during our trips to Europe. Must be the continental air or something..." Nyles threw in a wince for good measure.

"What? You took her to Europe?"

"Twice—Paris and Vienna, to be precise."

"Fuck's sake, Nyles! What if Terry finds out?"

"Look, Terry's most certainly not going to find out. No one is going to find out! And even if they did, it's not like I've broken the law—I had an affair with a married woman, for God's sake, and that's it." Nyles placed his wrists together and raised them, simulating mock handcuffs. "The only people who know are me and her... and now you. And it's not in any of our interests for anyone else to find out. Look, I know it was a bit underhand and deceitful, but it was an essential measure undertaken on behalf of Terry's Deconstruction. Without it, this would simply not have happened. Terry was at the health farm for most of the affair—there was little to no chance of him finding out."

"So you shagged his wife to *help* him? Fucking hell!"

"Well, I wouldn't quite have used that turn of phrase, but it certainly came close at times..."

"Jesus... So, what—you blackmailed her?"

"What? No! Of course not. Why would I? I didn't need to!" Nyles appeared genuinely incredulous in the face of my accusation. "I simply called things off, and the only time we met again was with her lawyers and ours when we all met up to broach the idea of selling the company... and the divorce, of course. Our little affair simply helped to grease the wheels of negotiation. That, and there is the existence of a certain videotape, capturing some of our more adven-turous moments."

"Jesus Christ! So you *did* blackmail her!"

"Not at all! The amateur filmmaking was all her idea. True, we both kept a souvenir tape from our *One Night in Paris* production, but that's always the way that sort of thing works. Imagine that—she effectively co-produced her own downfall! I didn't even have to mention its existence—though I'm pretty sure she now knows I couldn't get rid of such a high-quality piece of cinematic gold."

I sat back and downed the rest of my champagne. Speechless. Utterly speechless. But was I completely surprised? If I'm honest, probably not—I'd always suspected Nyles was a deeply cunning bastard.

He leant forward and topped up my glass with a sympathetic smile. I hadn't the energy to protest. At this rate I was going to be plastered by the time we met the Russians.

"Mate, I hope to fuck you know what you're doing..."

"Will, brother, I do. I've admitted what I did was a little unscrupulous, but no more dishonest than what she's been doing for their entire marriage! The whole thing really has a beautiful karmic element to it, if you look at it in the right way..."

He was clearly quite pleased with himself, and nothing I said was going to change that. "Just shut up and tell me what I need to do when we get there."

"Very simple—as I said, you're just there for appearance purposes. All you need to do is stand behind me and look intelligent. No offence, but it's not like you're here as hired muscle!"

Nyles cracked up as I flipped him a two-fingered salute. He was a complete arsehole at times.

"As soon as the papers are signed, I'll hand them over to you and let you get back to the office. We need to get them couriered over to Terry's lawyers by close of business today."

"Right. Limo-ing it back as well?"

"Uh-huh—we've got this chap for the whole morning, brother!"

"Nice one. And you—you're coming back with me...?"

"Alas, no. I'm going to save you from having to partake in the obligatory tiresome Russian celebrations—it's all vodka, gambling, hard drugs and harder-faced hookers. I think you're probably best off out of it."

"Right—you're the boss. Suits me."

I was honestly relieved. Another midweek Nyles-sized bender was not what I needed right now.

THE LIMOUSINE PULLED up outside a fairly unassuming townhouse on a side street in Kensington. I moved to get out of the car, but Nyles held up the palm of his hand to stop me. I shrugged, sat back and waited for the chauffeur to open the door.

We climbed out of the limo and the non-tinted daylight made me feel giddy—three glasses of champagne without a decent breakfast will do that. I felt wobbly but good. How could I not? Limo across the city, decent champagne—all before ten a.m. Any apprehension I might have had about meeting a gang of Russian businessmen, who might possibly be gangsters, had evaporated.

Nyles slipped his Armani sunglasses back on and grinned. "Let's get this bitch done, brother!"

We descended a flight of stairs adjacent to the pavement that led to the building's basement. Nyles rapped confidently on the large oak door. A muffled voice replied in Russian. Nyles snapped from grinning piss artist into serious businessman mode and, with a stern look on his face, replied—in Russian.

Nyles speaks Russian? Impressive.

The door was opened by a broad-shouldered man with a shaved head. He wore a black suit and his neck and hands were heavily tattooed. He looked every inch the stereotypical Russian doorman. He sized us up with cold eyes and an expressionless face. Wordlessly, he nodded us in.

Through the door a small hallway opened up into a much larger room. Inside, an equally broad-shouldered, slightly older man sat behind a large desk.

"Nyles! *Radushnyy priyem!*"

The man rose and greeted Nyles with a handshake of forged steel. He was in his late fifties with swept-back dark-grey hair that was receding at the temples. His face bore a couple of large scars, giving the distinct impression of a history of violence: one on his right cheek, one above his left eyebrow. This didn't seem like the type of man to upset, either.

"Jaroslav! How are you, my friend? This is my associate, Mr Will Harper."

"Pleasure to meet you, Mr ...?"

"Jaroslav. Please, just Jaroslav."

I went to shake Jaroslav's hand, but instead he nodded and smiled in my general direction. Slightly offended that I was too low in hierarchal terms to warrant a handshake, I shook my head in mock disbelief. Nyles shot me a look, but thankfully Jaroslav had turned his attention to the papers Nyles had handed him. My bad—I'd obviously overdone the Dutch courage.

Aside from the doorman, there were another couple of heavyset men draped over a well-worn green leather couch. I smiled and nodded, hoping I wasn't coming across as a twat. Nyles was now sitting across from Jaroslav, the two of them immersed in a conversation in Russian. Acutely aware that I was now the only one standing, I looked around for somewhere to sit.

The only available chair was by the two big guys sitting on the couch. I hadn't appreciated quite how massive they were until I approached. I smiled hopefully and one of them grunted towards me in a not-too-dismissive manner, which I took to mean *By all means, please sit down.* I thought about texting Catherine, but quickly decided against it. I needed to look professional for Nyles. Professional and not pissed—that was the game plan.

One of the Russian gentlemen on the couch, the elder of the two, turned to me and grinned through some fairly unique dental work: a number of teeth missing, with those remaining capped with gold or silver. After sizing me up as harmless, he produced a bottle from behind the arm of the couch.

"Vodka?"

"Erm, uh..."

Vodka. Vodka was my nemesis, avoided since a traumatic incident that occurred during a sixth form geography field trip. A vodka shot marathon had eventuated in me becoming immortalised in school folklore as a projectile vomiter with an unfortunate episode of incontinence. My relationship with the head of sixth form soured notably as a result. Ever since, vodka for me had been off limits.

"Vodka? You drink? Or no?"

"Erm, I..."

The younger of the two Russians had now also taken an interest in me and startled me by thrusting a cut crystal shot glass brimming with the evil tonic into my hand.

Vodka or no? Twist or stick?

Fuck it—the last thing I wanted was to look rude…

At the last minute, I remembered the only Russian phrase I knew. "*Za zda-ró-vye!*"

I drained my glass and gasped, but managed to stifle a retch. Not quite as bad as I thought it was going to be. The younger Russian slapped me heartily on the shoulder and offered me his hand.

"Will."

"Sergei! Pleased to meet—*Will*. Russian vodka is good, no?"

"Erm, I hear it's the best."

"Another?"

"Perhaps later. I should wait for the—business—to be complete…"

I was gesticulating wildly in an attempt to overcome any potential language barrier confusion. Sergei seemed to reluctantly accept this position. I looked over to Nyles and Jaroslav, who were now both nodding and smiling. Jaroslav reached under the desk, produced another bottle of vodka and began to pour two large glasses. The deal was done. My heart sank a little—more vodka was heading my way.

After the glasses were drained, Nyles beckoned me over and whispered under his breath, "So, it appears Jaroslav would like to have us *both* stay for lunch and some, erm, light refreshments."

"Ah, right… I don't suppose I could be excused, as per the original plan?"

"I'm… less sure that declining hospitality would be advisable at present."

"But what about the limo?"

"Don't worry—I'm sure he'll enjoy the rest of the morning off."

"Right. I suppose that means… more vodka?"

"Yes, but also a fair amount of caviar—swings and roundabouts. And of course, they'll probably be some quite decent Charlie."

"Right..."

"I'll let you draw the line at the hard-faced whores, though."

"Right. Thanks—that's, erm, extremely considerate."

Jaroslav was now looking at me with an altogether more welcoming expression. He clasped my hand in his and grinned, then began pouring my second of many, many more vodkas. I smiled and repeated my stock Russian phrase.

"*Za zda-ró-vye!*"

Jaroslav roared with laughter and slapped me on the back with such force that I tripped forward and had to steady myself with an outstretched hand on his desk. This was obviously also hilarious, and he roared some more. Still laughing, he reached into a drawer and produced a wooden cigar box crammed full of bulging Cohiba cigars.

"Thank you, Jaroslav, but I'm not a—"

"Better had, brother," Nyles interjected. "You know—for appearances' sake. God only knows what these cost." He was already smelling his cigar from one end to the other and nodding with the appropriate appreciation.

"Right, erm, okay then—thank you."

Jaroslav produced a fifty-pound note, which the younger of the two Russians from the couch duly lit. The burning fifty was proffered to Nyles, then to me. I inhaled on the gigantic Cuban while watching the remainder of Her Majesty go up in flames. Surely this now made me complicit in an act of treason? I sucked hard on the cigar. The smoke burnt the back of my throat, already tenderised by vodka. I stifled a cough while nodding my thanks.

While the cigars were being smoked, another round of vodka was poured. Following this, I'd be in the vicinity of being completely smashed. Why, oh why, had I not at least had something for breakfast?

After another toast, Jaroslav said something in Russian to one of his men, who disappeared. Shortly afterwards, an attractive Eastern European lady dressed in black beneath a white lace apron appeared, pushing a large steel service trolley laden with opulent offerings—including three ice buckets, each complete with a bottle of Cristal champagne. Jesus. This was going to get very messy...

Although it wasn't exactly what I'd have chosen, the trolley at least provided something to line my stomach. Small mountains of Beluga caviar, stacks of oysters and great swathes of gravlax were crammed between the ice buckets along with some dark, presumably Russian bread, which had the delightful consistency of concrete.

After what must have been an appropriate length of time, the waitress reappeared with two other similar-looking girls who wore little more than black lingerie. I caught Nyles' eye, and he raised his brow, confirming these were the anticipated prostitutes.

I was meant to be long gone by this point. A sober me would have found this extremely uncomfortable, but I was now too drunk to care. I carried on my conversation with Sergei, the younger of Jaroslav's compatriots. His English wasn't great, but seemed to improve with his level of intoxication.

The three Russian girls draped themselves around the room and sat in total silence with identical bored expressions. This changed when Jaroslav produced what I can safely say was the largest amount of cocaine I'd ever seen. A silver platter with what looked like a scale model of the

Matterhorn was placed on the coffee table. It remained there for the rest of the day, its magnitude unchanged despite everyone's best efforts.

The cocaine facilitated me to drink more and numb myself further to what was going on between the girls and the Russians in other basement rooms. I looked at my watch and saw that it was eight o'clock in the evening. By this point Nyles had disappeared and reappeared with at least two of the girls, maybe even all three. I had politely declined numerous times. Thoughts of STIs and human trafficking were more than sufficient to stop me being tempted. However, a tactical exit would ensure this remained the case.

"Nyles, mate, I think I might fuck off-ski..."

"Okay, brother."

Both of us were wasted, and the cocaine ensured we were now totally separate entities, each without any consideration for the other's wellbeing. Standing, I struggled to maintain balance. Jaroslav had sensibly disappeared some time ago, leaving his two men to keep Nyles and me company. I made my way towards the door. Slowly. Available furniture used in a supportive manner. A wave of nausea flooded my senses and I made a bolt for the door. There was no time to bid my new Russian friends goodbye.

I stumbled out into the small hallway and was amazed to see the doorman from the morning still standing there. I was caught by such surprise that I was unable to maintain my composure and retched. Rather than see me lose said composure completely all over the hallway carpet, the doorman acted with lightning-quick reflexes. In one swift movement, he opened the door and bundled me out.

I lost my composure all over the lower steps of the outside staircase.

I gained a few seconds of clarity—enough to mumble a weak apology before vomiting once again.

"Okay. I get car."

"I'll... Cab..."

"No cab. You take car."

In no position to object, I collapsed on the staircase while the doorman disappeared past me. The world span. Self-loathing crept over me as I noticed a damp sensation creeping through the seat of my trousers and realised I'd sat down in my own vomit.

This was a new low. I *had* to stop getting so fucked up.

I tired to focus my vision and decide whether I needed to throw up again. I decided I didn't. An unspecified amount of time passed before I was brought back to reality by a bottle of mineral water being placed in my line of vision.

"Here. Drink!"

"Thank you, that's very..."

The doorman half walked, half carried me up the staircase to a waiting car. Inside, another surly-looking Russian sat in the driver's seat, equally unamused at the state I was in. The doorman opened the rear door and I fell into the backseat of the car. The door had hardly closed before we sped off. I tried to open a window for some fresh air, but they were locked.

"Is there any chance..."

The driver turned back and fixed me with a look. I gave up. I was too drunk and too tired to wrestle with a language barrier. I resolved to concentrate all my efforts on not vomiting again. Streets passed in a blur of double vision and late evening light—I tried to focus on some recognisable landmark, but couldn't.

"Mate, I live in..."

"It's okay. I know where you live, my friend."

I was taken aback. This Russian spoke with almost no trace of an accent! Clipped, well-spoken English. Who was this guy? How did he know where I lived? I felt a fresh surge of nausea. My pulse pounded in my head.

Just. Don't. Vomit. Not in the car.

I focused on breathing. Inhale. Exhale. Slowly.

We were crossing the river again. *Not far now. Five minutes max. I can probably hold out. I'll be a hero if I hold out. In fact, I might not even be sick at all... I'll just give this mysterious and actually strangely good-looking driver an apologetic wink and a grin and stroll inside. All bad form forgiven—boys will be boys...*

We pulled up outside the apartment block, and shortly afterwards, my well-rehearsed plan fell apart as I opened the door and tripped on the curb.

Things happened in slow motion. The ground came up to meet me. My nose smashed into the cruel concrete. I lay facedown, my cheek resting on the cold pavement. Cold, but oddly no pain. Very slowly, I pulled myself up to a sitting position. I felt my nose. At least it didn't feel broken —just wet. With difficulty, I focused on my fingers. They were covered in dark red blood.

Blood... Christ...

My aversion to blood once again conquered all and I vomited. Again.

"Are you okay, my friend?"

The driver was now beside me with a supportive arm around me as I relocated the remaining contents of my stomach to the ground in front of him. He sounded genuinely concerned.

"That was some fall, my friend! My God! Straight to the face!"

"I'm... fine... I think..."

Still with his arm around me, the driver walked me up to the entrance door of our apartment building. The night doorman, Ned, was asleep at his desk. I really didn't want to wake him—Ned had seen me in enough states of disrepute over the last few months, but this was too much. I looked to the keypad on the right of the door.

"Mate. The code. The code is..."

The driver purposefully punched in four digits.

"*One-nine-eight-four*. Nice place, but not so secure."

"How did you...?"

He gave me a wry smile. "Come on, now. We don't want to wake old Ned."

As he walked me across the lobby towards the lifts, realisation sent my head spinning.

What the absolute fuck? Who was this guy? How did he know Ned's name?

The lift opened and I stepped inside. I turned to face my Russian Samaritan, who was still smiling. The ferrous taste of blood was dripping down the back of my mouth—extremely sobering. I returned his smile and nodded weakly. Something wasn't quite right. This guy was not just a driver—but who the fuck was he?

"How...?"

"Sleep well, my friend."

I watched him turn and walk confidently back across the lobby as the lift doors closed.

Nice place, but not so secure. That was a huge understatement.

18

A CHARMING BASTARD

"Well, I don't care what anyone else says—I say that larger nose gives your face some much-needed character! *Awww yeah!*"

Max. Always one for the rehearsed comedic opening line. Dickhead.

I performed an exaggerated eye roll and glanced at Catherine, who smirked affectionately in response. I had thought she would be unimpressed with my facial appearance following our meeting with the Russians. Thankfully she wasn't, and had actually found the whole story quite amusing. Admittedly, I'd felt it prudent to leave out certain details when recounting the events, but in my defence, the whole ordeal wasn't exactly the clearest of memories.

"Cheers, Max, great delivery—for once." I stood up and gave him a hearty handshake.

"What, no man-hug?"

"Nope—you don't deserve one."

On Max's shoulder hung a thin, large-breasted Eastern European woman: his current squeeze, none other than the unsuccessful secretarial applicant who he'd previously named affectionately *Tits-on-a-sticka Veronika*. Max and Veronika had now been an item for a couple of weeks and he was ninety-nine percent certain that she was *the one*.

He introduced her to Catherine, who stood up and gave Veronika a warm smile and a gentle peck on the cheek.

"Pleased to meet you, Veronika."

"Yes—also you."

Max smiled. I could see he was delighted with Veronika's interaction with Catherine. Brilliant—friends for life! Things really were that simple in Max's world.

"*Awww yeah!* Right then, I'll get the drinks in! What would you ladies like? Champagne okay? Will—a hand, my man?"

Max and I headed to the bar, leaving Catherine and Veronika to become acquainted. Catherine had already begun to sit forward in her chair, hellbent on making enthusiastic small talk with Veronika. She was really good at all that sort of stuff. In fact, she was really good at most things. Conversely, Veronika wore a panicked rabbit-in-the-headlights expression, immediately abandoned by Max and thrown into a social situation in a language she didn't really have the best grasp of. It was hard not to feel a little sorry for her.

"Any sign of Nyles?" Max asked.

"No, he's been pretty scarce since meeting the Russians over a fortnight ago."

"Really? Nothing?"

"Nothing more than a couple of phone calls to check in, but no *actual* physical appearance..."

"Do you think he just cracked on after you left? You know—week-long drugs-and-hookers bender type sitch?"

"It's certainly a possibility, I guess. Though I think he said he'd gone to the country."

"Hunting, maybe?"

"No, Max. He's not you. I don't know—maybe a retreat or something. You know, meditating or yoga."

"Hmmm..." This clearly wasn't quite rock-and-roll enough for Max. "Well, what about Terry's old missus, then?"

"What?"

"*Maybe* he's off slipping it to her again?"

"I sincerely doubt it, mate. I think that ship sailed as soon as he appeared next to Terry's lawyer."

"Right. Yep. Fair point. He's probably fucked that, hasn't he?"

Max ordered drinks and a bottle of Cristal at the bar while fulfilling his obligation to flirt atrociously with the barmaid.

"Jesus, Max!"

"What? Laying it on a bit thick?"

"Do you know any other way?"

"*Is* there any other way?"

"I'm sure there's a few..."

"Why change a winning formula?"

"Speaking of which, how's it going with fair Veronika?"

"Fantastic! She is an absolute animal in the sack. We're talking four times a night minimum—and some of the things she does! She can actually put her—"

"*That's* enough detail, mate."

Max flashed his well-practiced innocent-schoolboy-slash-sex-fiend grin.

"And the language barrier? Not much of a problem?"

"Not really, mate. She's a *really* good listener!"

"Right..."

We made our way back to the table to wait for our drinks to arrive. There was still no sign of Nyles, even though this celebratory meal had been his idea. Adriana had told me about it a couple of days ago. She'd been the only one to speak to him, and I'd tried pressing her for details on Nyles' whereabouts, but he hadn't told her anything. Either that or he'd sworn her to secrecy.

Nyles eventually appeared halfway through the second bottle of Cristal. Max had insisted we wait until he arrived before ordering food, which meant that the four of us were now deep in the throes of champagne joviality.

"Nyles!"

Max had picked him out from across the restaurant. He was dressed in a light cream suit and open-collared sky-blue shirt. He had the fresh, healthy, natural glow of someone who'd just stepped off a yacht somewhere in the Mediterranean. He was far more tanned than the last time I'd seen him, and his hair had been cut short. Very short—verging on a crew cut. He glided across the bar with the air of man so comfortable in his own skin it made you itch.

"Nyles, this is Catherine," I said.

"Pleasure to meet you." He took the hand she offered with an exaggerated camp flamboyance and planted a gentle kiss upon instead of shaking it—this made her giggle. "I've heard so much about you, it's so nice to finally meet!"

Catherine tilted her head to one side as though sizing him up. "Likewise, I'm sure. We've been waiting some time for you, Mr Henry—I do hope you won't disappoint."

"Ha! I'm so sorry. I was at the Nepalese Embassy—something I couldn't reschedule, I'm afraid."

"Well, that *does* sound intriguing—I'm afraid you'll simply *have* to expand!"

Nyles shrugged with mock reluctance and laughed again. His piercing blue eyes matched his shirt perfectly. He really was a good-looking bastard. Women were like moths to a flame with him, and Catherine unfortunately didn't appear to be any exception. I wasn't worried, though. Things were going well, and I was sure her flirting was purely in jest.

Well, fairly sure...

Catherine eventually managed to prise the details of where Nyles had been out of him. His reason for being at Nepalese Embassy: an audience with an eminent Tibetan Lama who was in London on both a spiritual and political mission. Nyles had apparently attended the Embassy at the Lama's request; it would seem that the two of them were rather close. I had my doubts. No one else seemed to.

Dinner was a feast of excessive proportions—a degustation masterclass. Countless courses, each more opulent than the last and matched superbly with an accompanying wine. Nyles held court throughout, making the seamless transition from one fascinating and humorous anecdote to the next while effortlessly involving everybody in the conversation—even Veronika. Interestingly, he declined any form of alcohol, despite Max's protests. Instead he sipped sparkling Swiss mineral water. He didn't even excuse himself to the bathroom to powder his nose. Not once.

Where had he been for the last two weeks?

My intrigue grew. I also had a thousand or so questions about the Russians—especially the driver. And I wanted to know about Terry, who seemed to have disappeared off the face of the Earth.

My chance came after dessert when the girls embarked on the clichéd joint bathroom trip. Max took this opportunity to visit the bar to "peruse their selection of cognac" and flirt with the barmaid again.

"So, off the booze and drugs this evening, mate?" I asked Nyles.

"Yes, brother—just good food and company."

"Really?"

"Honestly!"

"Have you been in... *rehab* or something?"

"Ha! No, Will—everything in moderation, brother. Always."

"Really?"

"Of course. Sometimes it's good to physically as well as spiritually cleanse oneself. Surely you must be beginning to understand that by now! Just look at the good it did Terry. Try it for yourself if you don't believe me—it may even wipe that sceptical look off your face."

"Sorry, I..."

I stared at him some more, trying to work out whether he was being serious. I gave up and shrugged—why not give him the benefit of the doubt? There didn't seem to be anything to be gained from lying in the present situation.

"So, Terry—I've got to know! Where the hell is he? We've had a few people try to contact him at the office—including Mrs Armstrong."

"Ah, Gloria, *Gloria*..." Nyles smirked and shook his head.

"Seriously, mate—where has he gone? I'm actually quite worried about him."

"All taken care of, mate. Just ask Adriana to forward any future enquires to me and I'll deal with them personally."

"And Terry is...?"

"*Il a quitté.*"

"Where to, though?"

"Reincarnated into a new life! I'm sure you understand that I'm sworn to secrecy on the exact details, but I don't think he'd mind me telling you that he's somewhere in East

Asia—keep that to yourself, though, brother. I probably shouldn't have told you that."

"Right... Doing what—the NGO thing?"

"Something like that."

"Well, that's good, I guess."

"Of course it is! He's finally free! A new life to start over again with a renewed sense of purpose. I feel rejuvenated just being part of the process—don't you, brother?"

"Well, yes, of course I do..."

"Jesus! Tough crowd." Nyles shook his head with an air of abject disbelief. He sipped his sparkling water and gave me a look of confusion and concern. "Is there something bothering you, brother?"

I sat back and thought about the incident with the driver again. Should I bring it up now? Would it ruin the evening?

Fuck it. I'd been replaying what scarce memory of the events I had over and over again—each time increasing my anxiety. It was time to share it with someone, but first, I wanted to know where the hell he'd been.

"Look, mate, what happened after the Russians?"

"God, Russians, always a bit rough—I take it you got home okay? I feel like I've spent the last two weeks recovering."

"Where, exactly?"

"I took a bit of time out—you know, went to the mountains."

"Which mountains?"

"Just this place I know in Austria, in the Tyrol. Been going there for years! Time in the mountains is always time well spent, brother. Being so far away from humanity and yet so close to the essence of it at the same time. It's exhilarating! Mind-expanding, even."

"Hmmm. I've never been great with heights..."

"Ha! So, what's up? What's the problem?"

I took a deep breath and began to recount the events, or at least those I could remember from the end of our evening of Russian hospitality. I told him about the well-spoken driver, his sobering *nice place, but not so secure* comment, him knowing the door code, him knowing Ned.

I finished talking and allowed a little gentle relief to seep into me. Nyles' expression had remained unchanged throughout my anguished outpouring. There was still no reaction. And then the corner of his mouth began to flicker slightly before he began pissing himself with laughter.

"Fuck you, Nyles! Christ!"

"I'm sorry, brother—but it's a bit far-fucking-fetched, isn't it? You make it sound like you're a marked man targeted by the Russian mob! I'm sorry, but you've got to see the funny side."

"Well—how did he know the fucking door code?"

"Well, my dear fellow, being the Sherlock that I am, I suspect it might have something to do with it being the year in which the building was built—which was...?"

"1984... Shit. And it's in great big fucking letters above the door..."

"It's not exactly a quantum leap in deduction, is it? Also makes it *not so secure*!"

"Fair enough. But what about Ned?"

"Ha! Ned, Ed, Ted—whatever, mate, I don't fucking know. A lucky guess? His name badge? You misheard him, maybe, in that hyperalert state you thought you were in?"

"Oh, fuck off!"

"Just relax, Will, please! You were probably just a little bit pranked—you'd done quite a lot of blow, as I recall. Those Russians can be scary bastards, but they're no more scary than anyone else—they get a bad rep from all the bull-shit media portrayals they receive. Seriously—even at their worst, they're all fart and no shit!"

I considered this for a minute. Maybe Nyles was right. I'd been on tenterhooks at the meeting, and although the alcohol and cocaine had seemed to help the situation, they probably hadn't. But there was still something about the evening that didn't sit quite right with me.

"You don't look convinced," Nyles prompted.

"I don't know, I guess it's possible... It's just..."

"Look, I put you through a weird situation. It was pretty stressful. I'm not afraid to admit that I was a little stressed out too—going into that fucking basement with all Jaroslav's homeboys hanging out and looking hard as nails. Personally, I'm just glad they didn't challenge us to a game of fucking roulette..."

"Shut the fuck up! You can't take anything seriously, can you?"

"I'm sorry, I couldn't resist. Please relax! It's all good! Everything's good. In fact, it's actually better than good."

"How, exactly?"

Nyles sat back in his chair and smiled. He took a long, slow sip of his water. "Before I go into that, I just need to know that *we're* okay, mate—you and me."

"Yeah, I guess."

"Will, this is important. You're more than some colleague—you're a friend. I can't have you being stressed out. I need to know that you're okay, or at the very least that you can put this behind you."

"Okay, okay, yes—I'm fine."

Nyles looked around to see where the other members of the dinner party were. No sign of the girls yet, and Max looked like he was in an engrossing conversation with the barmaid.

"Right. Well, I hate talking shop when we're meant to be out celebrating, but..."

"But what?"

"Well, I think we may have our next client."

"Really?"

Nyles beamed, his eyes glowing with fresh enthusiasm. "Yep. And I really think you're going to like her."

"Her?"

"Lady Ann Mei Golbourne, to be precise."

"A genuine *Lady?*"

"Yep. Well, a genuine hereditary title—I've always thought being a lady was more about how a woman conducts herself. Speaking of which, now *there's* a true lady..."

Catherine had reappeared from the bathroom and was walking through the restaurant, still elegantly picking her way between tables despite the large amount of wine we'd consumed. Her gold silk dress flowed gracefully behind her —God, she was beautiful. She reached the table and gave us both a warm smile. Nyles was already out of his chair as the courteous assistant, pulling her chair out. He could be a charming bastard at times.

"Thank you, Nyles. Very kind—and *very* smooth."

"Ha! Well, it wasn't me who said chivalry is dead." Nyles grinned and winked at me.

An exceptionally charming bastard—but we were okay.

Everything was okay.

19

LADY ANN

"Wow—those are some outrageous assets!"

The list of properties that Lady Ann Mei Golbourne owned spanned three entire A4 pages in twelve-point font. According to Nyles, these were just her UK properties.

Lady Ann had started buying property with her husband in the early 1970s. Lord Golbourne may have possessed the hereditary title and initial wealth, but it was Lady Ann who was the brains behind the operation. Over the following decades, her shrewd investment strategy grew into an empire.

Raised in British Hong Kong as the only child of hard-working parents, Lady Ann had arrived in the UK in the mid-1960s. Her parents' work ethic had rubbed off on her—she had been awarded a full scholarship to live and study in the UK.

She had met Lord Golbourne in her final year at Cambridge, when she was asked to tutor him as a struggling first-year student who was reading economics more as a result of family connections than academic prowess. For

Lord Golbourne, it was love at first sight—an exotic older lady from the Far East. Lady Ann took a little longer to fall for the charms of the wealthy, good-looking Englishman, but in the end succumbed. The pair tied the knot soon after she graduated.

Lady Ann initially pursued her interest in applied economics through investing in various stock markets. However, such heavy involvement and her competitive nature left the couple with little time to enjoy the finer things in life, to which they had abundant access. The Golbournes therefore switched their attention to the property market and began gradually amassing their sizeable portfolio. They continued in the same vein until Lord Golbourne died suddenly of a heart attack a little over a year ago, leaving Lady Ann a widow.

An extremely wealthy widow.

"I know! She owns half of Hampshire," Nyles said. "Plus she's still got a massive share portfolio—you can see why her kids are so avidly interested in her wellbeing."

"How many did you say she has?"

"Three. All complete arseholes—though they do vary a little in type."

Nyles was correct. Lady Ann's children were not nice people. Her eldest son, Simon, was the most comprehensively failed entrepreneur I'd ever heard of. He had been bailed out of numerous doomed business ventures by his family wealth, though he still remained in significant debt. Richard Branson he was not.

Lady Ann's middle child was her only daughter, Melissa Golbourne, who had kept her maiden name despite her marriage to a degenerate gambler called Mark Doyle. Melissa continued to cruise through life on the strength of the Golbourne name and remained one of London's most elite socialites. Her husband was a retired model and actor who looked good on her arm, but had little going on upstairs. This didn't serve him well as a passionate gambler, and massive debts had prevailed.

And then there was Daniel...

Daniel Golbourne was the youngest and most dysfunctional of Lady Ann's children—the blackest sheep of the family. Instead of gracefully accepting a life of privilege, it seemed Daniel had actively rebelled against it at every opportunity. As a young boy, he'd initially been the golden child. He'd been extremely likeable, although perhaps not the brightest of children. This may or may not have had something to do with Lady Ann's brief addiction to prescription pills that unfortunately occurred while she was pregnant with Daniel.

Things started to go badly wrong after he was sent away to boarding school, which was not a happy place for Daniel. The environment starkly contrasted with the warmth and love he had been surrounded by in his family home—albeit largely as a result of doting au pairs. Life at a British boarding school was a shock to the system. Keen to maintain the likeability he had fostered in his early years, he was eager to please.

Daniel's desire to fit in, combined with not being the smartest of boys, made him an easy target for some of the school's crueller characters, and he was duly exploited. His first major misdemeanour was being caught with his boarding house's drug stash, which he'd volunteered to safeguard. A swift expulsion saw him moved to another boarding school, where once again he fell in with the wrong crowd, found trouble and was expelled. A cycle had begun.

When he was sixteen, Daniel's parents decided enough was enough. This, and the fact that schools had started to decline him despite his parents' significant wealth, saw him sent overseas to a strict military-esque boarding school in Hong Kong. Lady Ann felt the only solution was some old-fashioned Cantonese discipline to set him back on the straight and narrow.

Alas, it didn't.

The decision to send Daniel to Hong Kong was one that Lady Ann regretted deeply, and was perhaps the reason that he remained the greatest source of her guilt regarding her children. His time in Hong Kong saw him graduate from naughty schoolboy to amateur criminal in impressive time.

"Triads?" I asked Nyles.

"Well, brother, that is the rumour."

"Rumour from where?"

"His mother, mainly. She thinks he's some sort of triad kingpin. Bless."

"So, he's not?"

"No. Most definitely not a crime lord—poor chap is widely perceived as a joke."

"But surely even a *casual* triad association is something to take seriously?"

"This is London, mate—everyone and everything is about two degrees of separation away from organised crime."

"I'm not!"

"Of course not." Nyles' grin was one of bemusement. "Look, I'm not saying that he's soft—of course he should be treated with a degree of caution. He's just overly anxious to prove himself, which has resulted in... outbursts."

"Outbursts?"

"Yes, you know, the odd bit of affray—he's managed to

get himself a police record. Something I'm not entirely sure Lady Ann is aware of."

"Okay, I get it. He's a bit of a bad lad, but not exactly one of the Krays?"

"Couldn't have put it better myself."

"And the triad connection?"

"It appears greatly exaggerated—the investigator I hired has come up with a low-level connection to an underground gambling ring, and that's it. I'm afraid this isn't going to turn into a kung-fu movie." Nyles got up from his chair and walked over to the window, shaking his head and chuckling to himself.

"But why is any of this a concern to us?" I asked. "What does Lady Ann want us to do? Fix her children for her? Surely we can't just start Deconstructing their lives?"

"Jesus, Will! Of course not. Haven't you been paying *any* attention?"

"Well, what does she want?"

"She wants her *own* life Deconstructed."

"Why? How will that help her sort things with her children?"

"I guess she understands you can't change others, but you can change your reactions to them."

Nyles paused and gazed out along the river while I reflected on what he said. I guess you really couldn't change people, could you—why waste time trying?

"So you're saying her Deconstruction involves cutting off her children?"

"Well, to some extent—if they remain the spoilt and dependent brats that they are, then why shouldn't she? In their present form, her children pose her nothing but misery —no source of joy, happiness or fulfilment in the slightest."

"And you think she'll go for that?"

"Well, that's only part of her Deconstruction, clearly."

"And the rest?"

"That's up to her to decide, and we'll have a better idea once we've met her."

"Right—so when are we meeting her?"

"In about... No! Hang on, what's the time?"

"Just gone half past."

"Well then, any minute now, I guess."

"Ah, for fuck's sake, Nyles! Why do you keep doing this? Any kind of warning or heads-up in future would be appreciated!"

I hurriedly began dragging the office furniture in place to create Nyles' familiar triangular *open-space arrangement*. Nyles conveniently excused himself in order to be ready to greet Lady Ann in person at the door. Shortly afterwards, I heard voices coming from the reception area. She'd arrived. I frantically looked around for my jacket, desperate for something to cover the many patches of sweat that had emerged following my bout of furniture wrestling.

The door abruptly swung open. Lady Ann entered as Nyles held it open for her.

"... and may I present our Executive Director—Mr William Harper."

"Lady Golbourne, it's an absolute pleasure to—"

"Please, call me Ann."

"Right, erm, of course—Ann. Please have a seat."

I took her delicate hand and shook it gently. Her appearance surprised me; my perception of a multi-millionaire was one of extreme glamour, high-end designer clothes, loads of jewellery—that kind of thing. Instead, she wore a plain white linen blouse and blue jeans—a Lady in *501s?* She had a pleasant, round face that was naturally youthful.

She gave me a brief smile that vanished as quickly as it had appeared, and sat down.

Adriana gracefully entered the room and took tea and coffee orders. Lady Ann asked for Earl Grey. This was a relief, as I was struggling to get my head around her. Earl Grey at least seemed the correct choice for a Lady of the realm.

"She is a *lovely* young thing, isn't she? So vibrant. Where's she from? Her accent sounds Latin American."

"São Paulo—I knew her father," Nyles answered. "He was keen to get her out of the favelas, so we sponsored her visa. She's settled into the job and life in London very well indeed."

He was absolutely full of it! Nyles shot me a fatherly look to ensure my raised eyebrows descended into a look of mutual acknowledgement.

"Now, Lady Gol—"

"Please—just Ann."

"Sorry—Ann. I know we've shared a lengthy correspondence, but I've kept the content of our letters largely private."

Letters! Nyles had been writing letters? I tried hard to mask my surprise as Lady Ann looked directly at me. I returned the most sympathetic smile I could muster, now unsure of what I was and wasn't meant to know. The best thing to do was to keep quiet.

Lady Ann looked around the office. "This isn't quite what I was expecting. It's a little..."

"Corporate?" Nyles supplied.

"Yes. That's it."

"Yes, I know—it's a shame. Will and I choose the place more for its location by the river. It was important for us to be by flowing water because of what it symbolises."

"Oh, I see."

Bizarrely, this explanation seemed to suffice. Perhaps Nyles and Lady Ann had established themselves on the same wavelength through all the letter-writing.

"So, Will here knows you're unhappy, and of course that's why you're here. But maybe you could start by telling us how long you've felt like this?"

"Well, I guess you can trace it back to the death of Simon."

"Your late husband."

"Yes, my soulmate."

"Once again, I'm so sorry."

"Thank you. Simon's death hit me hard. It was so sudden. I just wasn't at all prepared. It pulled the rug out from under me. I've never felt so..."

She broke off and looked out towards the river. I decided that this was the opportunity to involve myself in the counselling session.

"Alone?"

"Not just alone—more... empty. Yes—empty, totally empty. I looked around me for support and saw that there wasn't any. I was surrounded by wealth and fortune, but none of it helped. I thought I could rely on my children, but it turned out I didn't know them anymore. They were worse than strangers to me. Isn't that awful?"

"My God—yes. But why...?"

"Well, none of my children—I have three, you see—have really turned out as I would have... liked."

"I see. So you're not close?"

"Each of them now seems to be counting down the days until I join their father. They're like starving vultures, already circling my carcass."

"So you think they're after your wealth?"

"I don't just *think*, young man. I *know!*" Lady Ann took a few seconds to compose herself before giving me a tired smile. "I'm so sorry, William—please forgive me. You see, I know that they've already tried to get hold of their inheritance. My lawyers are very open and honest with me. They've told me that enquiries have been made. The silly thing is—I no longer have any interest in any of the money or wealth. Simon's death has put things into perspective. It's just... their behaviour has really brought it home to me."

"Brought what home?"

"How much I've failed."

From where I was sitting, it didn't look like she'd failed at much in life. I was trying to appear empathetic, but the blank look on my face gave me away.

"Failed as a mother, William. I have failed my children, and that's perhaps the greatest failure a woman can have."

"Right. Sorry—of course. I'm sorry."

"Looking back at my life, it's now very clear to me that I have sacrificed my children's upbringing for my own life—my career, my social life... All for myself."

Lady Ann broke off as her eyes began to well up. Deep, dark pools of tears looked ready to overflow. *Oh God! Please don't cry!* I was very bad at dealing with crying women—I was highly likely to go to pieces myself. I began to panic and looked desperately at Nyles for help. Thankfully, he came to the rescue with a seasoned sympathetic smile and an offer of one of his tailored handkerchiefs, taken from his breast pocket.

Lady Ann graciously accepted it and gently dabbed her eyes. "Please forgive me."

"No. I'm sorry—I'm afraid Will doesn't know a great deal about your situation. I felt that everything you've shared with me was done so in the strictest confidence. It wouldn't have been right to discuss it with him."

"No, it's fine. I'm very grateful for your counsel so far. Really, I am."

"Ann, I can assure you so far I have merely been an open ear and nothing more."

Nyles continued to nod sympathetically as he slowly walked back to his chair. Lady Ann finished with the handkerchief, folding it neatly into quadrants as she regained her composure.

"Will and I have often discussed parents' relationships with their children—it's something we've been reflecting on here a great deal," Nyles went on. "It's absolutely key to the process of Deconstruction, as it's often a source of so, so much tension."

This was, of course, nonsense. Nyles had never asked about the relationship between my mother and myself, which could be described as distant at best. Thankfully, Lady Ann continued to hold his empathetic gaze, so missed my expression of bewildered surprise as Nyles' bullshit level reached an uncomfortable new height.

"I believe your relationship with your children could actually benefit greatly from your own Deconstruction."

"How, exactly?"

"Well, as I've said before, Deconstruction can be a process of purification through simplification. It involves separating oneself from each element in one's life a step at a time. It sounds like you have already begun this process to some degree by yourself—you've reached an epiphany regarding material wealth and what is more important."

"But I can't get my children to see that! I mean, it's taken me virtually my whole life *and* the loss of my soulmate for me to do so!"

"Very true. You can't change people. But what you *can* change is your reactions to them, and that is central to Deconstruction. It *is* possible to separate everything from everything else—your wealth, your children, your relationship with them, and most importantly, your future and theirs."

Cue pause for dramatic effect. Lady Ann looked like she was going to need a little more convincing than that.

"May I run a scenario past you to see what you think?"

"Of course, Nyles—that's why I'm here."

"Very well. Now, this is just one of many possible scenarios. Your assets could be placed in a trust and managed independently. The trust will, of course, generate profits, and these could be used purely for charitable purposes—good work undertaken anonymously or in your family's name. Your children could even be afforded access to some of the trust's resources, should they fulfil certain conditions."

"Conditions?"

"Requirements that would need to be satisfied in order for them to have any association with the trust."

"And what might these be?"

"Well, given that you yourself are beginning to follow a certain path, I think these should be entirely up to you."

Lady Ann appeared to consider this for a moment, then allowed herself a small smile. "What you're suggesting, Nyles, is not going to be popular."

"Of course not."

"But it might be for their own good in the end."

"Exactly. Your relationship with them *will* change—that is certain. Perhaps not for the better initially, but in the long run, it may be closer to something you actually want."

Lady Ann fell into silent contemplation. Nyles sat back

in his chair, compassion painted all over his face. Finally, Lady Ann cleared her throat.

"So you're saying I can decide under what circumstances they receive income from the trust."

"Precisely—or possibly even the right to manage the trust itself in order to continue its good work."

"If they decide to follow the right path, that is..."

"Of course—and if they're on the right path, *really* on it, then they'll know exactly how to use the money wisely and justly to help others."

And there it was. Simple, really. Simple apart from the fact that there was no way on Earth her children would let it happen.

"If it's okay with you," Nyles added, "Will and I can begin work on a preliminary proposal—with your blessing, of course."

Lady Ann gave a shrug. "You may—it is, after all, a proposal and nothing more. I shall of course compensate you for your time if I decide against your proposition."

Nyles smiled warmly. "That won't be necessary—the opportunity to help others is fundamentally why we exist. The only fees we charge our clients are those to handle the logistics of their Deconstruction should they choose to proceed."

"Very well. Then if I may ask—how do you afford all of this?"

"We have been fortunate enough to receive a number of donations from those we've helped Deconstruct and find their own paths."

"I see."

I was staying well out of this. Surely this particularly stretch of the truth could easily be revealed if Lady Ann decided to look into it.

"Well, in that case, I shall leave you gentlemen to your work. I'm sure you're very busy, and I'm afraid I have another engagement."

Nyles and I stood up and exchanged handshakes and goodbyes with Lady Ann before Adriana showed her to the lift.

"Donations, eh?" I asked.

Nyles grinned shamelessly. "Well, okay, you got me there, brother—just the *one* very generous donation so far from *one* very grateful Deconstructee." Seemingly vindicated, he nodded and jumped up. "Right! So, we'll need to come up with the goods quick smart over this!"

"We will?"

"Absolutely. The longer we leave it, the more chance there is of one of those bastard vultures finding out."

"Right. Well, shall we chat over lunch?"

"Sorry, brother—another day. Unfortunately I've an appointment."

"Right now?"

"'Fraid so—really need to shoot. Look, why don't you take a wee butcher's at this little puppy and let me know your thoughts?"

Nyles produced an A4 manila envelope from thin air and flung it across the desk towards me, accurately missing the cafetière and assorted empty cups. I picked it up and pulled out a document recognisable as one that Adriana had neatly bound. I began flicking through it as Nyles was putting on his suit jacket, one foot already out the door.

"When the hell did you come up with this?" I asked.

"Adriana bound it this morning—she's done a lovely job, hasn't she?"

"No, I mean—"

"Look, brother—there's weeks of research in there. Have

a look and tell me what you think, but right now I need to combine sex and travel."

"Sex and travel?"

"I need to fuck off!"

"Right. Well, goodbye, then."

I settled into Nyles' comfy chair to digest the lengthy tome. It began with an outline for Lady Ann's tailored Deconstruction. She would initially embark on a two-month stay at a remote Buddhist monastery in the Khumbu Valley, right in the heart of the Nepalese Himalayas. It sounded idyllic, complete with easily accessible views of Mount Everest if you didn't mind a short trek. Immersion in spirituality and reconnection with nature. Simple.

Following the stay at the monastery, Nyles felt that Lady Ann would be better placed to make a decision regarding the particular path she might choose to take. Meanwhile, the two months would be spent finalising the details of her family trust—the foundation that would channel its profits into charitable causes.

I flipped through the pages listing her assets in greater detail and arrived at the section regarding her children. There appeared to be three proposed conditions that they would have to fulfil in order to receive any sort of income from the trust. The preconditions were laid out on a page interspersed with quotations from His Holiness the Dalai Lama:

1. Involvement in charity work. *Our prime purpose in this life is to help others.*
    1. Productive community members. *Be kind whenever possible. It is always possible.*
    2. Sustained commitment to meditation and Buddhist teachings. *Happiness is not*

*something ready-made. It comes from your
own actions.*

I had to admit there was a certain charm to it. Through
the trust, her children were being offered a chance of salvation: self-improvement with the added incentive of lifelong
support.

They weren't going to have a bar of it.

20

A TRUST THING

One of many issues with Nyles' proposal for Lady Ann's Deconstruction was that he had absolutely no idea how to go about setting up a trust or charitable foundation. These details had been glossed over in the otherwise very detailed document he had produced. Predictably, it fell to me to research how such things were done, and the remainder of the week was spent painfully doing just this.

A brief phone conversation with Nyles the day after Lady Ann's visit left me with little doubt that he was relying on me entirely to produce an overview of how the trust would function and support the attached charitable foundation. Nyles automatically presumed that, as a qualified accountant, I could pretty much turn my hand to anything relating to finance and the law. This was not the case. I could have explained to Nyles in great depth the many not-so-subtle nuances of different types of accountancy, but there's no chance he would have let me.

Not wanting to disappoint him, but mainly because there was nothing else to do, I embarked upon the extremely tedious process of finding out what it would take to create a trust for Lady Ann. All the while, I was cognisant of the fact that this was merely a proposal and would likely end up being a complete waste of time. This did little to motivate me.

Having gleaned a rudimentary knowledge of family trust law from the internet, I put what I'd learnt into practice. Painstakingly, I began organising Lady Ann's vast resources to produce a very basic document detailing how, *hypothetically*, a trust could be structured.

During that week, to escape the boredom, I periodically scoured the internet, trying to find out more about Terry. Nyles had reassured me that he was fine, but had been typically vague with the details. This made me more intrigued. I had to find out for certain—not just because I didn't completely trust Nyles, but because I felt partly responsible and wanted to be sure that we'd really made a difference. Confirming he was now living a better life would surely generate some enthusiasm for the mind-numbing task at hand.

Unfortunately, I'd come up with nothing. Terry had vanished without a trace. I looked for details on the sale of his business empire, but found little—the odd story in a local paper from a town where a warehouse was based, but nothing more. A Google search trying to connect the sale of the business with Jaroslav came up with absolutely nothing. It was strange that the sale of such a large company had gone unnoticed, but then again, Jaroslav was probably the type of businessman who favoured a degree of privacy.

Towards the end of the week, I was craving the weekend. Catherine was going to be away, and for once Max was going to be around. It was time to hit the beers and enjoy a weekend-long session with my main amigo. After a week of utter tedium that had begun to remind me what having a proper job was like, it was exactly what I needed.

Max and I were still living together in Canary Wharf—it wasn't exactly bohemian living, but it was easy. Maybe too easy. Despite only putting in the occasional appearance as a housemate and landlord, the sight of him lazing around in his tight white Armani boxer briefs had distressingly become something I'd grown to accept. I no longer even voiced an objection.

Living with Max was not only easy; it was familiar. Sometimes it felt like stepping back in time to my second year at Durham University when I'd briefly lived with him before moving in with Lucy. Max's father had bought him a swanky flat near the town centre. Our cohabitation had been filled with harmony and good times. Things weren't so different now.

Our Sundays in particular were almost carbon copies of those we'd spent together hungover in Durham. The university hangover remedy still worked: couple of joints and then endless hours of PlayStation until hunger drove us out of the house in search of the most easily accessible greasy food.

All the pubs around Max's flat catered to the Monday-to-Friday city commuter crew. Consequently, they were soulless, overpriced establishments lacking entirely in ambiance. On Sundays they were deserted and at their nadir. However, wrapped in the warm, cotton-wool fugue of hangovers and marijuana, we didn't care. Max and I enjoyed strolling around the streets clad in our student-esque tracksuit bottoms and hoodies with an ironic air like we owned the place. On Sundays, we might as well have.

Today we'd walked slightly further than usual, to a bar that was still part of some godforsaken chain but at least had marginally better food. The main reason we went there, though, was because Max liked the barmaid. Sara was a student from Birmingham who only worked there part time, but was generally there on Sundays.

As Max and I strolled in, Sara almost looked grateful to see us. We were her only patrons aside from a couple of career alcoholics propping up the bar and attempting to put to right the wrongs of the world with their own unique brand of philosophical misogyny. Max, very much with his own rival brand, grabbed a couple of menus off the bar and tried his usual sleazy wink at Sara. She returned it with the usual roll of her eyes.

"*Awww yeah!* Northern birds, eh? Gotta love 'em!"

"That poor, poor girl."

"Any day now, mate, any day."

"Yep, she looks *so* close to cracking."

We sat down at our usual table, positioned strategically by the window but also giving Max a good view of the bar and the entrance to allow him maximum *reconnaissance potential*. He enthusiastically flicked through the menu we both knew intimately.

His analysis came to an abrupt end and he tossed the menu down. "I think I'm going to eat something just a little bit special today."

"Really?"

"*Awww yeah!* Gonna hit something up that might be considered pretty radical in the world of pizza."

"Go on."

"Meat feast—with avocado!"

"Avocado on a pizza?"

"*Awww yeah!*"

"You're going to have to ask for that specifically, and I'm afraid Sara's going to think you're mentally unwell, mate."

"A-ha! But that's what all geniuses are told! Take Nyles, for example—at times you've got to think he's pretty close to being a genius and mental at the same time."

"Hmmm... still not made my mind up on that one."

"Really? But you work with the guy!"

"But as I've told you—I hardly even *see* the guy."

"Right, yes, true. So, what're you guys working on at the moment?"

This level of interest was rare for Max. Although nominally one of the company's directors, the backseat he'd taken wasn't even in the same vehicle.

"Well, *I'm* still trying to sort this bloody trust. As for Nyles, I couldn't tell you—he's... an enigma."

"Fair enough. I guess it doesn't matter. Damned good work on that Terrence chap. We only really need one client like that a year and we're laughing!"

"You know how much we made from that? I don't even know that!"

"Well, no, not exactly. I mean, Nyles just hinted that we were in line for a rather handsome little profit!"

"Uh-huh, the exact details of which still remain a mystery."

"Jesus, Will, chill out. I'm sure it's just not been finalised yet. So, you going for your usual—steak sandwich?"

"Yeah, why not. Best play it safe. I'm not exactly feeling a hundred percent."

Max grabbed the menus and bounded over to the bar in a puppy-esque fashion to hassle Sara with our order. I'm sure on some level his relentlessness was endearing, and maybe it would even eventually work. But not today. From our position of *maximum reconnaissance potential*, I was able to clearly see Max's business card once again being rejected. He shrugged, returning to the table with his grin already back in place.

"So, she didn't go for that number again, eh?"

"Getting closer each time, buddy! She definitely considered it for a bit longer this time."

"Dare I ask what's going on with Veronika?"

"Ah, yes, well, I think that ship may have sailed, old boy."

"Really? I thought she was very possibly *the one?*"

"I don't think I ever actually said that."

"I'm almost certain you did."

"Well, in that case, I *definitely* take it back!"

"What happened?"

"I'm not entirely sure. She may not have quite been all she seemed..."

"Wow! Really? I genuinely cannot wait for this."

"I think she may have been some sort of *spy* or something. Although I could possibly be wrong."

"A *spy?*"

"Well, working for the intelligence services at least..."

"For which country?"

"The Ukraine, or whichever godforsaken Eastern Bloc hellhole place she came from."

"And why do you think that?"

Max hesitated and clenched his jaw awkwardly. "Look, I guess she probably wasn't..."

"A spy?"

"Probably not."

"So, why would you even begin to think that?"

"Well, at first I thought I was just losing stuff— you know, the odd note here, the odd note there. You know I'm not great at keeping track of money like you are."

"Max—*anyone* is better at keeping track of money than you."

"True. Well, I guess that could have carried on for a while without me really cottoning on. But anyway, then I lost my Blackberry a couple of times..."

"I thought you lost that when you were pissed?"

"So did I, initially! But then my watch vanished..."

"You said it got nicked at the gym!"

"That's what I thought! But then last week I was at the office, and I thought I'd left my wallet at home... but then I got a call from one of my credit card companies."

"Oh shit—what did she do?"

"I'm guessing she intended to go on a shopping spree, but hadn't realised quite how close my credit cards are to their limit—*awww yeah!* You know how I like to roll. Anyway, the seven-grand Versace dress she tried to buy triggered a call to the credit card company. They called me, I cancelled the card, then tried to call her. Straight to answerphone. Then I got another call from a *different* credit card company—same story. So I cancelled that one, tried calling her again, same story. So I tried cold calling Versace stores, and bingo. First one, Regent Street, confirmed an Eastern European–looking woman had been trying to buy a dress— had two credit cards rejected and my gym card declined."

"Your *gym card?*"

"Well, it sort of looks like a credit card..."

"Fuck, mate. I'm so sorry."

"It's all good, mate—probably for the best."

"*Definitely* for the best—that's totally shit. But why the fuck did you think she could have been a spy?"

"Well, I got home that day and saw she'd taken my bloody laptop as well!"

"Fuck! That new MacBook?"

"Yep! Brand spanking new."

"And that's it? She took your MacBook?"

"Yep. Pretty weak evidence, I admit. But you know, gathering intel and that..."

"Not one of your best conspiracy theories."

Max nodded slowly in grim agreement. He'd been done. He shook his head and grinned. "Still, great shag though—*awww yeah!*"

Nothing more than a little collateral damage on the path to true love, then.

THE SECOND WEEK working on Lady Ann's trust was similar to the first, though even duller. Nyles had emphasised that the trust needed to be legally watertight and so put me in touch with a seemingly reputable law firm in the East End. I embarked on a cheerless correspondence with a number of lawyers with names like Brian who lacked even a suggestion of a sense of humour.

Lengthy queries from my end received monosyllabic responses from theirs:

> No.

Or if I was lucky, I sometimes got a:

> NOT POSSIBLE AND ILLEGAL.

The week wasn't all bad, though. Regular coffee breaks at Georgio's with Adriana were a daily highlight, and things were still going well with Catherine. Weekly dates and flirty texts had grown into daily phone calls and the very early stages of a relationship. Drunken snogs and fondles had now become fully-fledged sexual intercourse. And it was good—amazing, in fact!

I'd now even been introduced as her boyfriend at least once, and she'd done that with her usual grace and coolness and not a trace of awkwardness. No need to make a big thing about it. I suppose that's how we seamlessly came to be in an actual, proper relationship. Despite her office's proximity, I drew the line at visiting her at work—a sort of professional courtesy that I think she appreciated.

Things were going well. So well that it was inevitably time for us to have our first argument. There are few certainties in life, but arguments are one of them.

We'd gone to a new tapas bar near Carnaby Street on Thursday evening. I wasn't in the best frame of mind. I was frustrated about working on the trust without any support. I hadn't been able to get hold of Nyles since our brief exchange the previous week. I'd ridiculously even tried to run a few things past Max, which had been about as useful as I'd expected. Max was very much of the opinion that I should chill and wait for Nyles to turn up. I tried and failed. I just wanted to finish the task, regardless of whether it turned out to be a waste of time or not. Stressed and grumpy, I'd been looking forward to the evening with Catherine all week.

The bar had a good vibe—bustling but not hectic. Catherine sat across from me at a windowside table. She perused the menu while gently chewing her bottom lip, as she did when deep in thought.

"Look, Will, I honestly don't care, as long as there's a bloody massive plate of patatas bravas somewhere in the mix."

"Okay, I'll just order that then, along with an array of

dishes I can't pronounce, allowing me to humiliate myself in front of that tall, dark and handsome waiter."

"Sounds perfect, William! So you have a thing for the waiter? Now that is interesting."

"I just think he has a certain Mediterranean charm."

"Not really my type."

"Lucky for me."

I tried to catch the eye of said waiter and failed. Irritated, I sat back in defeat and allowed a sigh to slip out.

"Are you okay? I sense a little bit of agitation brewing."

"I'm fine—just work stuff..."

"Work stuff that you don't want to talk about with your adorable, highly intelligent girlfriend who is capable of providing unbiased expert advice at no cost?"

"Ha! Oh, it's just this fucking trust thing... I think I've nearly finished, but I don't really know what I'm doing, and I can't get hold of Nyles."

"That wouldn't happen to be a trust thing for a certain Lady Golbourne, by any chance?"

I froze and took a sharp breath, inhaling the sip of beer I'd been taking. What followed was a minute-long coughing and choking display for the benefit of the entire restaurant.

"Jesus, Will! Are you okay?"

"Sorry. I'm sorry."

I finished choking and saw through streaming eyes that Catherine wore a genuine look of concern. I gasped, coughed again and took another more cautious swig of beer, attempting a smile while my mind raced.

"How do you, erm, know about, erm, Lady Ann...?"

"Lady Golbourne?"

"Uh-huh. Yes, sorry—Lady Golbourne." I undertook another succinct bout of violent coughing.

"How do you think?"

A blank look was all I had in response.

"Nyles, you idiot! I thought you knew?"

"Nyles?"

"Yes, Nyles. Your elusive *supposed* boss. How do you not know this?"

I felt the colour seep out of my face like a slow tide drifting out.

"Will—what's going on? Why don't you know about this?"

"Well, Nyles can be pretty elusive, as you say..."

"Yes, but I presumed he'd have talked to you about this! I thought you'd suggested using my firm, for God's sake!"

I shook my head weakly. The waiter took this opportune moment to come over and try to take our order. Catherine politely asked for a reprieve. I'd suddenly lost my appetite.

"What's he asked you to do?"

"Will, you know I can't tell you that now."

"What? Why?"

"*Because*—you've just revealed you haven't a bloody clue that he's spoken to us! How is that even possible? Why hasn't he told you?"

"Look, I'm sure he had his reasons—he doesn't tell me half of what he does. Regular communication isn't exactly his forte. And besides, how can I even hazard a guess when you won't tell me what it's about?"

"What's going on, Will?"

What *was* going on? Did I even know anymore? Clearly I didn't know the full story, but I wasn't in charge. Nyles was the boss, so how could I be expected to know everything he was doing? I hardly ever saw the bastard!

"Nothing, as far as I know."

"Right—*nothing*. So, you've just thrown a complete

mental and almost choked to death on your beer because *nothing* is going on?"

"I guess I'm just annoyed at Nyles."

"For not running it past you?"

"Yes. Well, that and the fact that I'm being forced to work with some other law firm."

"What? He's using two law firms? What the hell are you guys playing at?"

"I... I guess Nyles must have his reasons..."

"Which would be? Will, this is really, *really* weird. Is there something you're not telling me?"

"No! Seriously!"

"Are you sure?"

"Look, all I'm doing at the moment is working on this stupid trust."

"Okay, well, you need to talk to him, then—sort this out! It's messed up."

"You're right. I will."

This was unbelievable. I couldn't believe Nyles would do this. What the fuck was he playing at? Catherine, sensing my anger, diplomatically decided to drop the subject.

"Shall we just bloody well order some tapas? I'm starving. Where'd that bloody waiter go?"

"He seems to have pissed off—I'm pretty sure if we start arguing again, he'll reappear."

"Ha! Not a bad strategy, William."

The rest of the evening thankfully passed in a more cordial manner. It always felt good just being with Catherine, and by the end of the meal I'd almost managed to forget about Nyles involving her firm. However, the resentment was still there, and I felt guilty about it, even though it wasn't my fault.

That probably underpinned my reluctant agreement to meet Catherine's parents for the first time. Sunday lunch at their house in Surrey. Over forty-eight hours of apprehension and anxiety stretched between then and now.

The rest of the weekend was absolutely ruined just thinking about it.

21

LIFE'S GREATEST REWARDS

A BRIEF but particularly hot spell of weather at the end of June convinced me and the rest of London that summer had arrived. Suit jackets were shed, shirtsleeves rolled up, and lunch breaks became liberally extended. Walking home from the office and enjoying the balmy evening air became a routine. I enjoyed the leisurely stroll and just being part of London with its injection of summer sunshine serotonin. Pubs were already rammed well before five p.m. as London skived off early, or perhaps never made it back to the office from that lunch break...

The much-dreaded meeting of Catherine's parents had gone well. We'd left the house late on Sunday evening with promises to return next time for an entire weekend. I'd combatted my preceding anxiety by spending the entire day before behaving like a monk: I ate well, I exercised, I avoided alcohol, and most importantly, I avoided swearing. The fear of developing a sort of sudden onset Tourette's and accidentally letting a *fuck* slip out weighed heavily on my mind. But the training paid off—good impressions were made, and the weekend passed without incident.

Back at work, the office was all mine, as Adriana was on a week's holiday in Barcelona with friends. I'd gotten as far as I could with Lady Ann's trust the week before, and I emailed Nyles the completed document on Monday morning. A huge sense of relief swept over me as I clicked *Send*. With that finished, I was able to look forward to a week of tranquillity: spending time killing time. Before she'd left, Adriana had diverted all her calls to a messaging service, so even the main phone wasn't going to ring. Throughout the entire week my blissful solitude was only interrupted by two phone calls on our other line—both caused me to jump out of my skin.

The first call was from Nyles, early on in the week. Suddenly hearing his voice on the other end of a telephone caught me by surprise. In fact, I was so surprised I momentarily forgot how pissed off I was meant to be with him for involving Catherine and her law firm without telling me.

"Morning, brother!"

"Holy shit! Nyles?"

"Indeed it is. How's life in the big smoke?"

"Good—I mean, I can't complain. Where are you?"

"N.Y."

"New York?"

"Yep. The Big, Big Apple. Weather's bloody awful for this time of year, but I'm dealing with it. Hitting the gym hard—going through a bit of a detox."

"Another one?"

"Ha! Yes, I guess so! Life is a series of detoxes, after all—feast then famine."

"And you couldn't possibly have done that here in London?"

"Had a spot of business Stateside as well, brother—a potential client, no less."

"And...?"

"Best not talk too much over the phone, mate. All will be revealed in good time."

"Okay..."

"Listen, in a bit of a rush—just checking in, really."

Then I remembered! Cue instant anger dialled up to ten.

"Fuck! Nyles! There is something, actually. Something I need to talk to you about."

"Can it wait until I'm back?"

Slow inhalation of breath. Pause. *Composure*.

"No. No, I'm afraid it can't."

"Okay then. What's up?"

"Why the fuck didn't you tell me you'd involved Catherine's firm with Lady Ann's trust?"

"What? Oh—*that*? That's it? Because I didn't think it was a big deal!"

"Not a big *deal*?"

"Yeah, I just wanted a legal opinion."

"What about the other firm?"

"Well, they're a bunch of pricks."

"You don't trust them?"

"I trust them entirely! They're the most scrupulous bastards you could ever meet. That doesn't mean they're not pricks."

"Then why use another law firm?"

Nyles sighed and took a deep breath before replying wearily, "Because, like I told you, it's crucial that this trust is legally airtight. Now, we're already using the best corporate and finance lawyers in town, but if I present a trust to Lady Ann that's been through two law firms, then that's twice the security. It doesn't really matter which other firm we use—I genuinely thought you'd be grateful that I was supporting your girlfriend's employment, especially in these times! It doesn't exactly strike me that her firm's doing that well."

"Well—why didn't you tell me?"

"Jesus, Will! It slipped my mind! I told Adriana, for fuck's sake."

"She's not here!"

"Right, shit, she's on leave, isn't she? Fuck! Sorry, mate, I totally forgot."

Convenient. Or was I now just being unreasonable?

"So we're cool?" Nyles prompted.

"Erm, yeah, I guess..."

"Good. Look, brother, I'm genuinely sorry. I should have asked you first. It won't happen again."

"It's fine. No hard feelings. When're you back?"

This was met with a long, drawn-out pause.

"Nyles?"

"End of the week, mate. No later. Promise I'll bring you back something nice. *Ciao!*"

THE SECOND PHONE call came midweek. By this time I'd developed a fairly solid daily routine. I would begin the day with an initial perusal of *The Times* and *The Guardian*, which were waiting on the doormat upon arrival. A brief emailing session followed in which I'd delete an inbox entirely of spam. Then I would conduct a brief bout of office-based exercise before heading down to Georgio's for a late-morning coffee, which I stretched out into an early lunch break. This would take me nicely through to the afternoon, where a more in-depth review of the papers was conducted in post-prandial bliss.

The phone call came midway through a bout of press-ups. I was using one of Max's *Men's Health* magazines that offered an "Extreme Office Workout". Throughout the day I got into the habit of attempting a variety of press-ups, squats and thrusts and an array of yogic poses aimed at strengthening that all-important core. Suffice to say I answered the telephone panting, and became acutely aware that I probably sounded like some sort of pervert.

"Hello. The... office of... Decon—Deconstruction."

"Good morning."

"Sorry... just... erm... catching my breath."

"That's absolutely fine. May I please speak to Mr Harper?"

"Erm... speaking."

"William Harper?"

The voice was familiar, but too distant to place.

"It's Ann Mei Golbourne here."

"Lady Ann?"

"Yes, that's the one. Please do try to call me Ann."

"Oh, sorry! Erm, lovely to hear from you, but I'm afraid Nyles isn't here."

"I know. It's you I wanted to talk to."

"Really?"

"Yes. I just wanted to thank you. Ideally it would have been in person, but I'm out of town and will be for some time, as I'm sure you understand."

"Oh, right, yes, erm... Thank me for what, exactly?"

"For all your hard work."

"Oh—on the trust?"

"Yes. I've decided to take it forward. I know it's not going to be popular, but it feels like the right thing to do. In fact, it *is* the right thing to do."

"Wow, that's great! Fantastic!"

"I know you must have already put a lot of time and effort into it, and I know that it'll no doubt give you a great deal of future hassle. For that I apologise in advance."

"I'm sorry, I don't quite follow..."

"My children, Mr Harper—I fear they will not take this lying down. I imagine they will cause you no end of grief."

"I see. Well, rest assured Nyles and I are quite capable..."

"I do hope so, Mr Harper. They can be quite persistent, and Daniel... Well, Daniel just has a reputation for making trouble, that's all."

"Thank you for the warning, but I'm sure we will be just fine."

"I do hope so, Mr Harper, and thank you once again. You've both really helped me see my life for what it could be."

"And what will that be, do you think, if you don't mind me asking...?"

"My life? Well, to quote Nyles, it's now a blank canvas!"

"Great! Well, erm, you're most welcome. It was a pleasure to meet you."

"You too, Mr Harper. Take care of yourself. Good day."

Was this for real? Was our second Deconstructee signed up and on board that easily?

I felt a strange mixture of elation and panic, but then a series of questions began to form in my mind. Questions that gathered momentum like an avalanche. What if there was a problem with the trust? What if we ended up facing lawyers? What if Daniel actually turned out to be a gangster? My anxiety began to turn to anger at Nyles again for not being around to discuss any of this with.

I decided I needed a pint. A pint or maybe two—that'd definitely put the world to rights.

FRIDAY AFTERNOON HAD ARRIVED. Today I was definitely leaving work early. I had a monumentally boozy lunch planned with Max and some of his city chums. I had now reached the definitive conclusion that one of life's greatest rewards was a job that allowed an individual to get absolutely rat-arsed at lunchtime.

Lunch was likely to become a protracted affair, so I'd only made the vaguest of plans to see Catherine later. She had a work thing that evening, and thankfully my attendance was not required.

I finished the *Times* crossword in record time with minimal assistance from the internet and spent the remainder of the morning going through my now well practiced *Men's Health* Extreme Office Workout. I was noticeably sorer than at the beginning of the week, but unfortunately no results were yet visible in the six-pack arena. However, I convinced myself that if I kept this up, I would eventually end up looking as ripped as the mug on the magazine's front cover.

Midway through my second set of push-ups, I heard the front door of the office burst open. I jumped to my feet, red-faced and breathing hard, and Nyles exploded into the office two nanoseconds later.

"SHIT! Sorry, brother! You weren't...?"

"No! Christ, no, I was... erm, just doing some push-ups..."

Nyles allowed a suitably awkward silence to pass before replying.

"Push-ups?"

"Yeah... It's this *Men's Health* office workout thing..."

"Right, sure."

"Honestly!"

"I believe you, brother. Thousands wouldn't. An-y-way —got you a little something."

Nyles nonchalantly tossed me a small box elegantly wrapped in striped off-white-and-gold wrapping paper. I hadn't even noticed he was holding it. I caught it with both hands. It was surprisingly heavy.

"What's this for?"

"It's an apology, brother."

"For what?"

"You know for what."

"What is it?"

"You could always open it and find out."

I slowly unwrapped the box, trying hard not to tear the expensive-looking wrapping paper. Inside was a box emblazoned with an instantly recognisable logo of a very expensive watch brand.

"A *Rolex*? Holy shit, Nyles! I can't take this!"

"Yes you can—and yes you will. Unless you want to hurt my feelings."

"But it must have cost a fortune!"

"It's a little crass to assign value to a gift, brother."

"But, I mean..."

"Please. In no way do I believe this makes up for what I did. I'm not trying to buy forgiveness. I'm just trying to demonstrate that I recognise I upset you and that I'm sorry."

"Yes, fine, apology accepted... But a *Rolex*? I can't..."

"Enough, brother. Enough."

Defeated without much fight, I opened the box. Inside was a silver Rolex with a white face. Very classic, very tasteful—very Nyles. I tried it on. It made my hand look slightly smaller than it was, but overall it looked—pretty good.

"Suits you, brother."

"Wow! Thank you—it's way too generous."

"Enough! Now, I'm going to be honest with you—I've been dry for a number of weeks and have just bought an extremely good bottle of duty-free Scotch. So, I was wondering if you'd join me for a small shot over a quick meeting?"

"Sure, absolutely. I've got lunch with Max in a bit—you should come along!"

Nyles disappeared into the reception area and came back with an unopened bottle of Scotch and a couple of glasses. I was admiring the new watch now adorning my wrist.

"I may have to pass on lunch, I'm afraid, brother."

"Sure. Other plans?"

"Happy without rocks?"

"Of course."

"Good man. I've taught you well." Nyles handed me a generous-as-ever measure of Scotch and raised his glass. "To our second successful Deconstruction!"

"Really? It's definitely in the bag?"

"It's in the bag."

"Well, in that case—to Deconstruction!"

We chinked glasses. Unsurprisingly, it was probably the best Scotch I'd ever tasted. Liquid gold.

"Wow, that's awesome!"

"Even better if you've been off the sauce for weeks."

"You sure about lunch? It should be a laugh."

Nyles had wandered over to the window and was leaning up against it with one arm while surveying the river. "I can't, mate. I'd love to, genuinely, but there's work to be done. Meeting a potential client."

"Really?"

"Yep. Main reason I was in the States. I didn't get the chance to meet them there, but now they're here in town—you're more than welcome to come along if you like."

I hesitated before replying. I'd been looking forward to writing off the afternoon with Max. True, his friends were mainly rich, entitled dickheads, but it was bound to be entertaining. On the other hand, a new client was important, and Nyles rarely invited me to do anything... And he had just bought me a Rolex.

"Sure," I said eventually. "Yeah—definitely. Lunch was just with Max—I see far too much of him anyway. What's the story with the client?"

"Well, I met with his agent a couple of times in New York and it sounds like he'd be an interesting case."

"Agent?"

"Uh-huh—we'd be broadening our horizons a little with this one."

"So, they're some sort of celebrity?"

"Yeah. Ex-A-list and now kind of treading water in that murky C-slash-D-list zone."

"Right. So who is it?"

"Chet fucking Long, brother."

"Chet Long?"

"No bullshit."

"*No fucking way!* Seriously? The eighties action hero?"

"Yep. That and those ill-advised family comedies that came after."

"Wasn't he in some Tarantino film after that?"

"No. Would have been a smart move, but no."

"Doesn't he *live* in rehab?"

"It would appear rehab ain't working, brother. He's looking to try an alternative approach, a different direction —*something fresh, something new* were his agent's exact words, I believe."

I chuckled at Nyles' fairly decent impersonation of a native New Yorker. "Wow! Chet Long—fuck!"

"Fuck indeed. I'm not sure it's exactly the right move for us, but I'm definitely up for hanging out with him for the afternoon. Things could get... interesting."

"Let me get this straight. You want me to come with you to hang out with Chet Long for the afternoon."

"Precisely. Keen?"

"Definitely keen!"

Max would almost certainly understand.

22

CHET. FUCKING. LONG

I WAS EXCITED. Very excited. I'd never met anyone famous before.

I suspected even Nyles was excited, but was just too cool to show it. In all fairness, he name-dropped enough to emphasise how different the circles he moved in were, but even so... this was Chet Long! He *had* to be excited.

The more I thought about it, the more crazy it seemed. I'd gone from a planned boozy lunch to standing in the now familiar lobby of the Savoy, on the verge of meeting Chet. Fucking. Long. Chet was the blueprint for the eighties Hollywood bad boy. He'd set the benchmark by dragging himself through three decades of drink, drugs and women. The tabloids may have grown weary of his exploits, but he was still a living legend. A completely indestructible living legend.

We stood waiting for the lift that the dutiful bellboy had called for with a degree of ceremony that seemed unnecessary. As we waited, I surveyed the surroundings: the Art Deco chequerboard floor, the tasteful marble pillars, the dark oak walls. This place wasn't bad.

I glanced at Nyles, who was chewing gum almost apprehensively—something was up. "You alright, mate?"

"Yep. Fine, brother—why?"

"You seem a little... on edge?"

"I'm fine—just jet-lagged."

"Not nervous?"

"Nervous? Come off it, brother—you must know by now that I don't do nervous! Excited, maybe, enthused, definitely, but never nervous! Nerves are a sign of weakness."

"And possibly humility?"

Nyles grinned and gave me a wink as we entered the lift.

It opened on the top floor of the hotel onto an opulent atrium, which funnelled us into an elegant corridor. I tried to follow Nyles' lead, casually strolling with an air of nonchalance towards Chet's room. Nyles rapped on the door with authority. He even managed to knock in a cool way—I still had a lot to learn from this guy.

The door swung open and a stunning model-esque blonde woman in her early twenties opened the door. She was dressed in a gold bikini that struggled to contain her, with a complementing sarong draped around her shoulders. It was hard to know where to look.

"*O.M.G.!* Nyles!"

The woman squealed her shrill orgasm-like greeting in what sounded like a Californian accent. She proceeded to literally throw herself at Nyles, jumping on him and wrapping her arms and legs around him in a tight embrace.

Nyles took a step backwards but managed to counterbalance the sudden addition without being knocked off his feet. For once, he seemed genuinely caught off guard. "Chanelle... Fancy seeing you here—my God!"

"O.M.G.! It's been, like, forever!"

"Yes... it's, erm, certainly been a while. Er, Chanelle, this is my good friend and business associate, Will Harper. Will, this is—"

"Chanelle!"

"Pleasure to meet you, Chanelle."

Chanelle dismounted from Nyles and took my hand while performing a mock curtsey. "*O.M.G.!* You guys are both, like, so adorable with those accents!"

"You're too kind, Chanelle," Nyles replied. "But, erm, may I suggest we move out of the corridor? I'm not entirely certain what the Savoy's policy on bikinis is..."

"Oh, Nyles! Would you, like, stop it already? You only just got here!"

"I..."

I was enjoying this. I'd never witnessed Nyles disarmed and uncomfortable before—I hadn't thought it possible.

We followed Chanelle into a large, dimly lit palatial suite. There was a heavy aroma of incense mixed with marijuana. Rays of brilliant sunshine snuck in through cracks in the curtains to pierce the haze. In the centre of the room was an assortment of couches and a huge glass coffee table. The room was otherwise empty. No sign of the big man.

"You guys, like, grab a beer or something—I'll go wake Chet!"

Chanelle disappeared through one of the two sets of large double doors that led off the suite's enormous open-plan living area.

"Wow—impressive to be sleeping after all that..." I pointed at the impressive quantity of cocaine and related paraphernalia on the coffee table. It had clearly been the centre of attention for some time.

Nyles grinned. "Maybe he's jet-lagged?"

"Really? Movie stars get jet-lagged too? Interesting..."

I walked over to what looked like the plushest couch and performed a quick reconnaissance glance for hypo-dermic needles before collapsing onto it.

"So, you and Chanelle—seemed like you'd met before...?"

"Yes... You astutely picked up on that, did you?"

"Getting shy on me, Nyles?"

"Hmmm. Look, brother, it was a long time ago."

"Wow! You mean you *actually* had sex with her?"

"Nice and subtle there, Will."

"Sorry, mate, I'm just in awe! She's... incredible!"

"She's certainly very attractive. I mean, she's a model—she's meant to look like that."

"So, what happened? If you don't mind me asking?"

"Look, it was just one of those holiday romances. It didn't work out. Not for want of me trying, either, I might add."

"Jesus! Where the hell do you go on holiday?"

"Different life, mate. Ancient history. Now come on—let's get a fucking drink."

Nyles clapped his hands together, rubbing them in jubilant anticipation as he went to grab a couple of beers from the impressively sized fridge in the adjoining kitchen. He handed me one and we sank back into the massive couches.

"Nice!" I sighed.

"Especially if you haven't had one in weeks."

"The couch isn't bad either."

"Yep, definitely sat on worse."

"So, you ever met *Monsieur Long* before?"

"No, not really. I think I saw him once in passing at some party, but I'd had a bit to drink—you know how it is. I don't remember actually talking to him."

"You'd probably remember something like that, though, wouldn't you.?"

"Ha—you're right. Probably!"

We sat in silence for a bit. I got the feeling my nervous chatter was getting on Nyles' nerves, so I sat back and tried to enjoy the moment. A couple of mates just chilling in Chet Long's hotel room. Completely surreal.

I took a huge swig of the crisp, cold beer to try to settle my nerves. It should have been the perfect antidote to the muggy atmosphere that hung in the room, but it just made me feel queasy. *It could really do with an open window in here.*

All of a sudden, the double door Chanelle had disappeared through swung open and the room erupted in light. Squinting against this new violent luminosity, I could just make out the silhouette of a man in a cowboy hat, who paused briefly before strolling into the room.

"'Sup, motherfuckahs?"

I'd recognise that thick Texan accent anywhere. Chet. Fucking. Long.

As my eyes adjusted, I could see Chet was dressed exactly how you'd hope he would be: barefooted with torn, frayed jeans and an open orange Hawaiian shirt that flapped around a solidly defined middle-aged paunch. Around his neck he wore a multitude of necklaces, pendants, feathers and beads. The look was topped off by his signature aviators and battered leather cowboy hat, complete with red-and-white feather sticking out of the hatband. Classic Chet.

He grinned first at Nyles and then at me. "How y'all doin'?"

It was amazing—he had one of those faces that was so well known and seemed to span decades in the public psyche. Occasionally, if looking sharp, probably with the assistance of hours of professional make-up, he could pass as a distinguished forty-year-old. However, when life had invariably... *gotten the better of him* when he was being snapped by paparazzi, checking into rehab or falling out of a limo, he looked well into his sixties. The latter appearance generally prevailed in people's minds. However, today, in the dim light, he looked somewhere in between.

I leapt to my feet, definitely with too much enthusiasm. Chet firmly shook my hand.

"Pleased to meet you, ma man!"

"Yeah! Absolutely! You too! I'm Will."

Nyles had gotten up from the couch in an altogether more dignified manner and shook Chet's hand with a far cooler uppercut-style handshake. "Nyles."

"Right on—Nyles! Ma man—heard a lot about you. You guys good for beers?"

"Another round would be sweet, brother."

Chet sauntered over to the fridge and grabbed three fresh beers. I was handed one. Chet Long handed me a fucking beer, as if it were the most normal thing in the world! I was so speechless I could only nod a thank you.

"I gotta apologise about the state of this fucking place, man... I'm sorry. I kinda roll with the *do not disturb* sign permanently on, if you get my drift."

"No apology necessary. Welcome to London, brother."

Nyles toasted and the three of us chinked our bottles together before collapsing back onto the couches. Chet drained half his beer in one long gulp. He looked from Nyles to me and back again.

"You guys get high?"

"Sure, brother," Nyles replied, and I nodded frantically in agreement.

"Cool. Well, there's a shit-ton of blow there, but I always start the day with a joint—have done since ma teens."

At that moment Chanelle breezed back into the room, sarong flowing behind her like one long exhalation.

"Shit! You guys met Chanelle, right? She's... a friend of ma wife's."

"Yes, brother, we've met," Nyles replied. I just nodded. I think this was technically called *being star-struck*. I nervously downed the rest of my beer in a desperate attempt to loosen up. But then I started to worry about over-cooking things, getting too smashed and making a total dick-head out of myself. Jesus! I needed to chill out.

Chanelle draped herself over the only remaining free couch. "Damn! This is, like, sooo bachelor party."

"That make you uncomfortable, babe? I can sure get some more female company around any time you like..."

Chanelle threw Chet a sulky pout and grabbed a half-drunk glass of champagne off the coffee table of depravity. Surely he wasn't shagging his wife's friend quite this openly?

Chet returned a grin and a wink. Clearly, he was.

An awkward pause followed where nobody spoke, though perhaps it was just me who found it awkward. Chet downed the rest of his beer and immediately appeared restless.

"Look, I just rolled a fat one, and I say we go smoke it on the balcony—enjoy some of your rare Brit sunshine. Nyles, ma man, you down?"

"Absolutely, brother—it'd be a pleasure."

Not being addressed myself, I felt this was probably a private invitation. And besides, the view from where I was sitting wasn't too bad—Chanelle didn't seem to be going anywhere fast.

Chet and Nyles extracted themselves from the couches and headed over to another set of double doors, which must have led to a balcony. Nyles looked back over his shoulder and rolled his eyes at me with a grin, closing the door behind him. I was left with Chanelle. Just me and a supermodel in a bikini, chilling out. Chilling.

Just chilling.

As my palms began to sweat, I felt I needed to at least try to start a conversation. "So, you're a friend of Chet's wife...?"

I'd grabbed the first thing I found in my head and immediately regretted it. Chanelle frowned and crossed her arms.

"Yeah, like, me and Tracy go *waaaay* back!"

Apparently not too much damage done. Maybe this was easy—maybe there was no such thing as an unacceptable question in these social circles. Perhaps I'd found my social niche—the lower levels of the Hollywood C-slash-D-list zone.

"Cool. So, how long have you known her?"

"From her modelling days, like, before she became Chet's wife. We're, like, such good friends!"

"Right, of course. So you're over just visiting, then?"

"To London? God, no! I'm, like, totally over for a shoot."

"A photoshoot?"

"Right, a photoshoot! God you're, like, *so* funny."

"I see—so you're a model as well?"

"Uh-huh! Can't you tell?" Chanelle tossed her hair back, shaking it in an exaggerated fashion. She was indeed an extremely attractive woman, and it was taking my full concentration to keep my attention on her face and not her assets, which threatened to jump out of her barely adequate bikini at any moment.

"Yes, of course. You are... erm, quite beautiful."

Dear God...

"Super cute! I, like, *love* English guys. So super, *super* cute!"

It genuinely seemed as if I couldn't fail. I barely had time to marvel at her response and how well this conversation seemed to be going before Chanelle sprang from her couch to join me on mine.

Maybe this was now going *too* well.

"So, erm, what might I have seen you in?"

"Lots! So, like, *Sports Ill* for sure—I didn't get the cover, but who cares, right?"

"The cover?"

"The cover! For like, the magazine!"

"Oh! A magazine cover."

I took a sip of my beer. Chanelle was now sitting very, very close to me. She fixed me with a look and tilted her head, holding my gaze. Slowly, she traced a finger across my right thigh, which had the adverse effect of making my entire leg convulse as though it was having its own secluded seizure. The jolt caused me to spill my beer.

"Shit! I'm so sorry, I'm extremely ticklish. Did I spill any on you?"

Chanelle giggled. "You're, like... *so* funny!"

"I'm sorry—it's just I—I have a girlfriend, and..."

"Cool! Maybe she can come by? What's her name?"

"Erm, Catherine."

"Super cute! Well, look, in the meantime, I'm totally sure Catherine wouldn't mind if you did me, like, an incy-wincy favour..."

Whatever it was, I was almost certain she *would* mind, and I was pretty certain that was written all over my face.

"Can you, like, blow a lil' coke up my ass?"

Yep. She would almost *definitely* mind. What the *fuck?* Was this really happening?

"Erm, *what?* I, erm—Jesus!"

With exceptional and rapid dexterity, Chanelle had positioned herself prone on the couch. Her skimpy bikini bottom, already discarded, hung from the toes of her right foot, which pointed skyward. Her rather perfect bottom was proffered in the same direction.

"C'mon on, hun! You're, like, the only one here..."

This was true. Nyles and Chet were still smoking on the balcony. I could vaguely hear their murmurs, which seemed to be getting louder, as if they were verging on a heated discussion. They seemed preoccupied.

I considered the situation again. No one would ever *necessarily* find out... I was a little drunk, therefore *probably* making it slightly excusable... And it was *very likely* a once-in-a-lifetime opportunity... I'd almost certainly regret it if I didn't. And the act itself didn't technically fall into the category of infidelity...

But that didn't make it okay. Catherine most certainly *would* mind very much, as I was pretty sure any girlfriend would.

"Go on, hun—pretty please!"

Chanelle was now not only proffering her perfect, smooth, immaculately tanned behind, but also the tools with which to complete the task: a thin, hollow silver tube, which she waved towards the small mountain of cocaine on the glass-top coffee table.

"Pretty please what?"

Nyles had silently strolled in from the balcony, a shroud

of sun-kissed marijuana smoke following him. He'd taken stock of the situation and had a quizzical eyebrow raised.

"Nyles! Thank God!" Chantelle cried. "Your buddy is, like, having a problem doing me a lil' favor—I think he's, y'know, a lil' uptight?"

"Will? Uptight? Surely not! What's the favour?"

"Like, I just want a lil' coke blown up my tush!"

"Really? Well, that sounds vaguely reasonable. I'd be happy to oblige."

"I don't care what you do, as long as you blow some coke up my goddamn ass!"

With one swift movement, Nyles took the silver tube she was still holding and pipetted a small dent in the white mound on the table. He then deftly leant over Chanelle's exposed behind, placed the tube to his lips and precisely performed the necessary manoeuvre.

Chanelle squealed with delight. "Ooh! I *looove* that tingle! Thanks, hun! You're, like, a *real* gent."

"My dear, I believe it may have been more gentlemanly to refrain from such an activity—much like the right honourable Mr Harper did."

The right honourable Mr Harper was now feeling like a bit of a pussy, as well as being irritated at the situation that made him feel so.

"But nevertheless, I couldn't leave a damsel in distress. Now, will the good Mr Will Harper join me in a line? Chanelle, one down the top end as well for you, my dear?"

"Sure, hun!"

I nodded. Fuck it. If things were going to get this loose, I might as well be unable to remember them.

I enviously watched Nyles racking up lines in front of me. Why couldn't I be that cool? Surely all behaviour was just learnt? He made it all look so easy. He seemed to get away with anything and maintain dignity in the process.

"Where in the fuck has ma sweet beer gotten to?" Chet had appeared in the doorway.

"Ah, shit! Sorry, brother! Your charming guest distracted me."

Nyles smiled and rolled his eyes at me. He then arranged four very large lines of cocaine on the coffee table. Chet went back out to the balcony, shaking his head in mock disgust. Grateful at the opportunity to make myself useful somehow, I rose to get another armful of beers from the fridge and took one out to Chet.

"Mr Long."

"Ha! Ma man! You Brit guys crack me the fuck up."

"Well, we aim to please."

"Amen to that!"

We clinked beers and I join him draped over the balcony balustrade, following his gaze towards the Thames.

"Some fucking river."

"It's not bad, is it?"

"See, that's the trouble with L.A., ma man!"

"What is?"

"Ain't got a river worth a shit! A river is a city's soul—and L.A. don't have one worth a shit."

"There's no river in L.A.?"

"Well, there's the L.A. River, but she's a real ugly moth-erfucking bitch—and that's on a good day. They built that shit in the thirties, man—it's a goddamn manmade streak of shit that bleeds to the sea, all under the watch of a neon Christ."

"Right, I, erm, I see—I never knew."

Chet turned to face me. It was hard to see exactly where

he was looking through the permanent fixture of his aviators, though it seemed he was sizing me up.

"So what's your story, man? You been kickin' it with Nyles long?"

I hesitated. I genuinely had no idea what angle Nyles had pitched to Chet—if any at all yet.

"Awhile. I was out of work and he was starting up this new venture, and... Well, right time, right place, I guess."

"How about that, eh?"

"Yeah, it's been interesting. Very interesting."

Chet lit up a cigarette and inhaled deeply. I got the feeling he was now looking beyond me over my shoulder. My answer had probably bored him.

"And you? What're you up to these days? Any, erm, new movies coming up?"

Chet shook his head and sucked hard to inhale a monumental lungful of smoke. "Buddy, I'm kinda on sabbatical right now—a sabbatical in getting fucked up so I can get ma shit together. You follow?"

"Yeah, I think so."

Chet clearly thought I did, at least. He flicked his cigarette over the balcony. I tried not to wince and hoped he didn't see me checking that it hadn't hit some innocent pedestrian. His attention was now clearly focused on whatever was unfolding behind me inside the suite. Nyles and Chanelle were deep in conversation. It was impossible to hear what they were talking about, but Chanelle's high-pitched giggling regularly punctuated the exchange. It was difficult to tell whether Chet was intrigued or irritated by this behind the aviators.

"Ha! That young buck."

"Nyles?"

"Yeah! Kinda reminds me of maself when I was that age. Boy's a wolf for sure!"

Chet threw back his head and unleashed an almighty wolf howl. The conversation inside paused. Caught completely off guard, I must have appeared visibly startled. Chet cracked up and punched me on the arm.

"Ma man! You kill me! C'mon, let's go get fucked up."

Back inside the suite, a couple of lines were waiting for us on the coffee table. Chet dove straight in and handed me a rolled-up fifty-pound note after he'd finished. I looked at the cocaine. It was a massive amount. I hesitated, then shrugged it off. I was a great deal more used to this stuff now —plus, a heart attack while doing coke in a hotel suite with Chet Long wouldn't be the worst way to go out.

I snorted the line. The sharp, anaesthetic sting informed me that it was pretty strong stuff—and why wouldn't it be?

The four of us sat there while Nyles embarked on a particularly long anecdote about a yogi he'd met in the Himalayas. Chet and Chanelle were momentarily trans-fixed. I'd heard it before.

My thoughts began to race at the same tempo as my heart. This was unreal. I was hanging out with Chet Long—a bona fide Hollywood movie star. This was fucking it! Right?

But was it?

I looked over at Chet. He was slouched on the sofa, shirt open, his gut spilling out over exposed boxer shorts.

Perhaps not.

It was difficult to tell if Chet was actually listening to Nyles at all. He nodded occasionally, but his attention seemed to be focused more on Chanelle as he began to trace a finger along the sole of her outstretched foot.

Nyles was reaching a point in the story where he was

explaining the ritualistic significance of a shaman-like ceremony when Chanelle interjected.

"Like, that is so interesting, but I just powdered my ass
—so, you wanna come play?"

The question may have been directed solely at Nyles or
at the room in general. It was hard to tell. Nyles had been
telling his story with such intensity that the interruption left
him momentarily speechless, mouth agape.

After a half-second of silence, Chet decided the query
was open to the floor. "Sure, babe. You guys good here?"

"Erm, sure. Yeah, we're good!" I replied for us, as Nyles
looked as though he was still coming to terms with the fact
that his anecdote had been derailed so abruptly and with
such disregard.

The Americans jumped up and headed towards what
was presumably the suite's master bedroom. Chanelle
skipped across the room, Chet following at a saunter that
had a suggestion of reluctant inevitability.

The situation suddenly became too much for me not to
crack up with laughter. "I'm not entirely convinced you had
that audience, mate!"

Nyles had now regained composure and was at least
pretending to see the funny side. "Alas, it would seem not.
What can I say—fucking Septics!"

He shook his head and picked up a half-smoked joint
from the table. He looked at it thoughtfully before glancing
in my direction with a quizzical look.

"No, I'm good, mate. This stuff is pretty fucking strong."

"Yep, that is the one thing celebs are good for—they can
usually source good drugs."

"So, what did you and Chet chat about?" I asked. "He
seemed a little..."

"... distracted?"

"Yeah."

"Well, I did *try* to briefly explain the principles of Deconstruction."

"And? How'd it go?"

"Not great. I think he's very much wanting Deconstruction on his own terms—he wants a sort of metamorphosis into a younger, more successful version of himself."

"Right."

"I don't think it's going to work. He doesn't want to Deconstruct his life—he just wants another chapter in a ghostwritten autobiography, and I'm not sure we should give to him."

"Really?"

"Yeah. I don't really think we need that kind of attention."

"I don't understand. Surely raising our profile would be good for business?"

"Look, Will, there *really* is such a thing as bad press—we could completely destroy what little reputation we have."

"I know, but surely Chet presents a *challenge?* If we can Deconstruct him and give him a rejuvenated existence that's in the *public eye*, then just think! We'd be in massive demand. We could pick and choose our clients!"

"Brother—we *already* pick and choose our clients."

"You might do, but I've only seen evidence of two in however many months it's been!"

This may have pissed Nyles off. He sat forward, placed his elbows on his knees and began gently massaging his scalp. He took a long breath in, fixed his gaze on me and exhaled slowly.

"Look, brother, both our clients have been able to undergo successful Deconstruction because they were *specifically* selected. Not just *anyone* can do it. You have to have the correct psyche, the appropriate qualities. Yes, admittedly they were both wealthy, but that in itself isn't essential. If anything, their wealth drove them towards Deconstruction. Chet's not like that—he craves fame and money, and that's what defines him. He doesn't want to change these aspects—he just wants more! He's as motivated by greed as everyone else in this business."

"But don't you see? That's exactly why Deconstructing him would be such a phenomenal achievement!"

"What if we failed, brother? What then? We'd have absolutely fuck all to show for it—*and* we'd have raised our profile to the extent that we'd frighten off the very people we're trying to help. Nothing good ever comes from a celebrity profile. Believe me—*I know.*" Nyles emphasised this with his most sincere look to date. "Besides, this guy's a fucking liability—a time bomb. He's, what, early fifties? And still behaving like this? You think this is going to end well?"

"Maybe we could... save him?"

"Oh, please—are you serious?"

I'd begun to see his point. Saving Chet Long sounded like the plot of an unwatchable surrealist indie movie. It probably was a very bad idea to get involved with him.

"So, what are we going to do?" I asked.

"Leave it to me."

"Come on, mate—I want to know! I thought we were a team."

"Okay, well... We've agreed—last thing we need is bad PR. We don't want him badmouthing us, or being associated with us at all. So we try to distance ourselves from him via a third party."

"A third party?"

"Yep. I'll explain, gently, that we can't really help him.

He's too complex a case, too unique—we'd be out of our depth even beginning to Deconstruct someone of his... *calibre.* Then I'll put him in touch with an advisor or some shit, and I'll just, you know—throw together the usual introductory bollocks that we do, but no more."

"Bollocks?"

"Yep—health farm, yogi, lifestyle guru, etcetera, etcetera."

Bollocks. The word resonated oddly. It managed to pierce through the ongoing self-adulating euphoric state I was in. Was that what Nyles genuinely thought? Was this all bollocks to him? Was it all an act? I had to admit I had never quite understood how a flagrant cocaine habit and Zen Buddhism went hand in hand...

Nyles must have seen the look on my face. "Jesus! Relax, Will—you look like somebody's just shit in your slippers."

"Just fucking hang on a minute, mate!"

"Look, Will—I'm sorry, brother. I'm fucking tired. Too much blow, and that guy really got on my tits. With people like that, it's all an act—it's all it ever is."

"I kind of liked him."

"No, look, he's fine. Maybe it's just the conversation we had on the balcony. Maybe it's just seeing him with Chanelle."

"Oh! Right, sorry, I forgot... You guys were... close?"

"Come off it, brother—no one's ever really *close* these days."

He broke off as there was a knock at the door. We exchanged a rapid nervous glance. Nyles looked at the incriminating evidence on the coffee table and acted swiftly. He grabbed a copy of *Vogue* from the underlying shelf and placed it strategically over the offending article before vaulting towards the door.

Nyles gently opened the door on its security chain half an inch and peered out. He turned back to me and winked.

"Room service...?"

Laughing, he opened the door and three stunningly beautiful women strolled in. Friends of Chanelle's? Fans of Chet? Prostitutes? Either way, I was now certain that whatever happened this evening, Catherine would definitely not approve.

Fast forward many, many hours and things had gotten far, far hazier. Flying across the London night in an illegal minicab. Loud hip-hop courtesy of some crew from Los Angeles pounding from over-stressed speakers. Chet had given up trying to educate me with mock exasperation. Hip-hop 101 with Chet Long. Fucking hell—what a night!

We were heading to some member's club in the East End. Probably Shoreditch. Chet rode in the back, sandwiched between two of the girls from the hotel. Not Chanelle. Chanelle and Chet had fallen out. The girls that arrived turned out not to be hookers, but friends of hers. She'd disappeared with Nyles out of protest.

I rode shotgun. Open window. Warm air on my face like a humid hair dryer. Chewing gum. Frantically, manically, chewing gum. The ecstasy I'd taken an hour ago was now in full effect. Everything felt good.

Adolescent giggling flowed in bursts from the back seat. Nige, our taxi driver, was shaking his head. He had to shout above the blaring music.

"Fhack me! Chet Fhacking Long. How long you know this khant for, then?"

"Couple of hours, mate. Only a couple of long hours!"

"Fhacking hell—wha's he been in recently? That fhacking shite pirate film, wonnit?"

"Yeah! I think you're spot on there."

"Fhack me, that was shit!"

"Didn't catch it."

"Don't fhacking bother. I should charge the khant double! Fhacking hell!"

Safe to say Nige was not a fan.

We continued on, music screaming out of open windows. I chewed gum with a fevered enthusiasm, mesmerised by the sea of light, London at night. Chet was necking with the two girls in the back. I could quite happily have driven round the East End until the end of time.

A small queue of people standing on the pavement. We'd arrived. Chet let out a wolf howl in acknowledgement. He jumped out of the car with the two girls.

"Will, ma man, you gotta get this, bro—I have none of your English dollars on me."

"Sure, dude! Of course—no problem." I grabbed my wallet and gave Nige a twenty. "Keep the change, mate. Sorry for being so fucked."

Nige thanked me, nodded at the note and gestured at Chet, who was now entering the club. "See, told you he was a khant!"

I giggled. He was spot on again.

As I walked towards the club I began to feel woozy. I tried to focus on my watch—was it 4 a.m.? Christ in a teacup! An aura of impending daybreak had crept into the sky. Morning equalled the unwelcome element of reality. I needed to get inside the club before that happened.

With chemically charged confidence, I strode straight up to the bouncer, ignoring a queue of about ten people. Arrogant but fair. Chet had just walked in, and it was clear we'd arrived in the same cab.

Clear to me, at least.

"I'm sorry, sir. This is a VIP event."

"I know! I'm with Chet!"

"Of course you are, sir."

"I am! I just paid for his fucking taxi!"

"His taxi? Of course you did, sir."

"Listen—please just call him back. I've been with him all evening."

"Of course you have, sir."

"I fucking well have!"

The bouncer's jaded expression became one of mild irritation. "Sir, if I could make a suggestion?"

"Erm, okay, what?"

"If I may, sir—why don't you fuck off home?"

"Sorry?"

"You've had a lot to drink, and, I'd wager, by the look of your pupils and your general demeanour, a lot of drugs too."

"I—"

"If you don't piss off now, one of two things is going to happen. I can give the Old Bill a call, or I can do things the old-fashioned way and give you a damned good thrashing. I'll tell you what—I'm going to leave the choice entirely up to you."

"Right, erm, okay."

Defeated, I turned around. The bouncer's calm tone, along with the glint in his eye, suggested he wasn't joking. Suggested maybe he was a psychopath. The invitation of violence cut through my warm, buzzing glow. I was not getting into the club—end of story. Probably for the best, all things considered.

A quick survey of the queue confirmed this. A man close to the front—shiny suit with slicked-back hair and an undercut that screamed *khant*—flicked a lit cigarette at a homeless man shuffling past. The punishment paid out for an outstretched hand plus desperate optimism. The homeless man flinched as the cigarette flew past his face. Embers sparked as it landed in the kerbside gutter. He scrambled to pick it up. Haircut let fly with a well-aimed glob of phlegm that hit him squarely on the back of the head. A chorus of appreciation erupted from Haircut and his friend standing beside him. A friend with an identical haircut.

Some people are poison.

The venom of London—vital to its survival, but toxic to everything around it.

23

THE LIST

July arrived and summertime was in full effect. The first was an absolute scorcher. Temperatures soared briefly in a classic one-day British heatwave and the office felt like a sauna. I'd given Adriana our single fan, an act of chivalry I now deeply regretted.

In comparison to me, Adriana was actually doing some work—continually manning the Deconstruction enquiry line was a significant ongoing chore. I felt guilty about my comparative lack of activity, but not guilty enough to take a shift on the phone. My chivalry, it would seem, was ankle-deep at best.

Lady Ann's trust was now in the hands of the lawyers. Chet had been bundled off to a health-farm-slash-yoga-retreat—something he'd apparently been only too willing to attend after the excesses of the previous weekend.

I leant out the window, desperately seeking the non-existent breeze coming in off the river. This was insufferable. The only course of action left was to go and hang out with Adriana and our single fan. Eventually she was bound to get irritated and suggest I go home.

"You mind if I sit in here, mate? I'm dying in there."

Adriana rolled her bloodshot eyes before sniffing and stifling a sneeze. Her particularly brutal hay fever that emerged with the intense heat wasn't exactly helping her mood.

"Of course, Will, you stay here as long as you like. It's quiet today, anyway."

"Quiet? Isn't it always quiet?"

Adriana gave me an incredulous glare. "*Puta merda!*"

"I'm only joking!"

"There are calls, many, many calls, calls all the fucking time! And so many crazy questions!"

"Like what?"

"Most are the confused, stupid people, but I find some real ones for the list."

"There's a list...?"

"Of course! Jesus, what do you think I do every day?"

She had a point. I knew she was on the phone a great deal, but thankfully a very thick door separated us, so I couldn't hear actual words. I also tended to have the radio on—it was always possible to find a test match being played somewhere or other.

"Sorry, I didn't realise—about the list. And Nyles, he... reads this list?"

"Of course! Every day I do the list for Nyles, add the names. I find some information here, some information there. I update everyday! The *filho da puta*—he better read it!"

"I'm sure he does. But, erm, can I? Read the list?"

"Of course! Why not? Nyles said if you ever ask to show you."

"If I ever asked?"

"Yes! I thought you knew!"

I was speechless. I don't know why I was surprised, though—things should really have stopped surprising me about Nyles by now.

Adriana minimised a couple of windows on her desktop and opened a document. It appeared to contain a number of half-page summaries on potential Deconstructees.

"May I?"

Adriana wheeled her chair back and embarked on a violent round of nose-blowing as I crouched down and began skimming through the pages. Even with the occasional fan breeze, it was too hot to concentrate on anything in depth.

There were at least twenty summaries. Each individual was identified presumably by their initials. Their lives were neatly dissected by various subheadings: *Employment, Marital Status, Family, Social Network, Problems, Aspirations, Assets* and finally, *Deconstruction Potential*. Under the final subheading, the vast majority were labelled as *unsuitable*, but one or two were listed as *pending*.

This was unbelievable. Absolutely unbelievable.

"May I get a copy of this?"

"*Não!* One copy only! On this computer. Those are the rules from Nyles."

"What?"

"The rules, Will, those are the rules. But you can come and read anytime. I work all the day every day on this fucking list!"

"Okay, okay!"

I stared, engrossed, aware my legs had gone to sleep from the crouching position I was skilfully maintaining. Even from a cursory glance, it was understandable why most of names had been designated *unsuitable*. For example, *KP*, who appeared to be a wealthy businessman from

Wolverhampton conducting multiple extramarital affairs, whose aspirations were simply listed as *power*. Or *JP*, an individual who appeared promising but worked as a journalist for a London newspaper.

One name labelled as *pending* caught my eye: *LB*. In terms of Deconstruction potential, LB seemed to tick a number of boxes: a depressed and stressed city trader, recently *amicably divorced* with no children, distant family, aspirations stated as: *Re-evaluating—?Humanitarian work.*

"Who's this one? LB?"

Adriana sniffed loudly and hesitated.

"You can't even tell me their names?"

"No. I can, of course. But you must promise not to write the name—for the security."

"Okay, I promise."

"This one is Lewis Bennett."

"Lewis Bennett, huh? He sounds like he might have potential?"

"Yes, he sounds."

"But?"

"But nothing—I just get the vibe off him when I talk on the phone."

"A vibe?"

"Yeah, you know? Like a feeling."

"Yes, I know, I mean... Never mind. Does Nyles know about Lewis?"

"*Puta merda!* Of course! Nyles knows everybody on the list! He decides who stays on the list! I think maybe he meets them all for the fucking cup of tea!"

"What? Really? And what does he think?"

"He is thinking."

"Thinking about Lewis as a Deconstructee? Why only thinking?"

"I don't know, Will, that question only he can answer. Hey! I have what we *Brasileiras* call a *boa ideia*—maybe you talk to him instead of me!"

"Or maybe I should go and meet Lewis myself...?"

Adriana raised an eyebrow and laughed, which provoked another uncontrollable sneezing fit. She was right. Nyles called the shots on everything, despite his perennial absence. Adriana still gave the impression she was in daily contact with him, though I suspected this was not the case and she was doing it to maintain appearances—perhaps even for my sake.

Regardless, there really was no point rocking the boat, and I had to keep reminding myself of this. I had a job and was being paid. This was not something to place in jeopardy.

I came back to the list a number of times over the next few days, quizzing Adriana about each candidate in turn until she got irritated enough for me to retreat. My first impression regarding Lewis Bennett proved to be correct. He seemed to be a solid candidate for Deconstruction. In fact, he was the only individual on the list who seemed to be. I was convinced—surely we needed to at least talk about Lewis?

I GOT a chance to confront Nyles later in the week. I had decided that talking to him required a little cunning and initiative on my behalf. My strategy was to leave my office door ajar and shamelessly eavesdrop on Adriana's conversations until one of them was clearly with Nyles. Admittedly, it was crude, and I was sure she knew what I was doing, but she didn't seem to mind. Her relationship with Nyles was now strained at best and her loyalties towards him were not what they had been.

It was obvious Nyles was calling when Adriana exchanged her irritated though professional tone for a mildly flirtatious one with a great deal more swearing. Upon hearing this, I swiftly darted out of my office and positioned myself directly in front of her, gesticulating wildly that she put the call through to my office once she'd finished.

"Nyles?"

"Will, brother! How're things?"

"Fine. No, good—really good! Where've you been, mate?"

"Oh, you know, here and there."

This was clearly going to be one of those times when even the continent he was on was a closely guarded secret.

"And how's that enviable creature, Catherine?"

"Also really good, mate. We're both looking forward to catching up with you again soon."

"Well, the pleasure will be all mine, I can assure you. We should do dinner again next time I'm in town. It'd be good to catch up with Max as well—how's that reprobate, anyway?"

"He's good! You know Max. Actually catching up with him later for a game of squash and a pint or two."

"Great! Tell him I'll give him a ring later in the week RE an update, would you?"

"Sure..."

"That okay?"

"Sure. Yep! I just, erm, didn't know he liked being kept in the loop."

"Ha! Well, he doesn't. You know what he's like—total space cadet most of the time. I'm just trying to maintain at least some sort of professionalism, given he's supposed to be the bloody Managing Director!"

"Fair enough." That phone call would never happen, but he had a point.

"Anyway, brother, how's the home front? Anything else up?"

"Not a huge amount. There was one thing, though..."

"Shoot."

"It's just, Adriana told me about the list..."

"The list?"

"Yep, the *list*."

"And?"

"It's just, well, I didn't know anything about it."

"It's hardly a secret, mate—what do you think Adriana does all day?"

"I..."

"I mean, we've got to keep some sort of record on our enquires. God knows we spend a small fortune on advertising."

"True. I just didn't know it was so... well-researched."

"Yes, well, that has taken a fair amount of time—hopefully proves to you I'm not completely idle!"

"Do you need any help? With the research, that is? I'm pretty much at a loose end since finishing all that trust stuff for Lady Ann."

A lengthy pause followed as Nyles gave this some deep consideration.

"Nyles?"

"Yes! I'll definitely have a think about it."

"Great!"

Another pause.

"So, do you want me to dig around, find out a bit more info on this Lewis chap?"

"Lewis...?"

"Lewis Bennett."

"Ah, Mr Bennett."

"Yeah, I thought he seemed, you know—promising?"

"Well, you may be right, brother. I've had a few people look into him already. We'll chat next time I'm in London. To tell you the truth, I'd been thinking about pressing forward with an introductory meeting."

"That's great!"

"Well, we'll see. Remember how the last one went?"

"Ha! Fair point."

"Actually, there was one thing I need to warn you about."

"Really? What?"

"I got a call from the retreat we sent Chet to..."

"Oh..."

"Yeah. Well, it seems he might not have been the most... exemplary of students."

"Oh, shit."

"I sort of figured this might happen, so I sent him to one I'd used before, which wasn't great. You know—in case we burned any bridges."

"And...?"

"Well, credit to him, he's absolutely incinerated them. Looks like it was a good decision."

"What did he do?"

"There've been a number of complaints—allegations of sexually inappropriate behaviour towards staff and provision of illicit substances to other guests being amongst them."

"Oh."

"Look, if anyone calls, best just decline to comment—actually, maybe just deny any association at all."

"Right."

"Nice one, brother. Look, best chip off. I'll catch you in a fortnight or so."

"A fortnight?"

I looked up to see Adriana in the doorway. She was gesturing impatiently about another call.

"Sorry, Nyles, just a minute. Who is it?"

Adriana blew her nose and shrugged. "Some rude American man."

"Right, Nyles, I have to—Nyles? You there...? It would appear not."

"The man—he is upset," Adriana went on.

"Chet?"

"I don't know. He is a very rude man."

"Okay, I'm sorry—please put him though."

The dial tone burst into life.

"Hello? Will Harper here."

"Will, you fuck!"

"Chet...?"

"Damn fucking straight it's me!"

"And to what do I owe the pleasure of—"

"Don't fucking get cute with me, ma man! You fucking Brit pricks are all the same!"

"Chet, calm down—what's up?"

"Like you don't fucking know already!"

"Chet, I—"

"They fucking threw me out, man!"

"What happened?"

"I don't fucking know!"

"Really? No idea at all...?"

"Maybe it was that uptight bitch from the tantric session..."

"Tantric session? Are you sure that was—"

"Fuck you, buddy! Fuck you and that other smug prick. You motherfuckers are going to hang for this shit, y'hear? I'll see you cunts in court!"

"Chet, I—"

He was gone.

I thought about calling his agent to smooth things over, then decided against it. Nyles was right—it probably was best to deny any association with him. Anyway, Chet's rage would probably dissipate as soon as he got some good-quality drugs and booze back into him.

24

LEWIS BENNETT

MONDAY MORNING A FORTNIGHT LATER, Nyles and I sat in matching high-backed cream leather armchairs in the Notting Hill residence of Lewis Bennett. The room was an exercise in chic minimalism, though more like an upmarket dentist's waiting room than somebody's actual lounge. Four identical armchairs were positioned around a wooden sculpture that looked like a flourishing brushstroke of mahogany. Perhaps it doubled as a coffee table?

Nyles had arrived unannounced in the office a week after our last phone call. In the intervening time, it seemed, he had decided to press forward with an introductory meeting with Lewis. In the taxi on the way over, he'd handed me another weighty ring-bound document with pages of details concerning Lewis' portfolio of investments.

A cursory skim through the document was enough to drop the jaw. There were endless pages of itemised investments: properties in Monaco, shares in just about every company you'd heard of, even a forty-nine percent stake in a superyacht. Landing Lewis Bennett as a client might allow us to take the rest of the year off, or possibly even retire!

On paper, he was the man every twenty-something city worker had aspirations to become. I'm not going to lie—I included myself in that cohort. Lewis was a young, ruthless hedge fund manager who had hit the big time so hard he'd broken it. In this financial climate, it was going to be some time before anyone would do that kind of damage again. Maybe they never would.

A striking secretary in her early thirties had let Nyles and me into the house and offered us tea or coffee before informing us that Mr Bennett was in his office and would be five minutes. It appeared Lewis worked from home these days—and why the hell not? His home was incredible.

Nyles had insisted we wear blue suits with light-blue shirts and no ties. He was big on the psychology of first impressions, and the colour blue purportedly produced an air of trust, loyalty and understanding. The decision regarding ties was my contribution. I had reasoned that Lewis was from a world populated by men wearing ties and we should therefore try to appear different—representing an alternative path. Nyles seemed to like this, and I began to wonder whether I was a natural at this psychobabble thing.

We sat in silence. Nyles seemed to want to keep any conversation between minimal and zero. I had finished my coffee. Nyles hadn't touched his sparkling mineral water. We must have been there for at least twenty minutes. There were no clocks in the room, just four bare walls, and neither of us wore watches or had our phones on us, at Nyles' insistence.

He stared out the window with a serene expression on his face. Here was a man perfectly content and at one with himself. He looked a million miles away from my own mental state of boredom and creeping irritation. I failed to stifle a small sigh. Nyles shot me a millisecond glare. No further sighing, then.

Suddenly the door was swung open by a short, plump man in his mid-thirties, unshaven and wearing what appeared to be a set of 1980s prescription NHS spectacles. He wore dark-green baggy corduroy trousers and a beige shirt with brown pinstripes. He looked more like a physics teacher than one of the city's most formidable forces in finance. I glanced over to see Nyles' reaction, but if he was surprised, he did an impressive job of not showing it.

Lewis shook hands with both of us wordlessly as Nyles introduced us. He nodded solemnly in acknowledgement and collapsed into another armchair positioned across from the coffee-table-sculpture thing. He looked tired. Exhausted, in fact. An anxious face with dark rims under the eyes peered out at us through thick lenses. An awkward silence crept into the room until Nyles took it upon himself to try to start a conversation.

"Thank you for inviting us to your home, Mr Bennett. You truly have a beautiful house."

Nothing. Nyles cleared his throat and almost adjusted a non-existent tie.

"So, from our correspondence, it appears you're interested in learning a little more about Deconstruction? If you'll give me a couple of minutes, I'll outline the principles and explain their significance, then answer any questions you may have."

Lewis nodded.

Nyles gave the now familiar spiel. I was a well-trained sidekick, able to look interested and enthusiastic, and nod in agreement with key phrases: *Deconstruction challenges the key assumptions of Western culture*; *Deconstruction requires dismantling of any ideals that you presently hold to discover exactly what underpins them; Deconstruction allows a more simple permanent reconstruction with only inherent values important to you.*

Nyles finished his monologue, sat back and smiled gently. Lewis looked like he was going to stay silent, but then erupted with a barrage of high-pitched staccato speech.

"So what would it mean? Deconstruction? For me? Exactly?"

"Erm, well, essentially a completely new life, Mr Bennett. Resurrected somewhere better suited to your actual character. Better suited to you."

"Right, right, and my various... issues? What about them?"

"Organised and concluded as part of your Deconstruction."

"How long would it take?"

"That very much depends on how much control you wish to have over the proceedings. Deconstructees who are completely accepting of the process and entrust the practicalities to us have a more rapid Deconstruction. We tend to offer more objective, less sentimental solutions than a Deconstructee themselves is capable of."

Lewis nodded furiously, scratching his head, presumably performing numerous *issue*-based calculations. He switched his rapidly blinking gaze from Nyles to me. "And Mr Harper?"

"Sorry?" Nyles replied.

"Where does he come in? Does he talk?"

I was slightly offended by this, especially given that he hadn't exactly been brimming with chat prior to this recent exchange. Feeling that I needed a quick retort, I cleared my throat to defend myself.

"Mr Bennett, I assist Nyles with the logistical side of Deconstruction. I feel it's important to meet a Deconstructee as early as possible in the proceedings. I only talk when absolute necessary. I'm sure you of all people can appreciate the value in this."

This appeared to suffice. Lewis began nodding furiously again and turned his gaze away from me. Nyles looked like he was about to say something, but stopped himself. Another long, uncomfortable pause followed, and that appeared to be the end of the conversation.

"So, Mr Bennett, if you don't have any questions, we'll leave you to reflect. You have our details, so please don't hesitate to call us day or night if you wish us to clarify or repeat any of the theory or practicalities we've discussed today. We look forward to hearing from you if you decide this is something you would like to explore further."

Nyles gestured towards me with an affectionate smile, presumably to emphasise me as part of *we* and *us*. Once again there was no verbal response from Lewis, whose nodding had now slowed to that of contemplation.

"Good afternoon, Mr Bennett."

A half-smile, half-frown in return. We saw ourselves out.

I GOT into the back of the hackney carriage with Nyles, dying to know what he'd thought of Lewis.

"Wow, that was..."

"Interesting, brother, very interesting."

"I was going to say *painful*, but yes, interesting is... fair."

"So?"

"So... What do *I* think?"

"Yep."

"Well, what do *you* think?"

"I can see... potential, brother. Plenty of potential."

"Really?"

He didn't appear to be joking. "Yep. I see a man so trapped by his circumstances that the weight of them is crushing him."

That sounded familiar.

"Nyles—he barely said anything!"

"He didn't have to, brother! It was obvious—just look at the guy. Empty, drained by his own existence—absolutely miserable."

"He didn't exactly strike me as the sort of guy who'd once *been* the life of the party."

Nyles chose to ignore me. "This is the sort of person we set up Deconstruction for, brother!"

"But you're not entirely certain—are you?"

"Well, I have the odd reservation. My main concern is that he may be resistant to the spiritual element, but that doesn't have to be a huge problem."

"*That's* your main concern?"

Nyles gave me a bemused look, as if there couldn't possibly be anything else.

"So you're telling me that a high-flying city trader with everything going for him suddenly wants out? In a climate where you can't get a job for love nor money. And we think nothing is suspicious?"

"Well, I wouldn't have said he has *everything going for him*—and plus, he's not really your typical high-flying city trader either, is he?"

"True—but even so!"

"Look, he may have come across as a tad eccentric, but

it's certainly not a quantum leap in reasoning to suggest that he might want and benefit from a simpler existence, is it?"

"True, but..."

"But what?"

"I just think we should look into this a bit more. He wasn't exactly what either of us were expecting, was he?"

"Will, brother, I have done so much background research on the guy. Just compiling a list of his assets in the public domain took ages! Here, feel free to go through it with a fine-tooth comb, by all means." Nyles opened his briefcase once more, grabbed the folder containing his research on Lewis and dropped the dead weight of it in my lap. "Voilà!"

"Ouch. Okay, I will—it'll keep me out of trouble."

"Speaking of trouble, I know quite a nice members' club around here. It should just about be opening for lunch. The... *waitresses* are quite remarkable creatures. Fancy a spot?"

We were heading to a strip club before midday? I thought about questioning the acceptability of this, but Nyles was already barking instructions at the driver.

25

SMUG CONTENTMENT

THE FRESHLY SHARPENED KNIFE BLADE, purported to be Japanese steel, made short work of the assortment of raw vegetables before me. I was a kitchen samurai. I looked around me. This place was superb! Catherine's kitchen had everything. Although modest in dimensions, it was packed with high-quality implements and utensils that I suspected had been bought with good intentions, but never actually used.

I'd been spending more and more time at Catherine's. Now with my own key, I'd become accustomed to arriving at hers before she finished work. I enjoyed playing the supportive partner role and having dinner waiting for her when she eventually got in. She worked the standard long office hours of a trainee lawyer and brought the obligatory mountain of work home with her. I felt guilty about how little I worked in comparison, especially considering that I was almost certainly being paid substantially more. Cooking dinner seemed the very least I could do.

I'd spent the rest of the week after meeting Lewis Bennett going through Nyles' research on him. I'd cross-checked everything as well as I could. To his credit, Nyles had been meticulous. All the information regarding Lewis' assets corroborated with the independent sources I used, and I couldn't really find much in addition to what Nyles had.

It seemed that Nyles had already decided Lewis was a suitable candidate for Deconstruction, so it was really just a case of whether Lewis himself was keen. I kept asking Adriana whether she'd heard from him or his people. She hadn't. Nor had she heard from Nyles, who had once again decided to vanish and become uncontactable.

I heard a key in the lock. I checked the oven one last time and confirmed the lamb was cooking well. I scooped up the elegantly sliced crudités and began arranging them around a pale China bowl of tzatziki. Presentation is everything.

"Hiya!"

"Hey, sugar plum!"

Catherine screwed her face up. I was sure on some level she found my deliberately Americanised platitudes endearing. Pretty sure.

"Christ, is there any wine open?"

"No, but I'll open a bottle—red or white? Bad day…?"

"The worst—either's fine. I'm just going to jump in the shower."

I went with white. I was avoiding red after Monday's impromptu lunch with Nyles. Four or five bottles had transformed lunch into a session that lasted well into the early evening. I could barely remember getting back to Max's place. The next day I'd felt suitably wretched.

Catherine emerged from the shower, towelling her long auburn locks. She was chewing her bottom lip, deep in thought.

"*Voici ton vin, ma chérie!*"

"Oh—*merci, ma... knoight in shinin' arma!*" She grinned and clinked her glass with mine.

"So, what's up? You wanna talk about it?"

"God, no! It'd bore you and myself to tears." She took a large gulp as she sank down on the couch. "I thought we could talk about something way more fun instead."

"Like what?" I vaulted over the back of the couch to land beside her—a deft move that went awry as I squashed her leg on the landing.

"Ouch! Will!"

"Sorry! I'm so sorry! That wasn't meant to happen quite like that. Here, let me rub it better... or maybe get some ice...?"

"It's fine, really."

"Okay. What did you want to talk about?"

"I thought we could *talk* some more on the subject we discussed the other night."

"Which was...?"

"*Gawn on 'oliday, Bill!*" Catherine's cockney accent was definitely one of her worst.

"God, that really doesn't get any better, does it? Yes, though—of course we can."

"Did you ask Nyles?"

"I haven't seen him since we spoke."

"Well, can't you call him?"

"He's not *amazing* at answering his phone—believe me, I try at least twice a day."

"Well, email or text, then? It is 2009, after all."

"That has an even lower success rate."

"Oh, Will! This is really annoying—how can we book anything when you don't even know whether you can go?"

"It'll be fine! I'm ninety-nine-point-nine percent

certain. Work is slow—we're between clients, without much on the horizon..."

"You're certain? I *need* a holiday—in fact, I need it so much I'll just go without you."

"Well, where would the fun be in that?"

Catherine grinned at me, her eyes twinkling in the long light of the summer evening. She really was beautiful —I still had to pinch myself at times. "Maybe not *as* much fun, but at least I'd be less likely to get physically injured."

"Okay, okay! Fair point. Look, let's decide tonight, get flights and accommodation on hold—as soon as I get the final okay from Nyles, we'll book it instantly."

"Oh, so we're flying somewhere now, are we? I thought *I* was allowed to decide the destination?"

"Well, we don't *have* to leave the UK. We could always go and visit my mum in *Rotherham*...?" Even joking, I felt a brief dash of guilt. I hadn't visited her in ages. Come to think of it, I couldn't remember when I'd last spoken to her on the phone. I made a mental note to call her at the weekend.

Catherine screwed her nose up.

"Oh, so Rotherham's too good for you now, is it?"

"Oh, shut up! I was actually thinking maybe Morocco...?"

"I'm pretty sure the most conventional way to get there would be to fly."

"I didn't actually say we *weren't* flying."

"Sure, okay. Morocco, eh? That'd be amazing. I've never been to Africa."

"Hate to break it to you, Will, but Morocco's not in Africa."

"It's not? I'm pretty sure... Ha! Okay, good one. Right,

I'd better serve this dinner before you decide to be any more hilarious."

Dinner was a resounding success. Afterwards, we lay on the sofa, limbs entwined and Catherine's laptop balanced across our full bellies. Multiple windows filled the screen. Flights were easy and cheap—we were officially Marrakesh-bound.

Catherine yawned. It was eleven o'clock.

"Tired?" I asked.

"Yep, but just give me a minute longer."

She was scrolling through some traveller's blog describing a trek through the Atlas Mountains in unnecessary detail. Thankfully, I could see even her interest was waning.

"William—I'm sure you realise this is the next step on the ladder, don't you?"

"Trekking in the Atlas Mountains?"

"No!"

"You've lost me, then. What ladder?"

"Clearly, the ladder is an analogy."

"For...?"

"Us!"

"Strange analogy..."

"You know what I mean."

"Okay, yes, I know what you mean. But that's cool, right?"

"I suppose it is—very *cool*."

I stroked her hair and she lowered the laptop to the floor and hugged me.

"So, what other rungs are there on this ladder thing?"

"Well, some are hopefully a reasonably long way off— such as your midlife crisis that culminates in you having an unsatisfactory affair with your secretary."

"I think I'd prefer to get a motorbike."

"Ha! Leaving you permanently wheelchair-bound and being pushed around by some of our many grandchildren."

"Grandchildren?"

"It's a long ladder!" Her eyes were still twinkling as she looked into mine.

"Okay, well, what comes after a holiday together? I've met your parents, and you've refused to meet my mother and stepfather on account of being unwilling to travel north of Watford..."

"Oh, shut up now! I never said that. Of course I'll go to bloody Rotherham! It's just it's *soooo* far away."

"Not as far as Morocco, some might say."

Catherine pouted, sticking out her bottom lip as far as it would go. "What I was trying to lead the conversation on to, Will, was our next step—which is maybe..."

"Maybe...?"

"Maybe... moving in together?"

"*Moving in together?*"

"Yep."

Whoa! How did that happen? We had now wandered into the realm of a dangerously serious conversation.

"You practically live here, anyway," she went on.

"True, but... well... what about Max?" I knew instantly that this was the weakest excuse imaginable.

"*Max?*"

"Yep, you know... I'm pretty sure he'd be—"

"If you say lonely I will punch you!"

"Erm... *unsafe?*"

"How long are you going to freeload off Max, anyway?"

"As long as he needs me. I see myself as sort of like his carer... It's a bit like community service."

"He's never there!"

"That's precisely why he's such a good housemate—unlike you!"

I grabbed her and squeezed her tightly. She was right, of course. I'd been living off Max's generosity for too long. Although I now paid him rent, it wasn't anywhere near enough. And he *was* never really there—his dedication and commitment to chasing women took precedence over everything else. I'd probably see him just as much if I moved out.

"So, *whatcha fink?* Is it something you wanna do? Will you give it some thought?"

"Yes. I absolutely will."

And I would.

In fact, I'd probably already made up my mind, and I had to admit, it felt quite exciting.

THE NEXT DAY I carried a warm glow of positivity with me. The night before marked a turning point in my relationship with Catherine. Things were definitely moving forward. I sat in the office, enjoying the feeling of smug contentment while sipping a coffee and lazily leafing through the paper. I was barely reading, as the detailed daydreams of our long, happy future together were requiring most of my concentration.

There was a knock on the door and a flustered-looking Adriana entered, quickly closing the door behind her. Her usual cheerful demeanour was absent. She looked panicked. I was wrenched from my pleasant little daydream. Something was very wrong.

"Adriana, are you...?"

"Will, there's..."

"What's up? What's happened? Are you okay?"

"There's two gentlemen here!"

"What? Here? Hang on—physically here?" I frantically stabbed at the closed door with a finger that had already started to shake. I'd not heard anyone enter the office above the radio, which I slapped off in an effort to fully concentrate.

We had never had anyone visit the office unannounced. We'd gone to great pains to avoid disclosing our location to anyone. In all our publicity, we'd only ever given out a phone number and a website address.

Who was it?

"*Yes!* They are *physically here!*"

"Okay, well, erm, who are they? What do they want?"

"To see Nyles, but I cannot find him on the phone!"

"Well, can you... maybe ask them to come back later?"

"No, I don't think! One is very angry!"

Fuck. This probably wasn't good.

"What do they look like?"

"Well, the small one, he looks—fucking angry, and the big is maybe security? I don't know, Will!"

"Oh, I see... How did they find the office?"

"*Puta merda!* I don't know! All I know is they are here! Outside the door!"

"Shit. Fuck. Are they Russian?"

"Will! *Puta merda!* How do I know this? Maybe you ask them?"

Fuck. The Russians. It had to be. Jaroslav? Or maybe a couple of his heavies?

It'd been a while since I'd replayed that scene in my head with the Russian driver dropping me off at Max's flat: *nice place, but not too secure...* I knew it! Nyles had laughed it off, but even smashed, I'd been sure there was something sinister in the way he said it. I'd been right all along.

"I mean, do they *look* Russian?"

"I don't think so, but I don't meet many Russians."

"Well, are they police?"

"I don't think so—but you have many strange things in this fucking country!"

Any further discussion into the subtle differences between British and Brazilian police forces was curtailed by a heavy knock at the door.

Fuck.

"Well, I suppose I should speak to them..."

"You want me to stay?" Adriana asked.

"Yes! No! I mean, no. Please just show them in. And can you *please* try to get hold of Nyles again?"

Adriana opened the door with a perfect false smile and gestured for the two men to enter. They confidently half strolled, half barged into the room, causing Adriana to deftly spring out of the way and quickly exit behind them.

On first impression, they definitely didn't *appear* to be Russian. The two men both looked East Asian in appearance. They were sharply dressed in black suits and designer sunglasses, which seemed unnecessary given the ambient lighting and how cloudy the day was. They were as Adriana described—one little, one large.

The smaller man wore slightly more flashy Gucci sunglasses. His shirt was half open, displaying a hairless chest and an expensive-looking gold chain that was just big enough to appear slightly awkward.

The larger man positioned himself in the doorway. He had the air of a man able to handle himself in any situation. He was indeed the muscle. Just in case there was any doubt, he folded his arms over his broad chest, which effectively demonstrated how his large hands were barely able to clasp his gigantic biceps.

I quickly stood up, buttoned my suit jacket, and, in a desperate gesture towards professionalism, offered my hand to the smaller man as he approached my desk. "Will Harper, pleasure to—"

It was duly ignored. "Where is Nyles? Nyles Henry?"

"Nyles..."

"Yes, motherfucker! You're Nyles Henry?"

"Motherfucker" sounded slightly odd delivered in such a clipped accent. This was all a bit surreal—who the hell were these people? It was impossible to read their faces. Neither had removed their sunglasses despite the office gloom. Nyles had insisted on a *warm glow of ambient light* for the office environment to conjure a place of comfort for respective clients. Today it didn't seem to be working.

"I'm Will Harper."

"Who the *fuck* are you?"

"I'm an associate of Nyles Hen—"

Instant regret.

"Right! Well, in that case, you can give me some fucking answers! I know my brother has spoken to you, but I want to speak to you fucking arseholes myself."

"I'm sorry, but I don't know anything about—"

"Don't play games with me, Mr Harper!" the shorter man snarled, and his face began to redden as he seemed to reach a higher plane of anger.

"I'm s-sorry! I just don't—"

"I know *you* guys fucked with my mother's will! And I know *you* got a letter from my brother's lawyer!"

"Letter? I..."

The penny droppeth. This was Daniel Golbourne. The youngest prodigal son of Lady Ann Golbourne. The one that I'd been assured by Nyles had a bark worse than his bite. The privileged rich kid gone bad who may or may not be moving in murkier circles—notably those of the Hong Kong triads. Judging by the hulk of a man standing impassively next to him, it seemed there might be some truth to that rumour.

Daniel looked around the office with apparent disdain before continuing. "Mr Harper—be aware my brother and I are on the same side, but we have different methods of getting things done. Very different. Do you understand?"

"I am so sorry... This letter, I—Nyles might—"

"Where is he?"

"I'm not sure... My secretary is *desperately* trying to get hold of him right now, to get this cleared up..."

"Are you fucking trying to tell me you know nothing about my mother's will?"

"I... Look, Mr Golbourne—"

"Oh, so *now* you know who I fucking well am!"

"I—I'm s-sorry, but I don't know the intricacies of your mother's situation... You see, I only work for Nyles. But I promise I will..."

The rage simmering beneath Daniel Golbourne's sunglasses reached ignition point. He exploded and lunged at me, swinging a vicious-looking right hook.

Fortunately for me, the actual connection between his fist and my face didn't occur. The desk between us provided too large an obstacle for his reach. Nevertheless, I flinched so hard that I tripped backwards, falling into my chair.

Despite my humiliation, Daniel was clearly more embarrassed. He flushed red before trying to regain some composure as he hissed at me, "*Shut the fuck up!*"

Out of the corner of my eye, I could have sworn I saw the man-mountain occupying the door frame smirk, though he remained otherwise motionless. I sat in shock, my heart racing, unsure of what to do or say next. Standing back up didn't seem like a good idea. Silence was probably the best option.

Daniel, however, obviously felt he hadn't made his point clear enough. He snatched an object from inside his jacket. A gold-handled flick knife twirled around in his hand before he stabbed the desk in front of me with a clenched fist around the handle.

I felt what little colour remained in my face rapidly draining away.

Oh. Fuck.

How was this happening?

A total silence wrapped itself around the room. Daniel stood hunched over the desk, breathing heavily, one hand still gripping the handle of the flick knife. Eventually he looked up at me. Unable to see his eyes, I retreated into my own timid, shaking reflection. Daniel stood back, seemingly satisfied he'd made his point.

I was more terrified than I'd even been in my life. I'd never even seen a flick knife before, let alone been threatened by one.

"Tell your boss that if he doesn't sort this, I'll be back for both of you. Next time I won't miss!"

I searched for something to stay, finally gasping a breathless response. "Of course I will—I p-promise. You have my word..."

"You best understand me, Will Harper! I'm gonna find out everything there is to know about you, and if I have to come back here, it won't just be your shitty desk that gets cut!"

I SAT IN NUMB, stunned silence for some time. I was vaguely aware of Adriana poking her concerned face round the door. She asked if I was okay, then returned with a large glass of Scotch. She sat it down on the desk and asked me if I wanted to talk about it. I shook my head. She left the room.

I looked at the half-full crystal whisky glass for some time. It sat a couple of inches to the right of the splintered indent left by Daniel's flick knife. Eventually I picked the glass up and downed the generous measure in one.

The whisky helped me steady my nerves and process the situation. My disbelief gradually turned to rage. I was angry. Very fucking angry. Where the hell was Nyles? This was clearly not over, and Daniel Golbourne was clearly *not* okay with his mother's Deconstruction. It didn't matter that Nyles reckoned Daniel's bark was worse than his bite—*he* hadn't had to face him!

Adriana checked on me at regular intervals. She saw my glass was empty and brought me another Scotch. And then another. Each time she asked me whether I wanted to talk. I didn't. She'd overheard the entire conversation, but there was no sense in bringing her any further into this. Instead, I asked her whether she'd managed to get hold of Nyles. Each time she shook her head sadly in response.

I started to feel drunk. Hammered, in fact. At some point Adriana said she had to leave to meet a cousin who was in town. She apologised profusely and looked genuinely reluctant to leave me. She offered me another drink. This time I declined. I needed to think. She told me she'd left at least ten messages on every number Nyles had ever given her.

"How many numbers do you have?"

"Maybe, five..."

"Christ!" Even drug dealers don't have *five* phone numbers.

Gazing out the window, I watched the dusk roll in. Long shadows mixed with the gentle haze on the horizon. My mind was in overdrive. Too much booze meant I couldn't concentrate properly on anything for longer than a few moments. As soon as I'd convinced myself that every-thing was going to be okay and that I was overreacting, another doomsday scenario popped into my head. I was worried I had inadvertently stumbled into a dark and shady world—first with the Russians, now these guys.

Things seemed to be heading somewhere ugly. Really ugly.

Waves of anxiety washed through me. A sense of impending doom made my heart feel like it was being squeezed. I could hardly use the excuse that I was *just* working for Nyles; I was hardly just an accountant. I was implicated in all of this. We hadn't done anything illegal, but the people we were upsetting didn't exactly operate within the confines of the law. What if another incident like today's occurred? Nyles was constantly absent. I was the physical presence left in the office.

I thought about quitting, but being unemployed was not an option. There was the upcoming holiday and the fact that I was in the process of moving in with Catherine. I could hardly become dependent on her. That hadn't worked so well for me in the past...

I needed a distraction. Catherine was catching up with her girlfriends. I tried calling Max. Nothing. Probably still trying to find a hopelessly inappropriate replacement for the lovely Veronika. Listening to his answerphone message made me smile nostalgically. I felt bad about not having spent more time with him recently. I was rarely round his flat these days. I envied Max a little. Although he was technically a director of the company, he'd never met any of our clients. He could probably quite easily and legitimately deny any further involvement with this whole mess.

I looked at my watch; it had now gone nine. I was slowly coming out of the fog of Scotch and beginning to develop quite a fantastic headache. As I looked around for my jacket, my mobile buzzed on the desk.

It was Nyles.

"Thank fuck!"

"And a very good evening to you too, brother."

"You have no idea how fucking hard I've been trying to get hold of you!"

"I'd say I do, brother—there's a fair few missed calls on my—"

"Why the fuck do you have five phones?"

"Five phones?"

"Five phone numbers?"

"I'd say I have a few more than that, brother!"

"What? Why?"

"Well, at least two numbers for each country I'm in—business and pleasure. Roaming charges can be absolute murder."

"Fuck's sake—so there's literally no way of getting hold of you at any time?"

"Brother, please, just leave a message with Adriana—I check at least twice a day."

"That's bullshit!"

"Look, brother, you're clearly very upset. My travel arrangements haven't been a huge concern of yours in the past. What's up? What's happened?"

I paused and collected myself. There was no point getting angry with Nyles—he'd probably just become even harder to get hold of. Christ, he might even disappear altogether.

"Daniel Golbourne is what's up," I said eventually.

"Ah, Master Golbourne..." Nyles chuckled.

I clenched my teeth. "Yes. Daniel fucking Golbourne and his henchman paid me a little visit this afternoon. Threw a punch at me and waved a fucking flick knife in my face!"

I felt my face flushing as I tried to keep my incipient rage from boiling over. I urged myself to be calm.

"Oh, shit! How the fuck did he get into the office? How the fuck did he even find the office?"

"I don't know, mate—we're hardly in the fucking Yellow Pages, are we?"

"Fuck! Are you okay? Are you hurt?"

"No, I'm not okay!"

"Where did he punch you? In the face?"

"No—he missed with the punch..."

"Missed? What a complete cock." Nyles chuckled again. This was clearly a future funny anecdote for him.

"Fuck you, Nyles! This is not okay!"

"I know, I know. Brother—please, I'm trying to think!"

"Mate, you need to get back here and sort this out ASAP. He said his brother's lawyers had contacted you?"

"Well, I look forward to hearing from them! We've done nothing at all outside the law. Lady Ann's decisions are her business and hers alone. It doesn't matter a damn how either of her dickhead sons feel."

"Well, technically, they are the heirs to her *massive* fortune."

"Entitled wankers! They've had privileged upbringings

and should be extremely grateful for them. All her children have had more than they deserve, and it's up to Lady Ann what she does with her money from here on out—the law is on her side."

Nyles may have had a point, but it didn't really help with the reality I was facing.

"Okay, well, what about Daniel? He doesn't exactly seem to operate within the law. What's your plan there?"

"*Our* plan is to do nothing until I've made contact with his older brother. I'm pretty sure he'd be interested to know how Daniel's handling the situation. Any threat of legal action should dissolve if he's got any sense—you've been physically threatened and assaulted. Well, almost assaulted." Nyles paused. "As for Daniel, a bit of guidance from his brother should pull him into line. As I've said before, Daniel Golbourne's bark is worse than his bite. I can assure you his *triad connections* are piss-weak."

I detected he felt the situation was now sorted. "And what about you?" I asked. "When are you back here?"

"I'm just tying up one or two loose ends with this Lewis Bennett case and meeting up with another potential client, then I'll be straight back. Give me forty-eight hours or so."

"Where are you?"

Nyles paused, clearly deciding whether or not to actually tell me the truth.

"Cape Town."

The other end of Africa. Perfect.

"And if Daniel comes back...?"

"*If* that happens, which I very much doubt it will, then put him through to me directly."

"We can *never* get hold of you—you have five fucking numbers, remember?"

"Take this one down."

I scribbled a number with an international dialling code down on a piece of paper. Christ knew whether or not it would actually work. Nyles assured me it would.

"Call me anytime. We're practically in the same time zone, and I'm on a bit of a health kick—up early jogging and off the booze, and the rest."

"Right."

It'd have to do. I closed my eyes and uttered a silent prayer to the gods that I wouldn't need it.

"And Will, mate, if you don't feel safe there in the office, then it goes without saying—you and Adriana take a few days off until I get back. You know, until all this blows over. God knows you both deserve it!"

"You mean lie low?"

"Not at all! Like I said—Golbourne Junior is harmless. I just don't like the idea of you guys sitting in that office needlessly worrying yourselves to death. Take some time out and relax—can you let Adriana know?"

"Sure."

A few days off could be just what I needed. Let everything settle—clear the head.

26

SAFER TO IGNORE THE DOOR

CATHERINE WAS WORKING from home for a couple of hours before heading into the office. Ordinarily I would have loved her company, but today I couldn't wait for her to leave. I willed her with every ounce of my being to hurry up and finish whatever it was she was doing. It wasn't working.

I hadn't slept. I'd lain awake all night worrying, trying to get my head around the meeting with Daniel Golbourne. I kept replaying the confrontation over and over, synthesising a thousand potential future scenarios in which his sneering face reappeared, flick knife in hand. Catherine was oblivious to my state of exhaustion and my teetering on the edge of a nervous breakdown. Instead she focused on the fact I'd been given the rest of the week off—a fact she was less than impressed with.

"I don't believe it! Are you sure this isn't coming out of your annual leave?"

"I'm one hundred percent certain. Nyles gave both me and Adriana a couple of days off."

"But why? Surely business can't be *that* good?"

"Things are, erm, quiet, that's all."

"Then surely that's all the more reason for both of you to be at the office, trying to find more work!"

"Well, we *have* been flat out, and now there's a natural lull. So Nyles thinks it's the best time to, y'know, give us a breather..."

I was a terrible liar. Catherine glanced over her laptop at me, trying to catch my eye. I had pre-empted this and concentrated my attention on buttering toast with renewed vigour.

"And you're *sure* you're being paid?"

"Yes!"

That was easier—not *actually* a lie, so I looked up and managed to hold her gaze. I needed this Spanish Inquisition to stop. It wouldn't take long for Catherine to uncover all the facts if she sensed anything even sightly suspicious was occurring. The combination of female intuition plus a lawyer's instinct was deadly.

"I only ask because of the holiday—it's not exactly cheap, and I'm definitely not getting any sort of bonus this year."

"Look, I'm definitely being paid! Nyles offered us a couple of days off—we'd have been daft not to take them."

This seemed to temporarily satisfy her, and she went back to furiously reading whatever was on her laptop. Thank God. I wandered over to the kitchen bench with relief and began absentmindedly opening cupboards.

"Now, are you sure you're not hungry? I could maybe... cook a fry-up?"

"What? Are you crazy? *I've* got to go to work. Shit! Is that the time? I'm already late!"

In one fluid movement Catherine leapt up, grabbed the extremely proficiently buttered piece of toast from my hand and darted into the bathroom.

A fry-up for one, then. Actually, that would be perfect—a task to become engrossed in and then back to bed on a full stomach. I'd wait for Catherine to leave before commencing preparations for what would be a momentous achievement in cholesterol and grease.

I leafed through the morning's paper. There was nothing in it. A new element in the periodic table had been named and a new *Harry Potter* film was being released. Even the sport was rubbish—dominated in a lacklustre fashion by the Tour de France and tennis.

Catherine walked into the living room, tying back her hair. She had showered, changed and applied make-up in under ten minutes. She was an unparalleled force of efficiency when she wanted to be.

"Love, it looks like I'll be late again tonight—still working on preparing this case that now looks like it will go to trial. It's actually looking like it'll destroy my weekend too... Hope that's okay?"

"Sure, I'll catch up with Max or something."

"Be good!"

"I will."

As she left she looked back at me with a mocking pout. A-ha—she was just jealous! Hence the reason for the Inquisition. Thank Christ for that. I'd been paranoid she would sense something was up. The night before, I'd managed to get home before her and sneak into bed. When she got back, I'd feigned a deep sleep to avoid talking. I didn't want to talk to her about the incident with Daniel Golbourne. I probably would eventually, but right now I didn't want to her to worry. She'd freak out, and she had enough on her plate.

Christ, I was tired. I'd never felt so jittery and on edge. I felt like I could vomit at any moment. I wished there was something to calm my nerves. Why did Catherine have to be so anti-drugs? Why couldn't she at least have a tiny stash of marijuana or some Valium lying around somewhere like most people did?

Alcohol, maybe? It seemed too early and maybe a little too desperate. Plus, I still felt a little rough from yesterday's mid-afternoon whisky session. Then a lightbulb went off—Irish coffee! The perfect mix of caffeine plus hair of the dog. If this wasn't the perfect opportunity to start the day with one, there never would be.

I hunted in one of the kitchen cupboards for the bottle of whisky I'd recently bought Catherine. She'd graciously accepted it with a knowing grin that acknowledged I'd probably be the one consuming the majority of it. I flicked the kettle on, then broke the seal on the whisky bottle and unscrewed the cap. A single inhalation confirmed that the usually comforting vapours were just going to make me nauseous today.

A knock at the door made me jump out of my skin, almost launching said bottle of whisky across the kitchen. "Shit!"

Who the fuck was that?

My heart began to gallop. I glanced at my watch and tried to calm myself down. It was half nine. Probably just Catherine having forgotten her Oyster card. Or the postman with a parcel. Maybe that DVD I'd ordered... I'd recently been seeking out obscure French films in an effort to impress Catherine on movie night.

I anxiously tip-toed towards the front door, breathing hard. Maybe it was safer to ignore the door altogether...

Fuck! I needed to get a grip. It was hardly likely to be Daniel Golbourne with a machete at nine-thirty in the morning. Besides, I was pretty sure I hadn't been followed home from the Tube. I'd been paranoid enough to continually check over my shoulder and even walk an obscure route home.

I eyed an unknown individual through the peephole: a short, stocky man with a shaved head but visibly receding hairline, wearing a slate-grey suit with a blue shirt. Probably a property agent or someone involved in the apartment complex's management. I hesitated, then opened the door.

"Good morning...?"

"William Harper?"

"Erm, yes?"

"D.C. Alan Hunt. Mind if I come in?"

An official-looking identification card had appeared in his hand and was being proffered to me in a lackadaisical manner. He gave me ample time to read the details and observe the official-looking *London Metropolitan Police* emblem.

Shit. Shit, oh, SHIT!

The photo appeared recent. On reassessment, D.C. Hunt's features seemed a little too large for his face. His nose was slightly crooked, as if it had once been broken, and his ears bore the chronically swollen look of a once enthusiastic rugby player. Beneath his name and title, the I.D. bore a description of his department. My eyes widened further and my mouth gaped open involuntarily.

Oh my God.

Homicide and Serious Crimes Division.

My heart skipped a number of beats, stopped completely, then seemed to sputter back into life. My nervous system, however, had frozen, and I was unable to verbalise any form of response.

Oh fuck, oh fuck, oh fuck!

"Do you?" D.C. Hunt prompted.

"Do I...?"

"Mind if I come in?"

"Erm, no—p-please. I, erm, I think you better had..."

D.C. HUNT LOOKED me up and down, smirked and walked straight past me through the hallway and into the kitchen. He had the air of a man who regularly invited himself into strangers' houses without the remotest hint of perturbation. He positioned himself in the kitchen with his back to the sink.

He looked directly at the open bottle of whisky and chuckled. "A little early, isn't it, Mr Harper?"

"Erm, I—"

"Or perhaps we're having a rather late night?"

The question seemed rhetorical. This was good, as I was still struggling with the power of speech.

There was a policeman in the kitchen. A policeman—a fucking *detective*, no less—in Catherine's beautiful kitchen!

Fuck. What if she *had* forgotten something and came back now? I felt the blood drain from my face, probably giving it a jellyfish-like translucency.

"Are you okay? Please, Mr Harper, relax. It's not as if you've killed anyone, have you, for God's sake? Christ, man —maybe you should have that drink!"

"No, erm, thank you. I'm fine... Sorry, erm, can I get you a drink...?"

"I'm actually okay. I've already had some vodka on my cornflakes, and besides, there are some silly little rules about drinking on the job before midday."

Brilliant. A comedian and a policeman. Well, at least if Catherine did turn up, she might get a laugh or two.

"So—not at work today?"

"No, erm, day off..."

I didn't even believe myself right now. There was no way D.C. Hunt was going to.

"I see. And what is it that you do?"

"I work in a... It's a s-start-up company. It's fairly new..."

"Okay. And what does this company—sorry, *Deconstruction Ltd*—do, exactly? Some sort of wannabe dot-com thing, is it?"

"Sort of... I mean, no, not really—more of an... advisory service."

"I see. Well, this is particularly painful, so I'll cut to the chase. I'm quite interested in what exactly you've been *advising* a particular individual upon. A particular individual who is a person of interest in an ongoing investigation."

"Who? Erm, I mean, I... It's all confiden—"

"Confidential, eh? That's an absolute classic! It never ceases to amaze me just how many presumably intelligent, educated people think that's a reasonable strategy when facing a member of the police force. I blame television entirely."

D.C. Hunt grinned. He may have been attempting a joke again. It was difficult to tell.

"Look, I'm only joking with you. Please try to relax, for God's sake. You haven't been accused of anything—and I haven't even really asked you anything yet!"

"Right... So...?"

"So—who? Hmmm? Who indeed is this particular individual?" He studied the room, seemingly only for the benefit of dramatic timing. "A Mr Lewis Bennett is the particular individual."

"Lewis Bennett?"

"Yes, Mr Bennett—a gentleman, if I'm not mistaken, that you and your colleague visited last week."

"Right... Yes—we did." It seemed pointless to deny it at this stage.

"I know you did, and I also know that both of you have independently run pretty in-depth background and credit checks on him."

This was also very true. "Look, we've really only met him once..."

"I know."

"And we're not really *involved* with him, in a professional sense... I mean, we haven't agreed to Decon—to work with him yet on any level at all, really... That was just sort of an introductory meeting-type thing..."

"Well, okay, that may be true." D.C. Hunt looked less than convinced. "But you *have* met with a gentleman who is a person of interest in an ongoing surveillance investigation by the Metropolitan Police Homicide and Serious Crimes Division. And therefore you have yourselves perhaps inadvertently become involved in an investigation, and *that*, my friend, is why I'm here."

"Right..."

"Perhaps see it as a friendly heads-up—a walk-away-while-you-still-can sort of thing."

"I don't understand—why would you...?"

"Simple, really: I don't believe you know anything about the trouble Mr Bennett is really in. You and Mr Pearce may have been pretty thorough in your background checks, but Lewis Bennett doesn't hide things in plain sight. He's too good."

Mr Pearce? What the fuck? That was weird. Surely Max had nothing to do with the background checks on

Lewis. Did he think Nyles was Max? What the hell was going on?

"I've looked into you both and your records are clean, and your cryptic so-called *start-up company* seems to revolve around yoga retreats and health farms. High-end financial espionage and organised crime doesn't exactly seem to be your game."

This still didn't make sense—or did it? *Yoga retreats and health farms?* In fairness, Nyles controlled the bulk of the finances, and the majority of transactions Adriana and I made came under that umbrella. That and reasonably large lunches.

"How did you know where to find me?"

"You're under twenty-four-hour surveillance."

"*What?*"

"Of course not! Do you honestly think we've got the resources? Do you know how many officers we have investigating this Bennett thing? Something that may or may not represent one of the biggest corporate-backed crimes of the decade?"

"Erm, no... No idea."

"You're looking at the entirety of the task force."

"Right... How come—?"

"Let's just say we've had other priorities since those pesky 7/7 bombings. Which is part of the reason Mr Bennett has managed to get away with what he has for so long."

"Right, so... How *did* you know where to find me?"

"Well, I went to your office and asked your secretary. Not exactly the most complex piece of detective work."

"Adriana?"

"Yes, I believe so—lovely Brazilian girl."

"And she told you where to find me?"

"She said you'd likely be at your girlfriend's apartment. Asked her first thing this morning when I went to visit *you* at *your* office, but you had decided to skive off."

Shit! I'd totally forgotten to tell Adriana she could take a couple of days off. This little surprise home visit was completely my fault.

"In fairness to her, she was initially pretty reluctant to tell me anything. I may have had to bring up the issue of her working visa and how easily it could be revoked. Admittedly a cheap trick and not my finest work, but as I'm sure you can appreciate, I don't exactly have the luxury of time and resources on my side."

"Right... Of course, I understand. But why now? Why warn us now?"

"Well, it took a bit of time to look at your *company*—it often does with new companies; no tax return filed, etcetera. Anyway, *Deconstruct*—whatever the hell it's called—*looks* pretty clean. I mean, it sounds like a lofty load of old bollocks, and I doubt you'll see out a year, but what do I know?"

"But why warn us about Lewis at all?"

"Well, if I'm honest with you, my main concern is you lot fucking up this investigation with your own enquires."

"I thought you said Lewis was *too good*...?"

"He is. But you might get lucky by chance—even a stopped clock is correct twice a day. *Comprendre?*"

"I think so."

D.C. Hunt got up, brushing his suit lapel and raising an eyebrow. It seemed a well-practiced gesture. "So we're definitely clear?"

"Yes. Very clear."

"Clear about?"

"Steering well, erm, clear... of Lewis Bennett."

"There's a good lad."

And with that he briskly walked up the hallway and saw himself out.

A wave of nausea hit me so hard that I barely had time to make it to the bathroom.

AFTER VOMITING, shaking violently for five minutes and then vomiting again, I emerged from the bathroom.

This was completely fucked! Visits from a wannabe gangster and the police in under twenty-four hours?

I downed a glass of water and collapsed onto the sofa, clutching my head. I realised I was still wearing Catherine's dressing gown. Interrogated by the police wearing a woman's dressing gown. That had to be a new low. No wonder he'd smirked at me.

I thought again about the conversation. There'd been no mention of Nyles. Zero. Absolutely none. Just Max. Why? Surely D.C. Hunt had accessed all the records from when Deconstruction Ltd had been registered as a business—that was in the public domain. Surely the business had been registered with Max *and* Nyles...?

What if it wasn't?

What if Max *was* the only one officially registered as a Managing Director? Had Nyles deliberately kept his name out of things? He'd been pretty vague about his past business exploits—maybe he'd previously filed for bankruptcy or something...

Shit! Adriana was still at the office. I looked around for my phone and gave her a call.

"Hi, Adriana? It's Will."

"*Puta merda!* I know! I have your number!"

"Yes—of course. Look—I forgot to let you know you can take the rest of the week off, okay?"

"What? Why is this? Am I fired? *Filho da puta!* Because I talk with the police? Oh, Will! I'm so sorry, I had to! He made threats, and I was scared, so scared!"

"No, no, no—Christ! You're not fired at all. It's just, with this Daniel Golbourne thing hanging over us... I spoke to Nyles last night. He told me that *both* of us should take the rest of the week off until he comes back."

"You're sure I am not fired?"

"No! I mean, *yes*—yes, I'm sure you're not fired."

"So what are the police wanting you for? About Mr Daniel Golbourne?"

"No! Hang on—did you mention Daniel's visit to them?"

"No! *Puta merda!* Of course no! I only tell them where maybe you are... I'm so sorry, Will!"

"It's fine. Please, Adriana, don't worry about it—you did nothing wrong. Nothing at all. The policeman just wanted to talk to me about something else..."

"What? Will! Are you in the trouble?"

"No, I'm fine—*we* are fine. It was just about Lewis Bennett, that's all."

"The police want to speak about Mr Bennett? Why? We have done nothing for him, no?"

"I know, I know... Look, it's complicated. I'll explain in person on Monday. Can you do me a favour in the meantime?"

"Sure, Will—anything for you!"

"Just don't mention anything about the police to Nyles if he calls... I'd rather talk to him about it myself."

There was silence at the end of the line.

"Adriana? Are you there?"

"Will... I'm so sorry... I... I already tell him about the policeman."

"What? You've spoken to him already?"

"Yes—remember I leave maybe one hundred messages on the phone yesterday...?"

Shit! Shit! Shit! I'd wanted time to work out if Nyles was up to something. If he was and he now knew about the police, he might get spooked... The bastard might disappear completely.

"Hey, that's okay. Don't worry! I'll call him and straighten this out. Look, enjoy your long weekend, and just try to forget about this week altogether. I know I will!"

"Ha! You will, Will. Thank you—you are so kind!"

"Take care, Adriana. Bye."

"*Tchau!*"

Shit. I had to convince Nyles everything was cool. If he disappeared because he thought the police were somehow involved, we were in trouble. Max and I were going to be left carrying the can for this Golbourne mess, which had already taken an unpleasant turn, regardless of whatever Nyles said.

After a great deal of thought, I texted the number he'd given me the day before and prayed it would do the trick.

> HEY MATE! POLICE
> VISITED RE. LEWIS
> B - ALL GOOD - BUT
> SOME USEFUL INFO!
> CALL ME WHEN YOU
> GET THIS!
> CHEERS WILL

Hopefully I was just being paranoid.

I looked around at the familiar comforting surroundings of Catherine's open-plan lounge and kitchen. I let my eyes rest on the cork noticeboard adorned with coupons, photos and magazine recipes, then looked away, a pang of guilt making me start sweating again. The room had taken on a sightly alien quality. There had been a policeman standing in it just moments ago.

I felt like I didn't belong here anymore. I felt like a total stranger... An intruder... A fraud.

For fuck's sake! I needed to chill out. I needed to relax. Control the breathing, concentrate and come up with some sort of plan.

Right. Breathe in and out. Inhale and exhale.

My phone rang, and all my efforts to install any form of meditative calm exploded.

It was Max.

Fuck! Max! *What the hell do I tell him? Where do I start?* Daniel Golbourne? The police? The fact that I'm now worried Nyles will possibly disappear and shaft both of us completely?

As it turned out, it wasn't the right time to mention any of those things.

Max was in hospital.

27

THE HEAVY WEIGHT
OF REALISATION

I FELT NUMB. Totally numb. I was dealing with a level of exhaustion I'd never been anywhere close to.

How the hell had this happened?

I was sitting in a chair next to a heavily sedated Max on a surgical ward at St Thomas' Hospital. *Heavily sedated* was a relative assessment from the healthcare professionals; I'd seen him in similar states before.

Max lay in a four-bed room. The other three beds were occupied by an assortment of sleeping patients with various limbs clad in plaster. Max's hand was strung vertically upwards by some sort of pulley system attached to an overhanging bar, essentially fixed in a permanent royal wave. He looked ridiculous. Ordinarily I would have found this hilarious, but I no longer felt like I possessed a sense of humour.

Max had called me after he'd come round from the anaesthetic. He'd been in the operating theatre all night following a "spot of bother with the old hand". *A spot of bother* translated into an eight-hour operation that involved reattaching nerves and tendons and doing something that sounded both horrendous and curiously like a death metal band song: *exploring the wound*.

On account of heavy-duty painkillers and the residual effect of the anaesthetic, the phone call with Max had been fairly disjointed. All I could gather was: he'd had an operation, he was at St Thomas' Hospital, the nurses were *sensational* and he himself was *pretty damned fine*. I'd later find out that he had tried calling me the evening before, but my phone had been off. In a parallel universe where I'd answered that call, this morning's police visit wouldn't have happened. I pondered whether this would have been worse or better. Probably worse.

I'd turned up on the ward armed with the most recent issue of *Men's Health* and some Quality Street. The attractive nurse who'd gently calmed me down upon my arrival had rolled her eyes once she'd ascertained who I was there to see.

"Mr Pearce is in bed 4A. He's absolutely fine, love. A little... disinhibited, but absolutely fine."

Max had clearly already been trying to make friends, despite being somewhat chemically castrated. He had also been taking advantage of whatever additional pain relief was on offer. When I turned up, I had to poke him hard to check whether he was in fact still alive. Max groggily attempted to focus on me and smiled dopily. He then offered me a high-five by pointing at his royal wave—this was hilarious enough for him to laugh softly until he passed out again. Seeing that he was indeed *absolutely fine*, I began to envy his blissed-out state of unconsciousness. I would have traded my own functioning hand for it.

I idly flicked through the *Men's Health* while waiting for him to wake up. I couldn't think of anything else to do or anywhere else to go. I still had no idea what had happened to him and had given up asking the nursing staff, who'd only looked irritated and shrugged with disinterest.

"Just ask *him*, love, okay?" one nurse told me.

About an hour and a half later, Max opened his eyes, still completely stoned and slurring, his brain clearly wrapped in warm, honey-soaked cotton wool.

"*Awww yeah*... Hey, man!"

"Max! Christ! How are you feeling?"

"Pretty good, old boy... Pretty, pretty good..." He looked over at the box of chocolates on the bedside locker. "Quality Street... *Awww yeah*! Nice work, Willy boy, nice, nice work... You best not have eaten all those yellow fudge sticks, you little bastard..."

"No, mate, haven't touched them—do you want one?"

"Nope... Not hungry, just admiring them... I feel very fucking high, but I literally have no desire for munchies whatsoever... It's weird..."

"Right. So...?"

"So... I'm... I'm just not that hungry, mate..."

"No, I mean—*what happened?*"

"Right... Fucked if I know, old boy... Some Eastern European meathead oik got the better of me..."

Max trailed off and seemed to be desperately trying to focus on one of the nursing staff who'd just walked in.

"Max! What happened, mate?"

He grinned inanely and winked me as I tried to bring him back to Earth. "Sorry, old boy... What happened about what...?"

"What happened with the *Eastern European meathead?*"

"Right, well, spot of bother... He didn't take too kindly to me... Did an absolute number on my hand... Surgeon said

I was lucky he didn't have to amputate. Damned fine fellow, that surgeon..."

"But what happened, though?"

Max looked at me with a genuine air of disbelief that suggested he'd just answered my question. This was clearly going to take some time.

"Okay, okay! Where were you when this happened?"

"Oh, erm, just finished at the old gym... Thursday, so mainly arms..."

"And this guy just attacked you in the gym?"

"No... God, it's a members' gym, for Christ's sake!"

"So where? At home?"

"No, no, no... He just grabbed me as I was walking back from the gym to the flat... Pulled me into some alleyway, between a couple of those fucking massive Grundon bins... God-awful smell..."

"And the hand? What the hell did he do to it?"

"He did an absolute number on it, old boy... But don't worry... I mean, I feel fine, great, in fact..."

"But what *exactly* did he do to your hand?"

"Ah... Well, he had a big bastard knife... One of those African types..."

"A *machete?*"

"Yes! Absolute bastard of a knife..."

"And?"

"And...?"

"Did he stab your hand?"

"Well, I couldn't very well fight the bugger off... Arms were shot from the gym, you see... Big fucker as well... Had an absolute bastard of a knife... Slashed me good and proper across the old palm... Absolute bloodbath... Went through the damned bones, almost lost a bloody finger..."

Jesus! I felt physically sick as I stupidly tried to visualise this. I couldn't believe it. It was far too *Reservoir Dogs* for Canary Wharf.

"So what did he want? Your wallet?"

"No... God, no! Actually, I couldn't really understand the bugger, you see... Dreadfully thick accent... Was actually bloody lucky someone scared the blighter off..."

"He ran off?"

"Yep... Bloody lucky, too... Old language barrier could have resulted in a much worse outcome... He didn't seem awfully pleased..." Max smiled to himself with a degree of contentment before adding, "Did seem to know who I was, though... Kept muttering something about the old boy Nyles..."

Oh. Fuck.

I caught my breath before asking slowly and very deliberately, "Mate, you sure this guy was Eastern European? Do you think he was Russian, maybe?"

"Russian...?"

"Yes, you know, Russian, Ruski—like the chaps I told you about from the Terry Armstrong deal."

"Fucked if I know, old boy... Russian, Polish, German, all the same to me... Wait a minute, what was that Veronika creature...? Czech...?"

"She was *from* the Czech Republic, mate..."

"Right... Well... Czech-mate..." This sent Max on giggling spree.

"Max! Please!"

"Sorry, old boy... What's up?"

"The guy who attacked you! Do you think he could have been Russian?"

"Very possibly, old boy... Very possibly... Of course, fellow could have been Czech too..."

Oh God, oh God, oh God. What the fuck did the

Russians want? Another level of panic was unfolding, fresh tidal waves of nausea and angst beginning to swell.

"Didn't you think that was strange, mate? That he knew Nyles? Why the fuck didn't you call me?"

"Well, for one, my hand... Slight issue there..."

"You have two hands!"

"I know, thank God... Lucky I'm just as good at most things with my left, otherwise I'd be seriously pissed off... Imagine that, no wan—"

"Max! For fuck's sake, this is serious! Why didn't you call me?"

"I did... Your phone was off... Presumably you were sticking it to that lovely lady of yours... Catherine... Wonderful creature... Fantastic ars—"

"Max! Please! Would you just focus for a second?"

"Right, of course, old boy... Seriously, though... You really need to learn to relax... Always been your problem— damned highly strung..."

This was bad. Really bad. Surely it had to be the Russians? One of Jaroslav's men? Fuck! It could also be Daniel Golbourne... Nyles had already underestimated him —he could easily be connected to a mob of Russians-slash-Eastern-Europeans doing his dirty work for him. How the hell was I meant to know?

Either way—what did we do now? How did they know where to find Max? What if they came back to finish what they'd started?

Oh God—they know where we lived! That Russian, the driver—*nice place, but not so secure...*

Fuck this. Maybe it was time to give D.C. Hunt a ring. After all, this was a *serious crime*, wasn't it? Fuck, fuck, fuck! I needed to speak to Nyles—somehow get him back here to sort out this mess. This wasn't fucking fair.

I looked over to Max, enjoying his opioid-addled state of blissed-out rapture, totally unaware of any danger we might be in. I had to tell him.

"Max, I need to talk to you about something."

He stopped scratching his nether regions under the sheets. With both hands, I gently turned his head towards me to try to refocus his attention away from a nurse whose eye he was half-heartedly trying to catch on the other side of the ward.

"What is it, old boy?"

"I think... I think Nyles has landed us in some serious shit."

"What...? Nyles? No... Good egg, Nyles..."

I took a deep breath and, as simply and concisely as possible, told him everything: the visit from Daniel Golbourne and then D.C. Hunt; my concerns about the Russians that even he had discredited as paranoid—surely his present predicament suggested otherwise.

He seemed to follow me. Or at least partially—some of what I said seemed to get through.

"Shit..."

"I know, mate, it's fucked—and I can't get hold of him at all! Which, to be fair, is nothing new..."

"Hold of who...?"

"Nyles, mate! Jesus! Look, I need to know you understand what I'm telling you here."

"Okay, okay..."

"Right—so please, mate—tell me what you understand."

"Okay... Okay... So something's going on with maybe the Russians... Which is, well... It's not good, judging by the state of my hand... If they're responsible, that is... And, er..."

"And Daniel Golbourne?"

"Daniel Gol—? Oh, the little Chinese fellow... You

chaps have pissed off some little triad oik who threatened you... Also with a knife... Although you seem to have fared somewhat better than me... And, erm, and... The police... The police are involved somehow...?"

"Forget about the police for a second. D.C. Hunt's visit wasn't anything to do with the Russians or the triad... oik."

"Jesus... They're upset about something *else?*"

I convinced myself that there was a look of conclusive understanding gradually spreading across Max's face. Whether he really understood or not, or whether he'd remember in five minutes, was unclear. But he was nodding.

"So we're sweet, then... with the police?"

"Yes! For now, anyway—but that isn't the point!"

"It isn't...?"

"Max! I think we might be in some fucking serious danger here, mate, *and* I think Nyles may have managed to distance himself from all of it. For all I know, he could've fled already."

"Mate... This is Nyles, he's a good chap... Hardly likely to... He just wouldn't do that..."

"Mate! You said yourself something about his past business dealings being dodgy."

"Rumours and nonsense, mate... Just rumours, probably nonsense..."

"Well, look, until we can get him here in person and sort this out, we need to get you out of here. Go somewhere safe."

"What...? What's wrong with here, old boy? Nurses for one are top-notch..." He delivered his plaudit on the nursing staff at twice the volume in case any of them were in earshot.

"Mate, think about it. This is a public hospital—I basically walked in here completely unchallenged. If the Russians want to come back to finish their *chat* with you, they can do the same."

This *did* seem to register. Max finally began to look a little worried. "Fuck... What do I do?"

"I don't know, but you can't stay here. You need to get out—discharge yourself or something."

"Well... I did think about transferring to a private hospital... Get my own room, my own nurse..."

"Mate, if you transfer to another hospital, they'll find out where you've gone! I'm sure they keep records of that sort of thing."

"You make them sound like the bloody KGB, old boy..."

"Look, Max—please! You need to get out of here, jump in a cab—don't go back to the flat—go to one of your folks' places, or check yourself into another hospital or clinic or whatever."

"I'll think about it..."

"Max!"

"Okay... I'll do it. I just need to get my hand out of this... thing..."

He gestured to his permanently waving hand. Fuck it! I'd forgotten about that.

"How long does it have to be in that thing for?"

"Couple of hours... Maybe a few days... I have no idea."

I looked around. Max's gym clothes were in a clear plastic bag on the bedside locker. Maybe a quick exit right now would be the best thing? Get him out of here and into some secure clinic on Harley Street or wherever. I had to go with him. I couldn't trust him to leave on his own and not take further advantage of whatever painkillers were offered to him.

Fuck it! That was decided—we were doing one.

"Hey... What the hell? What are you doing?"

"Trying to get you out of this fucking thing!"

I began to wrestle with the elaborate scaffolding system. A thick rope cord was tied to a splint around Max's wrist and connected via a pulley to a stainless-steel bar with a knot that looked like it required a set of garden shears. I began to fiddle with the splint and it came free suddenly, dropping Max's hand onto the bed. With the additional mass of the plaster cast, it fell like lead.

"FUCK! Ouch! Christ, man, be careful! Actually, that didn't really hurt much at all..."

"Shhhh! Mate—we're getting out of here. Try to keep it down!"

"Well, that could have fucking well hurt, old boy..."

"Shhhh! Sorry. Where's your wallet and phone?"

Max gestured to the bedside locker, which had its key securely left in the lock. I pulled the curtain around the bed and helped him get dressed, which I'm sure he tried to make as difficult as possible. I looked around the bed for something I could use as a sling and my eyes locked on the pillowcase—turns out being a Cub Scout hadn't been a complete waste of time after all.

I JOSTLED Max out of the ward as stealthily as possible. I was pretty sure no one would give us a second glance once we'd made it out into the vast network of hospital corridors, and I was right. With one hand on Max's shoulder, I steered him towards the front entrance and outside. I looked around for a cab while anxiously glancing over my shoulder for anyone who might resemble one of Jaroslav's men.

I asked the taxi driver to take a scenic route to Harley Street and we swung out west through Fulham, Hammersmith and Shepherd's Bush. I figured that would give me ample opportunity to spot anyone following us. I was almost certainly being paranoid, but figured it couldn't do any harm, given the circumstances.

In the taxi I called Talking Pages and got the number for a private hospital on Harley Street. I called the hospital and spoke with a highly accommodating patient liaison representative. I explained that my friend was a little fragile and had self-discharged on account of receiving a level of care below what he'd expected, muttering something about the inadequacies of the NHS for good measure. It seemed to do the trick. They guaranteed me that they could give Max a private room and that it was secure. Meanwhile, Max slept soundly, slumped against the cab window, mouth ajar and drooling down the windowpane.

After dropping him off, I planned to head straight back to Catherine's and hide out—en route I'd make sure I wasn't being followed. As I stepped out onto the pavement, the coast seemed clear. I was being ridiculous. There was hardly going to be someone trying to look inconspicuous in Ray-Bans and a Ushanka hat, pretending to read a newspaper.

I decided the best plan was just to keep moving. I began to head north towards Regent's Park. It was just about sunny enough to be busy. Busy places seemed like a good idea.

A ray of late-afternoon sunshine struggled through the clouds, temporarily bathing me and the concrete paving slabs in warmth. I briefly closed my eyes to feel the sunlight on my eyelids, and as I opened them again, the heavy weight of realisation landed.

This had all been inevitable.

Mixing with shady people was bound to catch up with us—we were always going to land ourselves in trouble eventually. But there was something else that dawned on me. Another possibility. Perhaps it was an obvious one, but I hadn't considered it seriously until now. Even now I was reluctant to admit it...

Perhaps Nyles was an honest-to-God professional con artist.

I shook my head. There was no evidence that was true. Sure, he might bend the truth and be prone to making unwise business choices... but a con artist? Max had mentioned something about the lack of clarity regarding how a few of his other business ventures had turned out... But deceiving people professionally—well, that was entirely different.

Entirely different, but possible...

Could his entire Deconstructive philosophy be a farce? A construct designed with the single agenda of conning desperate rich people out of their money? Was all this *rehabilitation of the soul* and *beginning a new existence* stuff bullshit? Just something to distract them while Nyles organised their finances to line his own pockets?

No way. And besides, I didn't have any proof. No proof —just a nagging suspicion.

Or perhaps a realisation.

Right now it didn't matter. I needed to find some way out of this mess. If Nyles was going to disappear, then I was completely screwed. There was no way that when the time came I could feign ignorance like Max might be able to. I'd been an integral part of assisting Nyles with both Deconstructions. More importantly, I'd met everyone face to face:

Terrence Armstrong, the Russians, Lady Golbourne, her son and his henchman...

I was going to have to face the music—and probably from the whole damned orchestra.

So, should I just go to the police? It didn't seem a wise option. It wasn't like they were going to turn around, thank me for the valuable information, and offer me round-the-clock protection in return. Things may actually get a lot worse. What little I knew about criminal enterprises suggested that they took a dim view of involving the authorities.

I needed time. Time and somewhere safe to think. I started to walk towards Euston Station at the fastest pace I thought I could get away with without appearing unnatural.

I checked my phone again to see if Nyles had returned my text. He hadn't. *Quelle* fucking *surprise*.

As I walked, it dawned on me that perhaps going back to Catherine's was a bad idea. I didn't want her getting any more involved in this than she may already be after fucking Nyles had enlisted her firm's services. Plus, if the Russians knew I'd been staying with her, surely they'd have already paid me a visit there. There was a good chance they didn't know anything about Catherine yet and were waiting for me to show up at Max's flat.

I couldn't risk putting her in danger. Could I nip back to hers now and grab a few things? I had nothing on me apart from my phone and wallet... But if I was being followed, I'd lead them straight to her place.

If I was being followed...

On balance, I decided to forget about Catherine's place—I could always buy a toothbrush and change of underwear. All I needed was somewhere safe. Preferably with a bed. A slow realisation came over me that I'd been awake for over thirty hours. Last night's lack of sleep had been a slow, crushing weight I'd been carrying around all day, largely unnoticed due to a steady supply of adrenaline. Now things had calmed down a bit, that full weight was becoming apparent.

I walked past Euston Station's forecourt and continued towards King's Cross. I needed a cheap hotel—one that could be paid for in cash. I found a bed and breakfast on a side street off Euston Road. Fifty quid a night. Bargain.

I paid the surly landlady, who explained that the bathroom was shared and the full English breakfast was subject to an additional surcharge; however, the continental option, which seemed to be toast, was included. She paused, eyeing me for a reaction. I thanked her sincerely, genuinely grateful to have a roof over my head, and assured her I'd be more than happy to pay said surcharge. I hadn't eaten all day, but even the thought of a full English right now nauseated me. She nodded with satisfaction and asked if I wanted a wake-up call at seven o'clock, which I perhaps overenthusiastically agreed to. I may have even used the word *splendid*.

Christ, I was tired.

I entered the small, cleanish room and closed the door on the world behind me. The LED alarm clock blared the time at me: six-thirty. I collapsed on the bed fully clothed and shut my eyes.

Just as I felt myself drifting off, I remembered I hadn't let Catherine know I wasn't coming back that evening. I dug around in my pocket for my phone. A single bar of battery gave me the perfect excuse for a text over a call.

HEY SEXY! PHONE
ABOUT TO DIE!

GONNA HEAD OUT
WITH MAX & CRASH
AT HIS PLACE AS
YOU'RE NO FUN!
;-) W xx

It struck me that with Max as a hospital inpatient and me hiding in a cheap hotel, this was probably the biggest lie I'd ever told Catherine. A wave of misery swept over me and my eyes began to sting. It struck me that now was probably an okay time to cry, behind a closed door in an anonymous hotel. I looked around; the chipped furniture and peeling, damp-stained wallpaper seemed to agree with me.

How the hell had this happened?

28

A FULL ENGLISH

I was startled awake from a deep, deep sleep by the sound of firm knocking at the door. An alien environment surrounded me, and it took me a few seconds to remember where I was.

The clock informed me it was indeed seven a.m. The *splendid* wake-up call had been delivered. I garbled a *thank you* and heard the soft sound of someone sighing before shuffling off on the carpeted floor.

I had slept like the dead and felt a hundred times better than I had yesterday. A growling stomach suggested I had also regained my appetite. Remembering the option of a full English breakfast, I lifted the neck of my T-shirt and inhaled tentatively. A shower was the absolute least I could do before visiting a public dining room. I grabbed the highly complimentary hand towel and went off to explore the delights of the shared bathroom.

Back in the room after a very brief shower owing to a less-than-generous amount of hot water, I reluctantly put back on the offending T-shirt I'd slept in and went down for breakfast. The dining room was a cramped, cosy space with four tables crammed into it. A generically Northern European-looking couple were the only other residents present. They smiled briefly at me and went back to studying their guidebooks in silence.

The landlady emerged from a back room, wearing an apron. She seemed to have a slightly sunnier disposition than the previous evening, although perhaps it was just me being in a less fragile mental state.

"What you havin', now, darlin'? The works?"

"Yeah, go on—I will."

"Surcharge's a tenner, that alright?"

I nodded.

"Magic! Sorry 'bout the lack of papers—I've just stopped buyin' 'em!" She raised an eyebrow in the direction of the European-looking couple and dropped her voice. "None of these fhackers can actually read propa' English, see..."

"Oh, I see." I gave her the benefit of the doubt and wrote her decision off as an austerity measure.

Lacking a paper, I decided to gamble with whatever remained of my phone battery and turned it on. The backlight went on briefly before it promptly died. Great. I began to worry that Catherine might have tried calling me, or even worse, tried calling Max. Panic began to rear its ugly head once again.

I took a deep breath. I needed to stay relaxed. Even if she had rung, there was nothing I could do right now.

I looked around the dining room. Faded prints of oil paintings hung in ornate gold frames on the walls. Grease-marked satin tablecloths and folded cloth serviettes were a nice nod towards the B&B dining room standard.

An idea suddenly dawned on me. Perhaps I had overreacted to the attack on Max. What did I actually know? He'd been attacked by someone who clearly wasn't on good terms with Nyles. I'd presumed it was the Russians, but I had no proof. Wasn't it more likely to be someone connected to Daniel Golbourne? After all, he was the one who had *actually* physically threatened me within the last forty-eight hours.

I didn't have any solid facts. For all I knew it might have even been some coked-up nutter that Chet had paid to rough up Nyles' associate in the absence of being able to get hold of him.

Furthermore, there was still the question of what we had actually done wrong. Sure, Nyles' methods were a little... *unconventional*, but we hadn't broken any laws, as such... Had we? His affair with Gloria Armstrong was devious, but not illegal. The Golbourne saga had gotten us mixed up with Daniel, but again, no laws had been broken. Plus, we'd been warned off Lewis Bennett before we'd even really gotten involved in his Deconstruction. Maybe the smart thing to do was to go to the police.

The more I thought about it, the more it felt like hiding out in a B&B had perhaps been an overreaction. I smiled—it was a little bit funny, if you looked at it in the right way. Apart from Max being in hospital, of course...

As I mulled things over further, the landlady appeared and set my full English down in front of me. "There you go, darlin'."

It looked incredible. Fried toast, black pudding—the absolute quintessential lot! I was starving, and this might just be the greatest breakfast ever.

I'D TAKEN the Tube back to Catherine's in an upbeat mood. My paranoia had abated to a degree, and I'd even taken to looking over my shoulder a little less. I tentatively walked the usual route back from the Tube and was pretty sure I'd not been followed.

The flat was empty when I got in around mid-morning. There'd been no signs of anyone suspicious hanging around outside, and I began to relax. I enjoyed the simple pleasure of putting on a fresh set of clothes. I noticed the bed was unmade and smiled. Catherine had obviously been cutting it fine to make it to work on time again.

I wandered into the kitchen and flicked the kettle on. Catherine had left a note on the kitchen counter.

Hey Sexy!
Hope the head's not too sore!
Can't wait to see you!
Stay out of trouble!
Cat x

Thank God! Everything was normal on the home front. I was suddenly struck by an overwhelming emotion sweeping over me—was this love? I'd never felt this strongly about anyone before, and I'd do everything I could to keep that feeling.

Shit! I was actually one hundred percent in love with her...

I smiled again guiltily while rereading the note. What a relief! She hadn't tried to get hold of me or Max. I stuck my phone on charge and made a mental note to call her as soon as I had some battery. Right after I called the hospital and checked in on Max, of course.

Today's *Guardian* was on the kitchen table, still in its

protective plastic cover. I flicked the kettle on and prepared to crash out on the couch with the sports section. It wasn't too long until the start of the football season—surely there had to be some transfer news worth reading in there.

I settled down with a hot mug of a tea and opened the news section first. There had been another terrorist attack, this time a coordinated bombing of two high-end hotels right in the heart of Jakarta. I skimmed the article with what had now become an unfortunate standard protocol: how many killed? Where were they from? Who was responsible? The weary familiarity of feelings arose—anger and disbelief at the senselessness of it all, followed by a now accustomed anxiety that it could so easily happen here in London again.

I was about to abandon the news section for the much safer sports section when a story on the second page caught my eye.

Multi-Millionaire's Ex-Wife in Critical Condition

I glanced at the accompanying black-and-white picture of said ex-wife. It was an old photo, with the woman sporting a classic 1980s perm.

But there was a something about that photo—a vague familiarity, a flicker of recognition... I'd seen this woman before. A sickening feeling somewhere deep in my abdomen began to grow with a frightening malignancy.

I read the article's subheading:

Gloria Armstrong, 48, has been placed in an induced coma after a traumatic brain injury. She remains in a critical condition at Queen's Medical Centre, Nottingham.

Oh God...

Oh fuck!

I read on, paralysed, unable to breathe. Only the muscles moving my eyes seemed to be functioning. My heart rate began to surge to accompany the feeling in my abdomen that now approached a crippling nausea.

Details in the article were sparse, but something horrific was now very apparent. Gloria Armstrong had been assaulted, and her injuries were life-threatening.

... a horrific series of intentional, systematically inflicted violent injuries ...

Oh, fucking hell! Had she been fucking tortured? This had to be the Russians! It had to be—hadn't it? But why?

Shit! Shit! SHIT!

A surge of crushing chest pain hit me and I doubled over, breathing hard. My vision swam and I felt giddy. Unsteadily, I staggered over to the kitchenette sink and reproduced the entire full English I'd consumed so enthusiastically less than two hours before.

I stood hunched over the sink, hyperventilating, as time stood still. My eyes streamed and I blindly groped for a tea-towel or some kitchen roll to wipe my face with. Failing, I settled for the back of my hand.

My mind raced as I tried and failed to grasp the full horror of the situation. If this was the Russians, then *we* were responsible for this...

What the hell had Nyles done?

I sank to kitchen floor, still panting furiously. I heard my mobile phone vibrating on the coffee table. I ignored it. I tried to slow my breathing down. It didn't work.

Nyles must have done something with the Armstrong deal

that upset the Russians in a *big* way. Surely that was the only explanation for this level of violence—first Max, now Gloria. Why the hell would he do *anything* to piss off the Russians? Hadn't he heard of Gulags or the Cold War? Maybe that was why he'd been so hard to get hold of recently—even more so than normal. Maybe he'd already gone into hiding?

I wondered if the Russians had found Terry, wherever he'd ended up. I had to speak to him. I had to warn him. He needed to know about Gloria too... But I had no idea where he was. Maybe that was better—if only Nyles knew, then maybe he'd be safe...

What if there was something on the office computers, though? What if the Russians got hold of them? Should I make a mad dash to the office and delete the hard drives to protect Terry? Would that be undertaking a suicide mission? And destroying evidence in what was now surely going to be a police investigation?

I needed to forget Terry for the moment and focus on what I could do to protect those of us here in London who'd been involved with the Armstrong deal. Max, Adriana and myself, at the very minimum, were definitely now in danger. Me staying at Catherine's flat was possibly putting her in danger as well.

I had to go the police. Things had gone too far. The Daniel Golbourne incident was child's play compared to this. A woman had been tortured and might even die. We were up to our necks in this. It was time to face the music before someone else got hurt. There wasn't any other option.

My phone rang again. Maybe that was the police already?

I shot up from my collapsed position on the kitchen

floor and darted for the coffee table. It was a withheld number. It could be anyone, literally anyone... What if it was the Russians?

I hesitated, my finger hovering over the *cancel* button.

Fuck it. I took a deep breath and answered the call.

IT WASN'T THE RUSSIANS.

"Will...? Will, brother?"

It was Nyles.

"Nyles? Fuck! What the fuck is going on? Where the fuck are you?"

"I know, I know, brother. I'm afraid things haven't gone entirely to plan..."

"To plan? What plan?"

"Well, I take it you've read the papers...?"

"Yes, I fucking have!"

There was a pause. A long pause. So long I began to panic and thought Nyles had hung up.

"Nyles? Nyles—are you there?"

"Yep, sorry, brother... It's... It's fucking awful. I had no idea this would happen. I didn't know they'd do that to her... You have to believe me..."

"What did they do?"

Another pause. He sounded genuinely shaken. Nyles' usually calm and collected voice trembling was not reassuring in any way. In fact, it was terrifying.

"Nyles?"

He sighed deeply. "They're animals..."

"Who? The Russians?"

"They... They pulled out her fucking toenails and fingernails, and then they started cutting off fingers..."

"Oh God."

"I think they must have got disturbed... They shot her in the head and then fled. It was meant to kill her. She's... She's as good as dead, brother."

The nausea from before rushed back. I held the phone away from me as I dry retched and staggered back to the kitchen sink. A cold sweat began to wrap itself around me and an icy trickle ran down my back.

This wasn't happening.

"Will? You there, brother?"

"Uh-huh."

"Look, I—"

"Nyles... Why?"

"Will, I've got to go—this call could be being traced..."

"Traced?"

"Never mind about that. I'm gonna be honest with you, brother, I don't have time to answer questions. Besides, it's too late for that now..."

"Too late?"

"Will, things have definitely not gone according to plan with the Russians... It's all gone a bit Pete Tong, so to speak. Some of the details of the deal didn't work out in their favour."

"Did... Did they work out in yours?"

There was another, longer pause, and I began to get angry. My hand clasped around the mobile began to shake. He had screwed them, hadn't he?

"Will! Please, brother... Listen. Let me finish. I have about twenty seconds before I chuck this phone and then I'm gone. Gone for good. I'm getting out. Evasive manoeuvres. I think you've probably got a couple of hours minimum before this all blows up big time. I'm about to get on a plane. I would urge you to do the same, brother... Cut one's losses, so to speak..."

"So you're here in London?"

There was another pause. "No—I'm overseas already, but people know I'm here. I... We need to really disappear—savvy?"

"No! I've nowhere to go. What about Max? He's in hospit—"

"I know, brother."

"How?"

"I've just spoken to him... Look, he's safe there. If they wanted him dead he already would be. I've done my best to keep his name out of most of this, especially the Armstrong deal. He should be fine."

"*Should* be?"

"He *will* be fine. He was barely involved. He'll get some questions from the police and they'll realise his involvement was minimal—it'll be written off as a bad investment in a new company."

"But what about me?"

"Well, that's why I'm calling, brother... You I'm less certain about. You, I'm afraid, are probably very much in the same boat as me."

And there it was. Spelled out to me.

"Catherine and her firm will be fine, though, in case you're wo—"

Fuck! The bastard! "Catherine? You fucking CUNT! You deliberately involved her!"

"Will, seriously, there's no need for that. Catherine's *firm* gave me independent legal advice on a couple of documents that were nothing to do with the Armstrong deal. She *will* be absolutely fine. End of story."

"I fuc—"

"Will, calm down—please! I'm calling you because I like you and care about you. I don't want any harm to come to you. I didn't *have* to call you, but I did. I'm putting myself at great risk in doing so. I *really* think you should listen to what I have to say."

I was seething. I clenched my teeth hard to stop myself from screaming at him.

"Okay. Good. You need to get out of the country as soon as you can, brother. Immediately. Head straight to Heathrow, buy a flight there—the company credit cards should be good for at least another couple of hours or so. We'll almost definitely have our assets frozen as soon as we're linked to Gloria Armstrong, and that won't be long once this becomes a murder investigation."

"Oh, Christ... Where do I go?"

"I'm afraid somewhere without an extradition treaty with the UK would be a good start."

"Fucking where, though?"

"That choice is yours, brother. I'd recommend Southeast Asia—it's a lot easier to disappear there, and much easier to get a new passport, which you'll need ASAP. Thailand is always a good shout. Take *all* your money with you. In cash. Hide it safely, brother."

"I... What about Catherine?"

There was another long pause. Nyles, it seemed, didn't have an answer to that one.

"Look, brother, I'm really sorry. This wasn't meant to happen. All I can do is tell you what I'd do. If you stay put and you're lucky, then you're looking at a jail term as the very *best* outcome."

"But I didn't do anything!"

"You were... involved, to a degree. Perhaps you weren't

consciously aware of *all* the aspects of the Armstrong arrangement..."

"FUCK, Nyles! You've completely fucked me!"

"Look, brother, you're welcome to take your chances in front of the judge and blame everything on me. In fact, I'd encourage you to do so if you go down that route... But I don't think things will get that far. These Russians have shown their true colours. I underestimated them— massively."

"Oh God."

"I'm afraid with me gone, you're rather going to be left carrying the can. You'll be the only one anyone can pin anything on."

He was completely right, of course. My eyes began to well up. "You bastard!"

"Will, listen to me, brother. This is the last time I'll say it. Leave right now and you might just have a chance of getting away and salvaging some sort of decent life."

"You total fucking *bastard!*"

"Will, I've talked for too long. You can remain mad at me for the rest of your life if you like. It won't change the situation, though. Best just accept it and move on. Practice what we preached—hopefully I've taught you that much at least. Goodbye, brother, and good luck..."

And with that he hung up, the dial tone blaring a final *fuck you.*

In less than an hour, my life had completely fallen apart. Now I was entirely on my own. I wanted to scream in rage. I wanted to burst into tears.

I decided to do both.

29

THINGS FALL APART

AFTER FIVE MINUTES of sobbing uncontrollably and a general outpouring of anger, misery and desperation, I decided I had to pull myself together. Stiff upper lip and all of that. Focus.

But what the hell should I do?

Do I listen to Nyles? Or do I take my chances and stay put?

I knew that I was heavily involved, but I hadn't really done anything wrong... Had I? Surely I couldn't end up in jail just for working for a total bastard?

Of course I could...

But running? Genuinely doing one? To Southeast Asia? Was that really my best option? Was Nyles right—was it the *only* option? Surely if I went to the police now and told them about everything, absolutely everything, they'd understand. Surely...

Could the Russians get to me in police custody? Or in prison? Wasn't there witness protection for this kind of thing?

And Asia? I'd never even been outside of Europe! Was I

really going to attempt to spend the rest of my life on an alien continent under a new identity? That seemed like total madness.

And what about Catherine? Could she ever forgive me for getting mixed up in this? If I stayed, I'd definitely be putting her in danger. And if I ran... If I *fled*... Wouldn't she be in even more danger? Wouldn't they find her somehow? I was really only guessing the Russians didn't know about her...

But if I ran, then... Well, that was it, wasn't it? It was over between us. I was throwing it all away. Maybe I'd done that already. Still, running away was a step further—a clear admission of being a coward, a fraud—a *criminal*. Not exactly long-term relationship material.

I thought back to meeting Catherine's parents. Having a cup of tea with her mum and chatting in their conservatory, so much more easily than with my own mother. I remember thinking, *I could get used to this*. An overwhelming sadness spread through me as I pondered the wasted potential of the happy life I could have had. My eyes began to well up again.

And what about my own mother? I wasn't close to her, but never seeing her again? When she found out what I'd done, she'd be devastated...

God! Focus!

What do I do? Should I stay or should I go?

If I go, there will be trouble... If I stay, it will be double...

I let out a hysterical laugh—the insanity of the situation boiled down into a Clash song.

Fucking FOCUS!

Another deep breath in and out. Right. Decision time.

What choice did I really have? If Nyles was right, then staying here could be fatal, and worse—it could put

Catherine in more danger. To take a chance that he was wrong was a hell of gamble, possibly with both of our lives.

So, the coward's way out, then, was it? I'd justified running away that easily, had I?

I looked around the flat. Silence and stillness, apart from my own heartbeat thudding in my ears.

Things fall apart. Life goes on.

It was clear.

I had to go.

I HASTILY THREW my washbag and what few warm-weather clothes I had at Catherine's into one of her old rucksacks. A pair of shorts and two mismatched T-shirts was essentially all I had to start a new life. Great. The majority of my clothes were still at Max's, but going back there was too risky.

Thankfully I had my passport from when we'd been booking flights to Morocco for our holiday. A holiday that would never happen. Regardless, I had to acknowledge that not having to go back to Max's for my passport was a stroke of luck, and right now I was grateful for any small mercy.

I roughly calculated I had just under three thousands pounds in my bank account. I prayed the cash machines at the airport were well stocked and thanked God I'd increased my maximum daily withdrawal.

I looked around the flat and imagined Catherine arriving after work. Maybe whistling to herself as she put on the kettle, completely oblivious to the fact that her boyfriend was now a wanted man, a fugitive. I thought about leaving a note. What would I say, though? Nothing I could write would improve the situation. I'd text her, perhaps, tell her I was heading up to see Mum in Rotherham. Family emergency or something... I could tell her I'd forgotten my phone charger as well... That'd give me time to think and to get to wherever I was going. Unless the police visited again...

Shit! Adriana! I suddenly remembered her—she also needed to get as far from this mess as possible. I tried her mobile—straight to voicemail. Shit! Was she okay? Hopefully just sleeping in after a big night... Alternative scenarios were not worth contemplating right now. I didn't even know her address—somewhere in Clapham, but that was it.

I tried phoning Max a couple of times as well—also straight to answerphone. I considered leaving a goodbye message—letting him know I was fine, heading to Southeast Asia, and... What? I'd get back in touch, one day...?

I decided against it. Max had always been terrible at keeping any form of secret.

I drew a deep breath and took one final look round the flat. I saw my old Discman on the bookshelf and grabbed it along with a plastic wallet of CDs. Wherever I was going, at least I'd have music.

I eventually stepped out on the street looking like a reluctant celebrity: sunglasses and baseball cap. Thankfully it was approaching lunchtime and pedestrian traffic was getting heavy. I darted up a side street and made for the main road, occasionally looking behind me, searching frantically for a combination of menacing Eastern European men, undercover police officers and, for good measure, anyone who looked connected to a triad.

This was insane. It was hard to breathe. The air was muggy and suffocating. As I power-walked towards the

Tube station, my phone buzzed. Another surge of adrenaline as I saw a text message from a number I didn't recognise. I didn't realise I'd been chewing the inside of my lip. I could now taste that distinctive flavour of iron as it began to bleed. I opened the message.

WILL IF YOU STILL

HAVE THIS PHONE

YOU ARE A STUPID

MAN! I AM FOR

THE AIRPORT. I GO

HOME NOW. TCHAU

Adriana! Thank God! Nyles had clearly spoken to her long before me. He always did have a soft spot for her... I felt an overwhelming urge to talk to her. To be assured that I wasn't going through this nightmare alone. I was almost at the Tube station. I decided to give her new number a ring. No answer. I called again. Christ, why the fuck wouldn't she pick up?

"Hullo?"

Weird. A man's voice. Oh fuck! Had they got her?

"Oh my God! Adriana?"

"Sorry, mate, hang on..."

What the hell was going on?

"Will?"

"Yes! Adriana? Thank God you're okay! Who was that?"

"Some man, I borrow his phone to text you. Nice guy. Maybe American."

"Oh! I see—clever."

"Yes, Will—clever. You are not clever. Why you still

have your stupid phone? You need to throw away right now! Anyone can find you if you have the phone!"

"Sure, I will, I will... Where are you? How did you—"

"Home. I go home. I speak with Nyles this morning—he says to leave England. To run away and throw my phone. He gives me a little money—he says not to talk to anybody—even you!"

"What? Why?"

"I don't know, Will—I don't know what you guys get messed up in. Some shit with Russian gangsters? I don't know! I'm scared for myself. Very scared, Will. So I go home. Goodbye—"

"Wait! Please, Adriana, you have to believe me! I didn't know Nyles had gotten us into this mess until today either. He's a fucking bastard. He's fucked me over as well!"

There was a pause. Adriana seemed to be mulling this over, no doubt deciding whether or not I was as full of it as Nyles. Who could blame her?

"Really, Will? You have *no* idea?"

"Look, I thought the Russians were a bit dodgy, of course! But I had no idea Nyles had ripped them off. I don't know how much for, or what he did with money. I have no idea!"

"Well, you are stupid, then, Will. He's a bastard, yes, but you are just—*stupid*."

"I know... I... God, it's all such a mess. That poor woman."

"What woman?"

So she didn't know. That was probably for the best. It wasn't going to help the situation or Adriana's state of mind to tell her about Gloria Armstrong right now.

"It's a long story. Look, do you know where Nyles was or is?"

"No, Will, come on—you know him. He say nothing."

I was right by the Tube station now and didn't want to hang around for too long in the open, standing in one place. An idea hit me—Adriana and I were sort of in the same boat. Didn't it make sense to stick together? I could go with her to Brazil! Surely going somewhere as a team was better? She could maybe even help me get settled into a new life...

"Adriana? Are you still there?"

"Yes, Will, but—"

"One last thing! Could I... come with you?"

"What?"

"To Brazil..."

"Are you crazy?"

"I just thought it might be saf—better... if we stick together?"

"You are crazy! I don't wanna see you or Nyles again! You bring me big, big trouble! I leave my job, my home, my friends, and for what? Nothing! You guys leave me nothing! So—*não!* Goodbye, Will. *Tchau!*"

"But I—"

Adriana hung up.

She was completely right, of course. More guilt to be dealt with later... but much later. Right now I had to get to Heathrow. Buy a ticket to—Thailand? Singapore? Which countries had extradition treaties with the UK wasn't really the sort of thing you could ask about at the ticket counter.

Was I really doing this?

I looked around the street outside the Tube station and felt a pang of nostalgia. Who knew when I'd be back here again, or even *if* I'd be back here... I looked across the road and saw the familiar Costa Coffee that I'd never been into on some ridiculously held principle regarding franchise coffee shops. Catherine had teased me mercilessly for my pretentiousness. I had to fight a bizarre urge to go inside, simply because I might never get the chance again. My eyes began to gently burn and a film of tears began leaking out.

Christ! I had to get a grip. If I was going to burst into tears at the sight of a Costa Coffee, I wasn't going to make it.

I wiped my eyes with the back of my hand and realised I'd been standing outside the station for some time now, not exactly inconspicuously. I remembered I had to at least text Catherine.

Hi Love! family
emergency. Really
sorry! Phone DyinG
- Left charger.
Will call you WHEN
I Can. Wx

Another—this time probably final—lie.

I vowed that when I spoke to her I'd tell her the truth. Tell her everything. I knew she may never forgive me and almost certainly wouldn't want to see me again, but I owed her that much.

I felt the stinging of tears again.

Get a grip, man!

I looked around one final time. Saw a litter bin close by. I turned my phone off and, as surreptitiously as I could, strolled over and dropped it inside, before heading into the Underground without looking back.

A FRESH WAVE of panic swept over me as I entered the living hell of Heathrow Terminal 2's Departures on a Friday afternoon in summertime. The train ride had not exactly helped my state of mind. Every stop found me wrestling with the urge to jump off and turn back. At South Ealing I'd even gone as far as physically leaving the train, only to immediately double back as soon as I set foot on the platform.

As the throng of people bustled around me, I squinted up at the departures board, searching for any suitable flight to Asia. I was significantly disadvantaged by not knowing what continent the majority of destinations displayed were on. Why hadn't I taken geography more seriously at school?

There was a flight to Bangkok at six-thirty... That would do. Providing the credit card still worked and I could get a ticket, of course.

I made a beeline for the nearest counter displaying a Thai Airlines sign. I waited in line behind an elderly American couple who seemed to need the answers to their questions repeated multiple times. I tried to look relaxed and vaguely bored. My heart raced and the inside of my mouth was now raw from near constant chewing. Why the fuck were there so many armed policemen about? I didn't remember seeing quite so many last time I'd passed through an airport. Then I remembered the bombings in Jakarta—that was probably the reason... Simple explanation. *Just keep it together. Nice and relaxed.*

The couple finally shuffled off, leaving a weary-looking airline representative facing me. I gave her time to readjust her smile and stepped up to the counter. My heart rate rose even higher and I began to hyperventilate. I could feel fresh rivulets of sweat trickling gently down my back. *Just going to buy a one-way ticket to Thailand... Nothing unusual about that...*

"Hello, sir, how can I help?"

"I..."

The power of speech failed me. I doubled over, coughing violently in an attempt to mask the fact that my throat had constricted on me.

"Sir? Are you okay? Would you like a glass of water?"

I finally looked up to see genuine concern on the airline representative's face. "I'm so sorry, I... Hay fever. I'm fine, thank you."

"Are you sure I can't get you a glass of water? It's really no trouble."

I shook my head and gave another more composed cough. "Sorry, I... I'd like a ticket on this evening's flight to Bangkok."

"Certainly, sir. Which flight will that be? The six-thirty or ten-thirty?"

I was momentarily stunned. Surely this couldn't be so simple, could it?

"Erm, the six-thirty, please."

"I'll just check the availability. May I have your passport please?"

I quickly placed my passport on the counter in front of her rather than handing it directly to her. I didn't want her to see just how much my hands were shaking. She punched a few keys on her keyboard and looked up with a broad smile.

"You're in luck—that should be fine. Which class?"

"I'm sorry?"

"Which class of travel, sir?"

"Oh, erm..."

I thumbed the credit card in my hand. Unless Nyles

had burned it—and he'd implied he hadn't—I knew exactly how much was left before it reached its limit. And it was a lot. Almost certainly enough for any ticket anywhere in any class. This might be the last flight I ever took... Would a business class ticket look *less* suspicious, even? If I was going to go down, why not go down in style...?

I decided to play it safe. "Economy, please."

"And your return date?"

"I'm sorry?"

"I need the date you wish to return, or take an onward flight."

"Oh... erm... I haven't decided yet... I'm, erm, going travelling, you see... It's all a bit spontaneous."

"I appreciate that, sir, but in order to be granted a visa on arrival, you'll need to show proof of onward travel. I can make the ticket flexible so it can be changed when you've decided, but I do need a set date, I'm afraid."

"I see. Erm, how about... August the 8th?"

"Thank you, sir." A glance at my passport followed by a few more keystrokes and it seemed set. "Coming back on your birthday, I see."

"Erm... Yes, that should give me enough time..."

"Okay—including taxes, that comes to a total of six hundred and ninety pounds. How would you like to pay, sir?"

"Erm, card... please."

I wiped any sweat off the credit card on my jeans and handed it over quickly, very conscious that my hands were still trembling. The girl took it and smiled. She began to manually enter my credit card number. Christ! More suspense... The moment of truth...

Oh God, oh God, oh God! Hurry up!

"That's fine, sir. Could I just get a signature?"

The relief was like an orgasm. I could have leapt over the counter and hugged her. I signed the invoice she handed me with lightning speed.

"Will there be anything else at all?"

"No. Erm, which way to the gates?"

"Just up the escalator. Have a pleasant flight, sir."

"Thank you! Thank you so much!"

I headed towards the escalator. According to the large LED clock in the centre of the departure hall, it was four o'clock. I had two and a half hours until the flight. One hour thirty minutes until boarding. Having the ticket in my hand somehow made me feel safer. Two hours and thirty minutes to avoid the police, Russians and basically anyone who might recognise me. This might actually work... If I could clear security and just find a quiet corner of a bar... I should be okay. Should be.

Then it struck me: I had two hours and thirty minutes left in England. A country that had been my home for my entire life. I might never be able to come back. All at once I felt a crippling nostalgia for everything around me. I seemed to be swinging back and forth from blind panic to misery so quickly that they were beginning to merge into one. The fear of drawing attention to myself was the only thing stopping me from bursting into tears.

I needed a drink. Something strong to steady the nerves... and maybe one last pint of English beer. I remembered that my stepfather, following a business trip to Singapore, had once told me that beer in Asia was gnat's piss. Imagine never having a proper pint again...

Dear God—what was I doing?

30

FULL CONFESSION

I stop talking.

I've been talking for hours. Literally hours.

I'm even feeling sober again. I look at my new French friend, Claude, who is remarkably still awake.

"Wowee! That is more than a little story, my friend!"

"Sorry, I... I didn't mean to tell you everything quite like that."

"*Mais oui*—you did just that."

"Yes, I did—it just came out..."

"So tell me, how do you feel?"

"Erm, I mean, I feel awful about everything, but to get it all out was... good."

"Like a confession, no?"

Ah. Yes. There is that. I *have* just made a full confession to a complete stranger. So now it looks like my fate may *also* depend on what he decides to do with this confession. Maybe he doesn't believe me...

"Yes... like a confession. Erm, I—"

"Please, I have heard worse."

"What? Really?"

"Oh, plenty! In my line of work I see many things that are much worse."

"Your line of work?"

"*Oui.* I work for Interpol."

"Ha! Oh, imagine! Good one!"

"*Non*, really, this is not a joke."

Claude hands me a half-drunk glass of Scotch, digs around in his trouser pocket, and finally hands me his open wallet that displays an ID card.

"*Voilà!*"

CLAUDE CISSÉ. INTERPOL. DÉPARTEMENT DES ENQUÊTES SPÉCIALES.

FUCK!

My mouth remains open. I enter full-blown panic mode. Of course this was all too easy. Of course they knew I was trying to leave. All they had to do was give me enough rope to hang myself—I am so fucking stupid!

"Oh God! So... you knew?"

I can't breathe. I look towards the exit. Mental, absolutely mental—we're at thirty-five thousand feet.

Claude sees me looking and lets out a throaty laugh that suggests a long-standing appreciation of Gauloises. "You know, *mon ami*, you may be a little crazy, like all English-men! But, *non*, relax."

"But..."

"I could not care one bit, my friend! I am on holiday! By this evening I will be having my wicked way with some girl half my age, making me feel like a young man again! *Savoir?*"

"What? What do you mean?"

"*C'est bien*—with me, of course. Maybe if you keep going

on this path you will end up on our list one day, eh? Maybe not. Either way, it sounds like you are, how you say—a *small fry*? I work in the *Département des Enquêtes Spéciales*, my friend. You know the bastards we chase—war criminals, international drug dealers, human traffickers, paedophiles, etcetera, etcetera. You are not in the same league, I think! Also, you have, how do you say—remorse? I think your guilt will be your *peine de prison*! I cannot see you doing the same again."

Claude gives another throaty laugh. Christ, he must be dying for a cigarette.

"Shit! I'm so fucking stupid. I can't believe I just told you all that shit!"

"Yes, it was little stupid, true. Maybe you won't get so drunk to do that again. You are heading to Thailand, my friend—there are plenty of other drunk mistakes you can make there!" Claude chuckles.

I nod. He makes a valid point. But then again, looking at the tray table littered with miniatures in front of him, he's not exactly held back on the drinking himself. Probably makes him reasonably safe, from a confessional perspective.

"So you think I'll be okay? Getting into Thailand, through immigration and all that..."

"How would I know? I'm on holiday, remember? Also, I have no idea how much trouble you have stirred up in your own country. You may be okay, you may not. That is the only certainty."

Great. Another French philosopher... How perfectly ironic.

Claude smiles again. "Now, my friend, I am going to catch a little sleep, and it would be good for you to do the same if you can."

"Yes, you're right. And thanks."

"For what?"

"For listening, I guess."

"*De rien, mon ami.*"

Claude necks the rest of his Scotch and promptly falls asleep. I don't. His *you may be okay, you may not* line does nothing to settle my spent nerves.

No sleep till Bangkok.

I LAND in Suvarnabhumi Airport a seething, anxious mess. I've had no sleep, unlike my travelling companion. Claude wishes me well after we leave the plane. I head straight to the bathroom and vomit up everything I've consumed on the flight. I splash water on my face and try to look as calm and respectable as possible.

The last hurdle—immigration.

The queue is long. Very long. It's agonising, and I feel like I've been waiting for hours. The air conditioning is not as strong as it could be given our proximity to the equator, and I'm sweating buckets.

I'm finally next in line and trying to keep it together. Trying to look relaxed. I'm just here on holiday, after all. Back home on August the 8th with a tan and hopefully not an STD.

I walk up to the counter and hand over my passport, which is immediately scrutinised.

One last bit of luck is all I need.

"You come from London, England?"

"Erm, yes..."

A slow leaf through every page, a long look at my photo,

then a long look at my face from the Thai immigration officer.

"William Harper from London, England?"

"Erm, yes..."

The officer turns to another in the next booth and speaks unintelligibly. The language is like nothing I've ever heard before.

Jesus—what's going on? Is this normal? Am I about to be busted? The conversation has gone on for an uncomfortably long time. I try looking bored by staring vacantly around, despite the fact that I am now absolutely shitting it.

It's then that I see Claude standing at an immigration booth three down from me. He raises an eyebrow. I shrug and try to grin back at him. It looks like the game is up. He gives me a considered nod and a sympathetic smile and shrugs back.

C'est la vie, eh, Claude?

I look back at the immigration officer holding my passport. He's still talking to his colleague. Are they talking or arguing?

I look back at Claude, who's looking towards the two officers deep in discussion in front of me. Claude then gives me a wink and slowly turns back to the officer in front of him.

Then he does something I'm not expecting.

He explodes.

I mean, he completely explodes. With the type of anger only an inebriated Frenchman can expel.

"Oiya, mister! You're talking to *me*, mister? You fucking cocksucker! You know who I am? Stop this—this fucking around and let me through, goddamn you!"

Claude is so loud the entire mumbling chatter of the jet-lagged immigration hall is instantly cut down to total silence. The immigration officers either side of the one he's shouting at spring to their feet. The two that were in deep conversation in front of me follow suit. My passport is quickly stamped and miraculously thrust back to me as the official runs over to assist his colleague being berated by an angry Frenchman.

I'm stunned. I'm holding my passport—and it looks as though I can walk through. Just walk though. I don't need to be told.

I look over towards Claude, who's now being surrounded by Thai airport officials, all of whom he is comically towering above. His palms are outstretched in an apologetic gesture, but the roar coming from the assembled immigration department suggests his apology isn't quite working. I try to catch his eye, but it's impossible.

God bless that man!

I mouth a *thank you* towards him and walk quickly between the immigration booths.

I walk past the luggage carousel.

I take the green aisle and walk past a number of bored looking customs officials, who show no interest in me.

I walk past the barriers separating the arriving travellers from their welcoming families and upmarket hotel limousine drivers.

I walk out into the arrival hall and into a new life.

ACKNOWLEDGEMENTS

To the following amazing people without which this wouldn't have happened.

Sarah — for being the best sounding board I could ask for, the honest critique, the cover graphic — and of course all the artistic direction!

Jenny — for everything, the direction, the tips and the consistent encouragement.

My editor, *Claire Bradshaw* — thank you so much for all your help and the fantastic work you did on this. https://www.clairebradshaw.com.au/

Tania at *Getcovers*, a Ukrainian based design company — for all the work with the cover layout and for your patience! https://getcovers.com/

Michael Campling — thank you so much for all help and advice with editing, formatting and publishing. I am extremely grateful. https://michaelcampling.com/

The *Pencil Pack* - for the camaraderie and sharing the pain!

And of course last but not least, *Aenz* — my soundtrack to everything!

AUTHOR'S NOTE TO
SECOND(ISH) ED.

Many thanks to anyone who picked this up and read it, especially if I didn't personally bully, coerce or intimidate you into it. A huge thank you to those that took the time to review it on platforms, particularly *Amazon* or *Goodreads*. Without a publishing juggernaut behind me the importance of these reviews cannot be understated—you're all I have— thank you once again!

An extra special thanks to those that highlighted the typos... (the *actual* reason for a reprint). A special thanks to *CJB*—the runaway winner of the Typo Cup. (yes, yes— finding double the number of anyone else...) but also to the others with sharp eyes who kindly pointed them out to me, notably *Chops, Zaki* & *Katie B.*—much appreciated!

ABOUT THE AUTHOR

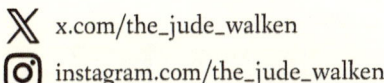

THE_JUDE_WALKEN

X x.com/the_jude_walken

instagram.com/the_jude_walken